FATED MATES

For J. My love, my heart, my world.

This is a work of fiction. Names, characters, businesses, places, events, locales, and incidents are either the products of the author's imagination or used in a fictitious manner. Any resemblance to actual persons, living or dead, or actual events is purely coincidental.

FATED MATES

BOOK 1 OF THE TRUE MATES SERIES

ALICIA MONTGOMERY

CHAPTER ONE

The club was dark and the music terrible. *Just like any New York club on Friday night,* Alynna Chase thought.

Blood Moon wasn't the type of place where she hung out regularly. It was, after all, one of Manhattan's hottest nightclubs, and she normally wouldn't be able to afford such a place or even get in. Of course, a flash of T&A helped usher her through the door. Her eyes grew wide at the price of a single drink. *Well, I'm not paying,* she thought as she brushed her long dark hair off her shoulders. She smoothed down the fabric of her very short pink dress and looked at the other girls around her, all similarly dressed in their flashy and even shorter attire. *Gotta blend in, after all.* But she wasn't here to snag a guy.

Well, technically, she *was.* Male, in his early forties, five feet, ten inches in height, thinning hair, with a slight paunch. Not her type exactly, but he was similar to many of the guys she had to tail as a private investigator. It was a suspicious wife who had hired her, of course. She came to her office the day before yesterday, afraid her husband was cheating on her. *Wife's instincts were probably correct.* Chances are, when someone suspects their spouse of cheating, they almost always are. Despite being only twenty-two years old, Alynna had been in the business for almost four years and she could attest to this truth.

Ah, there he is, she thought, as she took a sip of her beer. She watched as her target – a Mr. Greg Truman – approached a young, svelte woman about half his age. Alynna's bright green eyes tracked his every movement, watching as he slid a drink over to her, smiled, and leaned in close to say something. That wasn't a crime, or proof of cheating, but definitely a sign. She would just have to wait until Mr. Truman sealed the deal and then try to follow them. He seemed like a classy guy, and quite well-off, so he'd probably spring for a hotel room instead of getting a back alley blow job. This business was making her too cynical.

After twenty minutes of watching Greg Truman flirt with the younger woman, she was getting antsy. Also, her drink was getting warm and she needed something to cool her off.

"A glass of ice water, please," she asked the bartender.

He turned around and flashed her a smile. *Cute*, she thought. Well, everyone who worked in this club was insanely hot, from the beefy bouncer out front to the skimpily dressed waitresses. She was only human, of course, and she noticed these things. Many of New York's top clubs employed only the best-looking people.

The bartender handed her a glass of cold water. As she wrapped her hand around the glass, she could feel the condensation forming on the outside, wetting her palms. Alynna took a casual swig, keeping her eyes on her mark. Mr. Truman was definitely getting cozier with his sweet young thing. She could tell by the girl's body language she was definitely interested in what he had to offer.

"Typical," she snorted to no one in particular. Greg Truman

wasn't anything to look at – maybe once long ago he was hot – but he was slick and rich, one of those Wall Street hedge fund guys. Girls could smell the money oozing from him, and it didn't hurt that he was charming.

"Excuse me," a low baritone voice said from behind. "Is this spot taken?"

Alynna was shaken out of her thoughts by the deep, rumbling tone. Before she even turned around to face the speaker, a strange scent permeated the air. It wasn't bad, but she couldn't quite identify what it was. She breathed in deep – it was male, spicy, with tinges of an earthy, after-rain scent.

"What do you–" She stopped suddenly as a pair of hazel eyes stared back at her. They were almost luminous in the dim light of the club. The scent grew stronger. Not like a suffocating perfume, but she had a hard time concentrating on anything except the tall, handsome man in front of her. "It's ... fine?" she managed to choke out.

The man moved closer, staking out the spot beside her at the bar. "I'm sorry. I don't mean to be so forward. I mean, a girl like you at a club like this ... I'm sure you get lots of attention." He smiled at her, his eyes twinkling.

Alynna wasn't quite sure how long she stared at him, but then she finally snapped herself out of it. "It's not ... I mean ... you can ... it's a free country!" she stammered and took a sip of her ice water. The temperature in the room suddenly seemed to spike, and she fanned herself with her hand.

"Yes, I know," he said. "I'm –"

"Alex!" the bartender called out as he came over. "Nice to see you here, bro. Got the night off?"

"Yeah, Sean, it's my night off." He accepted a beer from the bartender. "How about a drink here for –" He looked meaningfully at Alynna.

"I'm ... uh ... Alice," she fibbed. It's not like she was an undercover cop, but her reaction to the man – Alex, apparently – made her uneasy. "And no, thanks, I'm fine."

He raised an eyebrow at her glass of water. "Not the usual drink around here."

"I'm not your usual girl, I guess," she said. He smiled at her, which, if it was possible, made him look even more handsome.

"I guess not." He took a sip of his beer, but his eyes never left her. It unnerved her, but she refused to be intimidated. She squared her shoulders.

"So, I hate to sound cliché, but ... what's a girl like you doing in a place like this?"

She nearly choked on her water, sputtering liquid down the front of her dress. Alex tried to help her, but he accidentally knocked her glass from her hand and spilled the rest of the water all over her.

"Oh fuck, Jesus! Sorry!" Alex said in a panicked voice. Sean the bartender laughed out loud, handing him a towel. "Here. Let me help." He tried to wipe her down.

Alynna grabbed the towel from him angrily. "No, it's fine. I'll be ..." She coughed, then wiped the front of her dress. "I'm – shit!" she cursed. Across the room, Greg Truman leaned over and whispered into the girl's ear. She giggled, then gave him a nod. He finished off his drink and took her by the arm, then led her to the back of the club toward the exit. "I need to go."

"Wait!" Alex grabbed her arm. "Where are you going?"

His hand on her arm sent small shocks up and down her spine. She gasped at the sensation, feeling her knees go weak. The warm feeling flowed through her, slowly getting hotter and hotter.

"Hey, what's wrong?" he asked, genuine concern on his face. "Are you sick?"

"I ... I don't know." She felt dizzy and steadied herself

against the bar. *What the heck was going on?* "What the fuck. Was there something in my drink?" She looked up at him.

Alex's eyes darkened and took her empty glass. He sniffed the rim. "Do you think someone spiked your drink?"

"I don't know. I didn't take my eyes off my glass," she said weakly. God, she was burning up, feverish.

"Shit!" he cursed as he felt her forehead. She moaned and recoiled from his touch. "Sean!" he called out. "Did she have any other drink?"

Sean nodded. "She had a vodka tonic, that's about it. Hey, is she okay?"

"I don't know, but you better give security a call. Might be someone causing trouble," he turned to the girl. "Alice ... are you all right?"

Alynna heaved and she felt her stomach rolling. "I think I'm okay. Don't call anyone. I mean, I just need to get out of here."

Alex nodded and took her by the elbow carefully. She didn't recoil from him this time, but clung to his arm instead, allowing him to lead her away.

She wasn't sure where she was being led, but she didn't care. She felt a little bit better once she got away from the noise and pulsing lights. She closed her eyes and leaned against a wall, breathing heavily.

"Feel better?" Alex asked, his face a mask of concern. He stood right in front of her, one arm braced on the wall behind her.

She nodded, then opened her eyes. "Where am I?" There were three twin beds in the room and several lockers.

"It's the staff break room," he said. "Do you want me to call a doctor or a friend? Boyfriend?" He leaned in closer, examining her face.

"I'm much better now." She shook her head, then gave him a small smile. "And no. No boyfriend."

"Good," he said in a serious tone. "I wasn't sure a girl like you would be single."

She raised an eyebrow at him. "Not from New York, are you?"

He laughed. "No. I just moved here from Chicago a couple of months ago. Were my Midwestern sensibilities showing through?"

"Hmph," she huffed. "Something like that." That same masculine smell filled the air again and this time, without the distraction of the club or other smells, it hit her nose sharply. "Shit! Do you smell that?" She felt her temperature spike again, though now there was no nausea or dizziness. In fact, she felt almost ... tingly. "Do you work here or something?" she asked, looking around again.

He chuckled. "No, not really. This is kind of a regular hangout for my, uh, workmates and me. My boss is part owner and the bartenders here treat us well."

"Ah, I see," she said. *God, was the A/C broken? It's burning up in here. Why was he leaning in so close?* Not that she minded. The smell was turning into something amazing, and it grew stronger as he came closer. *Was that smell his aftershave or something?* She looked up straight into his eyes, which seemed to have changed into a bright, glowing yellow. He also had the strangest expression on his face, which sent shivers through her. "I'm much better. I think I should go." She saw the door next to them and turned to leave.

"Don't!" he said in a low growl. Before she could open the door, she found herself pushed up against it, her back against the hard wood.

"What are you doing?" she asked in a shaky voice.

Alex said nothing, but instead pressed his body up against her. He leaned in, nuzzling her neck and letting out a guttural sound. Alynna froze on the spot. She could feel the hard planes of his chest and torso against her own body.

His lips grazed the soft flesh of her neck, moving up her jaw to her chin. Finally, his lips claimed hers. Alynna was surprised at the touch of his lips and perhaps even more surprised she responded. Her mouth moved against his, opening to let his tongue snake in to mingle with hers. She gasped against him when he pressed his hips toward her, his erection evident.

Alynna lost all thought, her body burning up, both in temperature and with desire. She clawed at him, tugging at his shirt. His hands, meanwhile, roamed her body, cupping her breasts and kneading them through the fabric of her dress. Her nipples hardened and she pushed her body up toward him. His lips moved against hers, practically devouring her mouth.

Alex's hands moved under her dress, inching up toward her inner thighs. Alynna gasped into his mouth when his fingers skimmed over her lacy thong, rubbing her dampening pussy through the fabric. She clung desperately to him, her arms wrapping around his neck as he pulled the scrap of lace aside to touch her core. His fingers traced her wet slit, moving up and down, which made her moan in pleasure. After teasing her for a while, he found her clit. She cried out against his mouth when his fingers started making lazy circles around the hard nub.

She moved her head back, her long dark hair falling aside to reveal her neck. Her pulse seemed to throb, and he immediately moved to her neck, licking her there.

Alynna felt him move his lips and bare his teeth. Two points grazed over the skin on her neck, and she opened her mouth to moan. But what came out was a loud growl, and she suddenly felt dizzy. She pulled back and gasped in horror. Alex looked up at her with golden glowing eyes, and it looked like the bones underneath his skin were moving on their own. His face was elongating, as if he was growing a snout. He bared his teeth, the canines showing prominently.

She screamed and tried to push him away. Instead, he grabbed her by the shoulders and pinned her to the door.

"Who are you?" he snarled at her. "Did someone send you here? You must know you can't just walk into this territory without permission! Which clan do you belong to?"

"What the fuck is going on? Who – what are you?" She struggled against him.

"Don't play dumb!" he snarled. "You hid your scent well, but you can't deny this!" He lifted her hand to her face.

Her eyes widened as she looked at her right arm. Much like his face had done earlier, the bones underneath were stretching and crawling. Hair sprouted in patches all over her skin, growing at an alarming pace. Her hands and fingers lengthened, growing out sharp claws. She let out a scream and pushed against him. Then, she blacked out.

CHAPTER TWO

"Oh god, someone turn off the sun," Alynna groaned as she slapped her hand over her eyes. Her head felt like she had been hit with a sledgehammer repeatedly. She let out a groan as her stomach rolled, and she ran to the bathroom in her tiny apartment to retch out what was left of her last meal.

Flushing the toilet, Alynna slowly stood up, steadying herself against the cold sink. *Holy shit!* She was fully naked. *And wow, how many drinks did I have?* Her skin was pale and dry, and her hair hung around her face in dark, stringy strands. There were dark bags under her dull, almost lifeless green eyes. She searched her memories, trying to remember what happened. Was she out on the town with friends? No wait, she didn't exactly have a lot of friends. None, actually.

"Fuck!" She slammed her palms on the counter. Greg Truman. Mrs. Truman. She was supposed to track him down and get evidence for her client. She racked her brain, trying to remember what happened. She followed Truman to Blood Moon, waited by the bar when he chatted up a girl and then ...

well, shit. Bits and pieces came to her. A handsome smile, golden eyes. Warm hands and then ...

With an annoyed sigh, Alynna grabbed a Tylenol from the medicine cabinet, swallowed it, then took a swig of water from the faucet. Was she drugged? Did she drink more than she could remember? She washed her face and then wiped it with a clean towel before heading out of the bathroom.

She grabbed her robe from her closet and wrapped it around herself. Aside from the headache and blackout memories, she felt normal. Actually, the awful headache was going away quickly. *Thank god for the miracle of modern drugs.*

"Sorry, Mom. Sorry, Uncle Gus," she said, looking at the two pictures on her work desk. One was of a pretty, smiling young woman with blonde hair who was holding a dark-haired toddler. The other was of an older man wearing an old-fashioned fedora and staring into the distance.

Uncle Gus taught her everything she knew about the PI business, and he had been like a father to her. In fact, when Alynna was fifteen, her mom passed away and Gus had taken her in, since Amanda Chase never spoke of Alynna's father. Her mother's brother was an old bachelor and worked late nights and long hours as a private detective, but he fought to get custody of Alynna despite only having met her three times. Needless to say, her teen years were interesting, and it only seemed natural she would take over for Gus when he died.

"Don't worry, old man," she said. "I won't disappoint our client. I always get my man, don't I?" It was strange to think of Mrs. Truman as "their" client, seeing as Gus passed away two years ago due to lung cancer leaving Alynna to run Chase Private Investigations. She had learned the business, but more importantly, a good work ethic from Gus. She was only twenty years old when she took over, but she had already been on her own stakeouts since she was seventeen. There was not enough money to go to college, but she already had a career and a business by the time she was eighteen, so she didn't need a degree.

Of course, there wasn't much time for anything else. Most days she worked fifteen hours and all she wanted to do when she wrapped up a case was crash in bed for some much deserved sleep. No time for hobbies, a social life, or even a love life. She wasn't sure this was what Gus and her mom wanted for her, but it was what she had.

Pushing those thoughts aside, she sat down at her work desk, trying to figure out how she would salvage this case. In the back of her mind also sat the mystery of what happened last night, but her client came first.

———

"Are you all right, dear?" Mary Truman asked as they sat down. "You look tired."

Alynna weakly smiled at her. "It's part of the job, I'm afraid," she fibbed. "But, I don't want to waste any more of your time." She handed the file over to the older woman.

Mary Truman was a beautiful, slim woman in her mid-forties. She had an ethereal, almost serene beauty about her, even though she was on the verge of tears. She was also very sweet. Alynna almost wished she had taken the chance and kneed Greg Truman in the balls. *Why the hell would a scumbag like Truman cheat on his perfect wife?* She mentally shrugged. In her experience, men rarely needed a good excuse.

"I ... I ..." Mrs. Truman pulled the pictures out of the manila envelope. "I can't ... I know these pictures show it. But, are you sure?" They were stills from the video she took of Mr. Truman entering the hotel with a hot young blonde. They were kissing and cuddling as they went into the lobby.

Alynna nodded. "Yes, I'm afraid so. I followed them to the hotel and all the way to their room. They didn't leave for at least four hours," she explained. "I have the full video and some, uh, audio I took from outside their room." Mr. Truman and his paramour were quite loud, and all she really had to do was stand outside their door and use one of her special microphones.

Mary's hands shook as she put the photos away. "Thank you, Ms. Chase," she said, then leaned back into her comfy armchair and took a sip of her tea.

Alynna didn't have a real office to work from, so she met clients at a coffee shop a few doors down from her apartment. She helped the owner with a big worker's comp case a year ago, and instead of charging her usual fee, the owner closed up a corner of the shop whenever she needed to conduct a private meeting.

"I'm happy to be of service, although I really wish it was under different circumstances," Alynna said sympathetically. As with all of her similar clients, Alynna gave Mary the business card of a great divorce lawyer she knew who always gave her a small commission, plus occasional free legal advice, before she escorted the older woman back to her car.

Alynna watched Mrs. Truman drive away before heading back to her apartment. It was a beautiful summer afternoon, but she hardly noticed. Aside from sleepless nights, she was tired from the case. After tracking Greg Truman for three days, she finally caught him. She almost wanted to jump for joy when she saw them enter the hotel room. Not that she wished all her clients were cheats – maybe ninety percent of them were – but she was just exhausted. Three days of no sleep took its toll. When she wasn't chasing Greg Truman around Manhattan, she was having these weird dreams. Although she wasn't sure if they were dreams, since she sometimes had them while awake. They started off pleasant enough. She felt good, wonderful actually.

She blushed thinking about it. There was a hot guy with a bangin' bod – tall, broad shoulders, abs, the works. She wasn't quite sure what was happening in the dream, but it was very nice. Then there would be flashes of golden eyes and something that made her skin crawl, followed by a terrible feeling. She shook her head, trying to forget. *I should really go to a doctor*, she thought. *Just to make sure I don't have any weird drugs in my system.*

Alynna reached her apartment building, a four-story converted brownstone in lower Manhattan. It had been Gus' place, small and tidy. It served its purpose well, and she had lived there ever since she was fifteen. She had taken over the single bedroom, as Gus would often crash on the couch after long stakeouts. She climbed up the stairs and said hello to Mrs. Anders, her neighbor on the third floor, before heading up to her own place.

As soon as she touched the doorknob to her apartment, she knew something was wrong. Gus told her she had strong instincts, *a natural,* he said. It wasn't magical, but she had learned to hone and trust her gut over the past couple of years. Right now it was telling her something wasn't right. With one hand, she took out the pepper spray from her purse and her keys with the other.

As quietly as she could, she slipped her key in the lock and turned it. Opening the door, she stepped inside. She froze as something hit her – a familiar scent. She couldn't quite figure out exactly what it smelled like, as if she had never smelled anything like it before. It was male and masculine, and the closest thing she could compare it to was like she was walking in the woods after the rain. Memories flooded back and she staggered backward, closing the door behind her. The man in the club. His hands all over her. Golden, feral eyes, and the claws. Closing her eyes, she remembered everything clearly, even the fact it was her own hand that sprouted those menacing claws.

"We're glad you've finally come back, Ms. Chase," a deep voice said.

Her eyes flew open. "What the – mmppphh!" A large hand came around her mouth and she was dragged up against a warm, hard body. The scent enveloped her again and instead of struggling, her body chose to sink against the person behind her. With wide eyes, she looked to her right where a man was sitting in her armchair.

He stood up and walked toward her, his stance imposing and strong. He was tall and lean, though Alynna suspected he was probably well-muscled and compact underneath his impeccable gray suit. He had blonde hair and sunglasses obscured his eyes.

"My name is Nick Vrost. If you promise not to scream, Ms. Chase, my friend will let go, okay?"

She nodded, realizing she didn't have much of a choice.

The hand on her mouth loosened its grip, as well as the arm around her waist. She moved forward, but curiosity got the better of her and she turned around. "You!" she exclaimed. The guy from the bar. Did something happen that night? Her memories suddenly came back, and she let out a sigh of relief when she remembered nothing had happened between them. *Nothing major.* At least, not before she blacked out.

"Yes, me." His hazel eyes twinkled. "Nice to see you again, 'Alice'."

Her eyes narrowed at him. "What did you do to me? Did you put something in my drink to make me hallucinate? How did I get home that night?"

The two men looked at each other, confusion on their faces.

"I should have you both arrested for breaking and entering!"

she shouted. "What the hell are you doing inside my apartment?"

Nick Vrost came closer to her and gripped her arm so tight, she didn't even try to struggle. He took off his glasses, revealing icy blue eyes. "You don't remember anything?" he asked, his gaze boring into her.

"Oh, I remember! This asshole drugged me and then pulled me to the back room to ... to ..." God, she really must have been under some powerful stuff if she almost had sex with a stranger! "But he must have used too much and I started imagining things. Then I blacked out. Did you bring me back here when you realized what you had done?" she snarled. "If you think I'm not pressing charges, think again!" She pointed a finger at the Alex's chest.

Nick Vrost raised an eyebrow at him and Alex just shrugged. The blonde man cleared his throat. "Ms. Chase, I think you should come with us."

"Come with you? Are you crazy?"

"If you want to know what happened that night, we can give you answers. But first you need to talk to our boss," Nick explained. "I promise it will be worth your while."

Curiosity pricked at her. Her instinct told her it wasn't a drug that made her see things, and she should at least hear them out.

"Lead the way, gentleman," she said. "But just in case, I'm keeping my cell phone handy." *And my pepper spray*, she added silently.

CHAPTER THREE

Alynna looked up at the imposing building in midtown Manhattan, right smack in the middle of Madison Avenue. She knew these guys must have been hired by some big guns, but she didn't realize *how* big.

Fenrir Corporation owned and was headquartered in one of the tallest buildings in New York City. The giant, black, obelisk-like structure rose to the sky, probably over seventy stories high. The ground floor was all luxury shops, restaurants, and commercial space, while the rest was devoted to offices for Fenrir, its subsidiaries, and related businesses. A lot of businesses. Fenrir had a hand in almost every type of industry, from shipping to manufacturing to retail. *Geez, I hope I didn't piss off anyone important,* she thought as the luxurious town car pulled into the basement garage of the building.

She sat in the back of the car, her arms crossed over her chest. "Where are we going?" she asked for about the hundredth time since she went with them. And for the hundredth time, her question was met with silence. Alex drove the car while Nick sat in front, so she couldn't read their faces. She was pretty sure the doors were locked from the outside, so she couldn't jump out even if she wanted to.

The car stopped and Nick stepped out, then headed to the opaque glass doors on the right. Alex got out and walked around to her side, opening the door. Ignoring his offered hand and cheeky smile, she followed right behind Nick.

The glass doors opened up to reveal a small receiving room, where a burly guard sat at a desk. He looked at Alynna, but when Nick nodded at him, he turned back to watching the monitors.

"You think Fenrir'd have better security than that, being a billion-dollar corporation and all. Am I right?" she joked as the elevator doors opened. Nick remained steely, stepping into the elevator car first. Alex held the door and motioned for her to get in, a grin on his face, though he remained silent.

Alynna stood in the middle of the elevator while Nick stood to her left, though slightly ahead of her. Alex stepped in, taking the spot to her right. Nick pressed his palm to the plate beside the doors, then keyed in the "P" button.

She swallowed a gulp, sweat slowly beading on her temples. Top floor, penthouse. Who could she be meeting that was literally and figuratively that high up? *And for God's sake, what the heck was that scent?* It was a little faint now, but she could still smell it. It wasn't unpleasant, but it was just too strange how it seemed to linger in the air. "Someone needs to tone down the aftershave," she muttered to no one in particular.

Finally, the elevator stopped. The doors opened and Nick walked out first.

"After you," Alex said, holding the elevator door open once again.

Alynna gave him a nod and followed Nick down the plush hallway. Everything was sleek, modern, and expensive. In her Gap blouse, skinny jeans, and worn boots, she suddenly felt scruffy. She spied views of the East River through one of the windows and had to stop herself from whistling.

At the end of the long hallway was a set of large wooden doors. A young man sat at the desk next to them. He was in his early twenties and wearing an expensive-looking suit that probably cost what she made in a month.

"Mr. Anderson is waiting for you and your guest, Mr. Vrost," he said, standing up and giving him a small nod.

The man kept his head bowed until Nick spoke. "Thank you, Jared. We'll let ourselves in."

He pushed the door open and walked inside the huge room. It must have taken up an entire corner of the top floor. The décor was intimidating and ultra-modern, the floor to ceiling glass windows revealing a spectacular view of New York and Central Park. Standing by the window was a tall, imposing man. The light from the outside made his form into nothing but shadow. Alynna didn't know who it was, but for some reason felt like she wanted to cower. *Don't be intimidated*, she told herself as she squared her shoulders.

The figure turned around to face them and as he came closer, she could make out his features. He was good-looking, older, maybe mid-to-late thirties, with thick dark hair and green eyes that glittered like emeralds and looked hard as diamonds. He wore a suit which probably cost what she made in a year. She instantly knew who this man was, having read a couple of articles and, admittedly, some gossip rags about him. She was meeting with Grant Anderson, CEO of Fenrir Corporation.

"Have a seat, Ms. Chase," he said, his voice strong and forceful. Of course he knew her name. "My name is Grant Anderson."

It was almost like she felt compelled to follow him, and she seated herself in one of the chairs by the large mahogany table in the center of the room. She crossed and uncrossed her legs nervously. A new scent drifted into her nostrils. It wasn't like the previous one. This one smelled like the beach. Clean, salty air. It was pleasant, and she felt strangely warm and at home.

The man moved closer and sat behind the desk while Nick followed him, standing on his right side, while Alex remained behind her. He sat back, placing his interlaced fingers over his abdomen. "Ms. Chase, do you know why you're here today?"

"You tell me, Mr. Anderson," she said, planting both feet on the floor and leaning forward. "You were the one who had a couple of your goons break into my home and then bring me here. Is that what CEOs do these days?"

His lips tightened. "Let's cut the bullshit. Tell me, does the Constanta Agreement mean anything to you? The Vaduva Wars?"

"What are you babbling about? And since we're asking questions, what about the drug your flunky gave me?" She nodded toward Alex.

"A drug? You thought you were drugged?" he asked, his voice carefully controlled. "That's a pathetic excuse, and you must know venturing into New York without permission from me and your Regal is practically asking for war."

"Dude!" she said, shooting up to her feet. "What the heck is going on? Maybe you guys are the ones on drugs!" She stiffened her shoulders. "That's it. I'm leaving." She turned toward the door and started to walk away, but Nick moved with almost superhuman speed and grabbed her arm. "Let go of me!" she said, her voice turning into a growl. *Where did that come from?* Alynna felt faint again, her stomach churning, much like it did that night she blacked out. *Oh God, was that scent some sort of airborne drug?*

"Primul." Nick turned to Grant. "Perhaps you should take shelter in the safe room."

"No," Grant said, coming closer. "She can't deny it now, not when she's in the middle of a shift. Tell me, lupoaică, where did you come from? Who is your Regal?"

Before she could say anything else, pain shot through her body. She didn't know why, but this time, it was worse. She felt dizzy too, and she crumpled against Nick. He let her fall to the ground, but kept his grip on her arm. She whimpered in pain, her arm twisting unnaturally. "Hurts ... don't ... help, please!" A snarl came from behind her and she looked up weakly as Alex approached her. Her vision started to go hazy, but she could see his eyes blazed in anger.

"Stand down, Alex," Nick said as he held onto Alynna.

Alex suddenly stopped, his fists clenched at his sides. He looked down at the girl half-crumpled on the floor, his face conflicted. "Yes, Al Doilea," he said, bowing his head.

"Ms. Chase," Grant said looking down at her, his eyes turning into dark green pools. "Tell me which clan you belong to and maybe we'll return you to them in one piece!"

"I don't know what you're talking about!" she snapped at him. Somehow, she found the strength to break free from Nick's grasp and lunge at Grant.

Surprised, Grant didn't have time to move away and Alynna's small frame tackled him to the ground. Her hands began to stretch and grow claws, and she swiped at him. This time, he knew to protect himself, and he grabbed her arms before she could do any damage.

"Primul!" Nick called out. He grabbed Alynna and pulled her off Grant. He cursed at her and then flung her away toward the wall with unnatural strength. She hit it with such force her brain rattled in her skull.

"Alynna!" Alex called. This time, he did not remain still, but sprang toward her.

Without warning, Alynna shot up at him, her claws bared, growling loudly. Her eyes were bright green and the bones underneath her cheeks moved and crawled. Alex caught her wrists. "It's okay, Alynna, fight it. It doesn't control you," he said in a soothing voice, his thumbs circling her wrists.

For a brief moment, her eyes turned normal. "Alex?! What's going on ... who ... what ..." Suddenly, she let out a pained whimper, her eyes rolled back and she slumped against him.

Alex's eyes widened in surprise, then he looked up at Nick. He stood there with his arm extended, his just-fired weapon pointing at them.

CHAPTER FOUR

Alynna awoke slowly, her eyes fluttering open. "Not again," she groaned, feeling the same uneasiness in her stomach and maddening headache. At least this time, she had remembered to close the curtains.

"Fuck!" she cursed softly. *I don't have curtains.* She sat up quickly, looking around her, but it only made her stomach worse. She looked to the side and saw a trashcan. It was close enough that she could bend down and throw up without leaving the bed.

"Are you okay?" A soft, feminine voice from somewhere in the room startled Alynna and she nearly lost her grip on the trashcan. "There're some wipes beside you."

Turning to the bedside table, she saw the wipes and grabbed them. "Who are you? Where am I?" she asked, cleaning her lips with the soft, damp cloth. She struggled to get up, throwing the covers from her body. A rattling sound came from somewhere in the dim room, and when she looked down at her feet, she realized there was a chain around her ankle.

There was a gasp from across the room and a figure emerged from the darkness. It was a petite redhead with a gorgeously delicate face, which was now a mask of shock when her eyes landed on the chain. "I'm so sorry! I told them this was totally unnecessary!" She looked down, grabbed the links, and tried to figure out a way to unlock it. "I don't know how to take this off."

Alynna yanked at the chain, but it seemed pretty solid. *What the fuck did I get myself into?* It was just like when she blacked out after going to Blood Moon, but this time she remembered everything. The memories flooded back to her and she let out a small cry, covering her face with her hands as tears flowed down her cheeks.

"Oh my. Are you okay?" the redhead asked, a concerned look on her face. She sat by Alynna, but didn't touch her. "What's the matter?"

"You tell me!" she said angrily, waving her hands at the woman. "I'm chained to a bed, probably in some dingy basement where no one will ever find my body, AND apparently I'm some sort of monster!" She sobbed into her hands.

"Alynna," the woman's voice was soothing. "You really don't know, do you?"

She looked up, her face confused. "What are you talking about? Why won't you just tell me what's going on here?"

The redhead sighed. "Alynna, were you adopted? Do you know who your parents were?"

Alynna nodded. "Of course I know who they were. Well, I know my mom's definitely my mom. When she died my uncle kind of adopted me; he became my guardian until I was of legal age."

"And your dad?"

"I didn't know him." Alynna went quiet. "I've learned to live without a father, so I don't think about him much. My mom implied she left him, but I never got a straight answer."

There was a brief spark of surprise in the other woman's eyes. "That may explain it! You see Alynna –"

Before she could explain further, the door flew open. A dark, shadowed figure stood in the entryway. "We need to take her to the Alpha," the figure said, looming inside the doorway.

The redhead turned her head toward the door. "Mr. Vrost, please. We need some privacy here, and it's my duty to smooth things over with Ms. Chase."

"It's my duty to keep our Regal safe and obey his orders, Ms. Gray. He wants her in his office now." His voice was even, but commanding.

She nodded. "Could you give me a few minutes please? She's not feeling very well, and I want to make sure she's presentable for Grant."

The man nodded and tossed her a set of keys. "All right. Five minutes. But if you're not out by then, I'm coming in here to get her myself." Without another word, he turned around and closed the door behind him.

The woman turned back to Alynna. "Look, I'm sure you're very frightened. But if you could please trust me, things are going to be okay. I'll do my best to help you, but you need to keep an open mind, all right?"

Alynna wanted to cry again, this time out of the small sliver of hope the woman gave her. "Th – thank you. I don't even know your name."

"Oh goodness! I'm sorry!" she exclaimed. "Cady Gray." She held out her hand. "Officially I'm Mr. Anderson's Personal Executive Assistant, but most people here like to think of me as VP of Human Relations." She chuckled, as if sharing a joke.

Alynna raised her eyebrow. "I've heard of Public Relations and Human Resources, but not Human Relations. Is that a combined role?"

"Err ..." Cady stammered. "Something like that. But I think I'll let Grant tell you more."

Cady helped Alynna remove the chains and get cleaned up. Alynna was shocked to find she had been out for almost ten hours, and it was already late evening. She was still wearing the rumpled jeans and blouse from that morning, and she cleaned up as best she could before following Cady out of the room. Nick was waiting for them outside, and he led the two women down a long hallway and into an elevator. Walking inside, Nick pressed his palm on the sensor and the elevator zipped up, how many floors, Alynna wasn't sure.

When the doors opened, Nick, Alynna and Cady were once again in the penthouse offices of Fenrir Corp. As they walked into Grant Anderson's office, Alynna heard two male voices talking.

"...Are you sure Dr. Faulkner?" Alynna recognized the low timbre of Grant Anderson's voice.

"I've run the tests thrice, just as you asked. Same results each time."

"This could complicate things."

There was a long pause. "It doesn't have to. You're still thirteen years older than her and Michael's chosen one."

"It's not that, Doctor," Grant sighed. "The clan's been after me to produce an heir. And now that –"

A discreet cough interrupted Grant. "Primul, she's here," Nick said as he entered the room.

"Thank you, Nick." Grant nodded to Dr. Faulkner who then sat in one of the chairs in front of his desk. He then turned to Alynna. "Please come in and have a seat, Ms. Chase."

The redhead ushered her into Grant's office, gave her hand a reassuring squeeze, and then left with a nod to the men, her head held high. She sat down in the other chair, giving Dr.

Faulkner an acknowledging nod. Nick took his place on Grant's right side.

There was an uncomfortable silence until Grant cleared his throat and began to speak. "Tell me, Ms. Chase ... Alynna," he began. "Did you ever meet your father?"

Alynna felt her anger begin to simmer at the deeply personal question. "I don't think that's any of your business, Mr. Anderson," she huffed. "But if it's going to make this interrogation go faster, then let me answer you. No, I have not. My mother died before she was able to tell me anything about him."

"And you didn't ask her? Before she died?" he pressed.

"She was a little too busy fighting cancer, so, no, I did not," she said in a defensive voice.

"I'm sorry for your loss," Grant responded, his tone sincere, "and for the nature of these questions. But perhaps we should just cut to the chase. Dr. Faulkner." He turned to the older man. "Could you please give Ms. Chase a copy of your report?"

Dr. Faulkner gave her a reassuring smile and handed her an envelope. "Hello, my dear. I'm Dr. Tom Faulkner, and I was the one who processed your test. There's a summary at the beginning, but you may skim through the whole thing if you wish and ask me any questions as well."

Alynna raised an eyebrow at the doctor and Grant, but took the report anyway. She opened it and started reading. She felt her hands begin to sweat and she felt faint. There was also a sinking feeling in her stomach, which seemed to grow as she read more of the report. DNA results positive ... non-human ... Lycan one hundred percent. *Lycan? That was like a werewolf, right?*

"No," she said softly, looking at Dr. Faulkner. It took every ounce of her control not to look at Grant. "It can't be. This is a joke, right?" This was some sort of hidden camera show and they were actors. She continued to stare at them, waiting for them to break character, but their faces remained serious.

Dr. Faulkner took his glasses off. "I'm afraid DNA tests don't lie, my dear. We have some of the best here, far more sophisticated than any human test."

Her hands shook as she closed the folder. "So let me get this straight ... what you're saying is my father ... was a werewolf?"

"Yes," the doctor confirmed. "We do prefer Lycan, shifter, or varcolac in our native Romanian."

"I'm half Lycan?" she asked. She couldn't say werewolf out loud, as if doing so would make it more real.

"On the contrary, Ms. Chase," he stated. "You are full Lycan. You have the same biology as any of us."

"But how can that be?" She already had a hard time believing she was half wolf. Or that werewolves existed. *Oh god, that sounded crazy.* Why wasn't she fighting this harder? "My mother was fully human according to these test results."

Dr. Faulkner and Grant looked at each other and the younger man nodded. "It's very rare. In fact, I believe you're the first one in about two generations, but ... uh ..." The old man struggled to find his words. "Your parents were what we call True Mates."

"True Mates?" she echoed.

He nodded. "You see, Lycans breed and have children much like any species. However, once in a while, a Lycan will meet someone – could be human or Lycan – that he or she is destined for." He shrugged.

"Like soulmates? That's like magic and stuff, right?" she asked. "Wait, what other types of people exist aside from Lycans? Witches? Vampires?"

"Er ... yes ... and no," he explained. "First, no, vampires aren't real I'm afraid, so I hope you're not too disappointed, especially if you love those novels and movies."

Alynna cracked a weak smile. "I was never a fan."

"But," he continued. "Witches and warlocks, yes. We have a tenuous peace with them, and they do tend to stay away. But I digress," he said. "We like to think magic and science are somewhat interconnected. Exactly how, well, we're not sure yet, but we keep our minds open and continue to do more research. The explanation behind True Mates, for example, could be magic-based or evolution-based. Sure, we could all be destined for that one person, but also our bodies, seeking the best possible partner, choose mates who are most biologically compatible and could produce the best and strongest pups. The past research on the subject is very limited, but some of the material we do have says that True Mates will know each other by scent, something particularly pleasant for them and gives them a physical reaction when they first meet. We do know one thing for sure," he said. "Not taking into account physical contraceptives, True Mates will always produce offspring with the first coupling."

Alynna gulped. "So what you're saying is my parents had sex once and nine months later ... surprise?!"

"Most likely, yes."

There was another pause. "I don't know what I'm supposed to do with all this information," she confessed. "I'm a were – er – Lycan. Do I get superpowers? Do I have to shave more?" she asked with a nervous laugh. She could have sworn Nick Vrost cracked a slight smile, but she chalked it up to her imagination.

"Well, it explains a lot of things. But, I'm afraid there's more." The doctor looked slightly nervous.

"There's more?" She could hardly believe there would be more to this story. "Wait. I'm not half-unicorn, am I?" This time she thought she heard a slight cough. Nick definitely had to stifle a laugh.

"Um, no. You see, there's the matter of who your father was. He was a ... the ..." Dr. Faulkner looked toward Grant.

"What he's trying to say, Alynna," Grant interrupted, "is your father used to be our leader. Michael Anderson."

Alynna practically jolted from her seat. "Michael Anderson?" She looked at Grant. "He's ... he was your ..."

Grant nodded. "Yes. Alpha of Clan New York before me. My father."

She sank back down to her seat and buried her face in her hands. "No. My mom never said ... she didn't even ..." Alynna felt tears forming in her eyes but mustered every bit of courage to stop herself. Michael Anderson. Finally, a name to a shadow that had loomed over her entire life.

"She probably didn't know," Dr. Faulkner explained. "It may be even Michael didn't know."

Shock, sadness, hurt, and anger went through her at lightning speed. She looked up at Grant. "There must be a mistake. Run the tests again." She stood up and began to pace. "No one knows about me, right? That's good. No one has to know. I'll live my life like this never happened. Or maybe I'll move to Alaska ..." she babbled, scratching her head.

"Ms. Chase, have a seat, please," Dr. Faulkner said. "You seem mentally stressed. I can prescribe you something to calm you down."

"I am calm!" she said, whipping her head around. "Listen, I'll just go okay? I'm not part of your ... group or clan. I don't want anything. I've been on my own for years and I'll be okay." She turned to Grant. "Hey, so, like ... thanks for keeping me on the up and up, and you have a nice life. I mean you are a billionaire, so that's no problem. Not that it matters to me. You're famous and everything, so that's not a secret. But like I said, I don't need anything, so you don't have to worry. I'll even sign a ... it's not a prenup I guess, but whatever would be the equivalent in this ... situation."

"I think we should bring you back to Medical." Dr. Faulkner stood up.

"No!" She turned toward the door. "I'll be fine. I can catch a cab."

The doctor and Nick looked at Grant, who just sat there, staring. "Take care, Ms. Chase," he said. "But do let one our guards call a cab for you."

"Uh, sure ..." She nodded as she walked out the door. She breezed past his admin, who looked at her strangely. Alynna ignored him and kept walking to the elevators, jabbing the down button repeatedly. *God, what a day.* She breathed a deep sigh as the doors opened and she stepped inside.

―――――

As soon as Alynna left and the heavy wooden doors closed, Dr. Faulkner turned to the younger man. "Grant!" Dr. Faulkner scolded, looking at him in disbelief. "You may be Alpha now, but I was your father's best friend and second-in-command. You know you can't let her leave and not just because she knows about us!"

Grant shook his head. "I'm not letting her go and forgetting about her, Dr. Faulkner. Nick will have someone keep an eye on her and then report to me. She seemed to have warmed up to Cady; we'll send her in later. But she needs time to process this new information."

The older man sighed and shook his head. "Maybe she's not the only one."

CHAPTER FIVE

"Don't worry, Mr. Garson," Alynna assured as she bid her new client goodbye. "I'll start right away."

"Thank you, Ms. Chase," said Tom Garson. "And whatever you find out ... just give it to me straight, okay?" He jumped into the waiting cab.

"Well, that was a first," she stated out loud. Her first male client. Mr. Thomas Garson suspected his wife, Lydia, of cheating on him. Mr. Garson seemed like an okay guy, and she really hoped Lydia wasn't cheating. But, she was paid to find out these things and report back to her clients.

She took the long route back to her apartment from the coffee shop, going up a block further so she could stop by her favorite bakery to get some bagels and cream cheese. Today was an asiago cheese bagel with honey pecan cream cheese kind of day. Of course, this was the fifth time this week she'd had that bagel, but who the heck was counting anyway? As she walked into the bakery, the delicious scent of fresh-baked bread called to her. Although the scent was familiar, today it seemed different. Aside from the yeasty scent, she could smell rosewater and something sweet, like sugar cookies.

"Good morning, Alynna," greeted Mrs. Aaronson, the kindly old Jewish woman who owned the bakery. "The usual?"

She nodded without a word. As the old lady began to prepare her order, she thought back to the report that was sitting in her apartment and some of the things she had read about being a Lycan. Enhanced senses ... particularly taste and smell. It seemed after she read that she began to pick up a lot more things. The first day had been almost overwhelming. She could not only smell her next-door neighbor, Mrs. Patel's, cooking, but also the scent of the patchouli oil she regularly rubbed on her wrists. She walked outside, which was a mistake, as New York City practically assaulted her nose. Garbage, food, people, animals all mixed together, and she almost passed out on the street. She was able to calm herself down enough to get back up to her apartment, and after some time she gained control and was able to keep some of the scents out of her sensitive nose.

She gave her thanks to Mrs. Aaronson and left with a paper bag in her hand. As she approached her apartment building, she felt a weird sensation, like a prickling along the back of her neck before that familiar, masculine scent hit her nose.

"What are you doing here?" she groaned. She really just wanted to go home and devour her bagel.

Alex stood on her stoop, casually leaning against the entryway to her building. He looked devastatingly handsome with that knowing smile on his face and his honey gold eyes twinkling. "Oh, you know. I was in the neighborhood."

"A likely story." She hopped up the stairs to get to where he was standing. "Can I get by now? Or is this not a free country anymore?"

"Alynna," called a soft voice from behind. "I apologize for the intrusion. Alex drove me out here and I asked him to wait for you while I made a call in the car."

"Cady." Alynna acknowledged the pretty redhead standing behind her, her demeanor taking on a less chilly tone. "Is there something I can help you with?"

"Well," Cady began, "I was wondering if we could talk? Sit down somewhere, maybe have lunch?"

Alynna crossed her arms. "Now seems like a good time. So, what do you want to say?"

Cady sighed. "Please, Alynna. I just want to speak with you and maybe we could come to an understanding?"

"Understanding?" she said in an incredulous voice. "I thought Mr. Anderson and I already had an agreement. I would stay away and not demand anything of him, and he would leave me alone."

The redhead raised an eyebrow and squared her shoulders. "Actually, I was told Mr. Anderson agreed to no such thing. You walked out without a by-your-leave."

Alynna's eyes narrowed, realizing she may have underestimated the woman. "I don't care much for Mr. Anderson or the flunkies he's had tailing me these last couple of days. Surprised? Yes, I knew about them; they had the subtlety of heat-seeking missiles. Now please leave."

Alex guffawed, but Cady paid him no mind. She opened her mouth, but before she could say anything, her phone rang. "Gray," she answered in a cool voice. Her face changed slightly and then put her hand over the receiver of her phone. "I'm sorry, I have to take this call." She walked back to the car and slipped inside gracefully.

"Heat-seeking missile, eh?" Alex asked, moving closer to Alynna.

"Do you mind?" she asked as she stepped back. Unfortunately, she miscalculated the distance of the next step and she began to fall backward. Before she could even let out a yell, strong hands wrapped around her waist pulling her back. The momentum shot her forward, and she fell against him.

A wonderful scent filled her nostrils, wrapping around her very being. It was obvious it was Alex she'd been smelling the whole time, something she chalked up to her newly enhanced senses.

They stood together for a moment, his warm hands on her waist. Her shirt had slightly ridden up, and the fingers on his right hand grazed her naked skin. It was like a hot brand, and her heart began to beat faster. She braced herself against his chest. "I'm fine now. You can let go."

She heard a soft growl rumbling from his chest, but he released her. They stood close to each other and once again, that delicious, earthy scent lingered between them.

"Alex," Cady called from the car. "We have to go. Now. I'm sorry, Alynna. I have an emergency. I'll come by another time, okay?"

"Duty calls," he said. Alynna stood aside to let him by. Alex winked at her as he passed, but not before he let his fingers brush hers slightly.

Alynna stood there, rooted to the spot by some unknown reason, and watched them drive away. She had a feeling this wouldn't be the last time she'd see them.

———

She wished she had been wrong, but a week later, Alynna spotted another tail. She put her camera away, tucking it into the large backpack she carried whenever she did surveillance. It was about one a.m., but it wasn't an unusual hour to be out when she was on the job.

She hopped down from the fire escape staircase and dusted

off the rust that had rubbed on her jacket. Her eyes were immediately drawn to the car at the end of the block, where it had been since she climbed up the stairs. A lone figure in the driver's seat was hunched over, trying to look inconspicuous. She strapped the backpack on properly over her shoulders and across her chest, then stalked over to the car.

"Hey," she greeted as she rapped on the driver's side window. The window rolled down. *Christ, just my luck.* She gave Alex a tight smile. *It had to be him.*

"All done?" he asked in a good-natured tone. Amber eyes seemed to glow at her in the darkness of the car.

"Yep. You can go home now." She turned and began walking down the sidewalk. A few seconds later, the car behind her roared to life. But instead of driving away, the vehicle simply rolled alongside her. She walked a few more steps, hoping he'd drive away, but he kept following her. She stopped and faced the car.

"Can I help you?!" she said loudly, putting her hands on her hips.

Alex grinned at her. "Aren't you hungry after two hours of sitting on that fire escape?"

"I'm gonna pick up a slice of pizza on the way home," she retorted.

"I know a place that serves a great key lime pie. They're open all night long."

Alynna's stomach decided it was a great time to gurgle hungrily at the thought of key lime pie. *Fuck.*

Alex cracked a smile at the sound of her hungry, traitorous tummy. "Hop in."

Alynna sighed in defeat and strode over to the passenger side, yanked the door open, sat inside, and sulked like a child.

———

They drove in silence, heading toward the Upper West Side. After a few minutes, Alex pulled up in front of a diner and put the gear in park.

"I don't think I've ever heard about this place," Alynna said as she slid into the booth seat across from Alex. The sign outside read "Elsie's Diner," and the inside was pure old school Americana kitsch – weathered Formica tables and counter, bright red vinyl stools and booths, a mosaic tile floor, and beautifully carved woodwork was all over the walls.

"Yeah, I discovered this place after working a couple of overnight shifts," Alex said, pushing the menu at her. "Try the burgers. They're huge and juicy. The shakes are pretty good too; they make 'em with malt and everything."

She pushed the menu back at him. "I was told there'd be pie."

"Your wish is my command," he said, standing up and heading toward the counter.

Alex put his hands in his pockets as he casually strode alongside the counter and over to the display of pies at the end. He wasn't quite sure what prompted him to invite Alynna out to eat. In fact, he wasn't even sure what he was doing. Who was this mysterious woman, or Lycan, and why did the Alpha order twenty-four hour surveillance on her? The Beta had only told the rest of the team that she was prone to uncontrollable shifts and would need to be subdued if she were to turn while in public. Other than that they were to stay away from her. Of course, he didn't tell the team about what he'd witnessed himself – she didn't even seem to know she was a Lycan, which was already strange to him.

He admitted he was drawn to her, from the first moment he saw her, standing there in Blood Moon. Okay, he was more than drawn to her. He wanted her. He wanted to touch her porcelain smooth skin and see desire in those green eyes. He wanted to taste her lips, to touch her, and make her moan again. He wanted to take her to bed and slake his thirst and desire until they both passed out. Did she even remember what happened to them that night? He sure did, and it haunted his dreams. It was strange, what he felt when they first met. He'd been with lots of women, Lycan and human, but never felt quite like that before. Even standing next to her, it was like he was drawn to her and he couldn't do a damn thing about it. And her damn feminine scent was driving him crazy. It was floral, but fresh and clean.

Pushing those thoughts away with a shake of his head, Alex concentrated on the task at hand, peering at the pie display case. "Oh damn," he cursed. There was one piece of key lime pie left.

"Any chance you have a whole pie in the back?" Alex asked to the figure behind the counter.

An older man with white hair stood and turned around to face him, his hands on his hips. His face was weathered, but he seemed to be quite cheery and awake for someone up at one in the morning. "Sorry, sonny." The older man shook his head. "Last one, I'm afraid." Alex groaned. "Can I give you some advice, son?"

The older man reminded Alex of his father, so he couldn't help but nod.

"When I was younger, I asked my dad what love was. I was six," he began as he took a plate from behind the counter and placed the lone slice on it. "He said, Eddie, love is when you have one last piece of pie, but you give it to her. It could be your favorite piece of pie. You could be hungry and your insides turning. It could be the best ever piece of pie you'll never ever have again. But, love is when you give her the piece of pie and say, 'No, you can have it.'"

Alex stood there, pondering the older man's words.

"So, my advice is," he handed him the plate, "let her have the pie."

Alex looked over to where Alynna was sitting. "Right."

The older man winked at him. As Alex fished out his wallet, the man reached over and put a hand on his arm. "On me."

He smiled at the man and thanked him, then walked toward Alynna. He sat down across from her.

"No more pie?" Alynna asked.

"Just one more slice."

"Are you gonna share with me?"

Alex shook his head. "No, you can have it." He smiled as he pushed the plate toward her.

"You sure?" Alynna looked at him suspiciously. "This isn't crappy, defrosted pie, right?"

"It's not," he laughed. "Go ahead. I actually had a burrito in the car while I was waiting for you."

She looked at the pie hungrily and dug in with her spoon. "Oh my god," she moaned as she took a mouthful. "This is pretty good pie."

"See? I told you."

"Hmm ..." Alynna replied, her mouth full of pastry and whipped cream.

The old man who had served the pie came over to them and brought them two cups of coffee. Alynna nodded her thanks and took a swig, washing down the last of the pie with the hot brown liquid.

"That was delicious," she declared as she dabbed her mouth with a napkin. "Thanks for bringing me here."

"No worries." He leaned over, his long frame allowing him to stretch across the table and wipe some crumbs from the corner of her mouth.

"You should have told me I had pie on my face." She pouted.

"I know, but you looked too cute with pie on your face." He gave her a flirty smirk.

Alynna rolled her eyes. "Right. With crumbs all over me."

"Too cute. Makes me want to lick it off." Alex gave her a hot stare, which made Alynna blush furiously.

She pushed the plate away and quickly changed the subject. "All right, I'm done. That was good pie," she remarked. "Thank you."

He gave her a bright smile, which made him look even more handsome and boyish. "You're welcome."

She yawned. "Well, I'm gonna go catch a cab and head home."

"No need. I'll take you home."

Alynna was too tired to argue. "Fine." She yawned again, then stood up and stretched. "Home, James!" she joked.

Alex stood up and offered his arm. "Well, my lady, your carriage awaits."

She guffawed and looped her arm through his. As they walked out and left the diner, the old man waved at the couple, then raised his fist in silent cheer at Alex.

"What was that about?" Alynna asked as she entered the car.

"Oh, nothing." Alex switched the subject. "So, are you always gonna be out this late?"

"Are you worried about following me cutting into your social life?"

"I'm worried about my pie budget." He smirked at her, which earned him a smirk back.

The trip to Alynna's apartment was relatively quick since there was no traffic. "Well, thanks for the pie ... and the ride. You should head home," Alynna said as she opened the car door.

"You sure you don't want me to walk you up?" he asked hopefully.

"I can manage," she said dryly and stepped out of the car.

Despite her shutting him down, he definitely saw the hesitation in her eyes for just a split second.

CHAPTER SIX

The next day, after running a couple of errands, Alynna came home to her door unlocked once again. Alynna sighed in resignation as she pushed it open with her shoulders, her arms around two large bags of groceries. A scent of cool, ocean spray hit her nose.

"You know, breaking and entering is illegal in the State of New York," she said as she set the bags down on her small kitchen counter. She didn't even bother looking toward the living room. "And this is the second time now."

"You wouldn't answer our calls." Grant stood up from her armchair.

"I thought I made myself clear from the beginning." She turned to look at him. Grant was dressed in one of his expensive suits, but his tie was gone. As usual, Nick stood next to him, ever ready for any possibility. "I don't want to be part of this."

"You are a part of 'this'," he stated. "Whether you like it or not." Grant let out a breath. "Nick, please give us a moment."

Nick nodded. "I'll be right outside, Primul," he said and then left the apartment, closing the door behind him to give them some privacy.

"Why does he call you that?" Alynna asked, hoping to change the subject.

"Primul?" Grant asked. "It means 'first' in Romanian. It's customary for my lieutenants under me or any Lycan to address their Alpha as such." He shrugged. "Anyway, Alynna, I think you must have misunderstood why I let you go. It wasn't because I was letting you walk away from all this. I wanted to give you space, some time to process, but I can't sit by and let this go on. You must come with me and take your place; come under my protection."

"My place?" she asked, her voice taking on a higher pitch. "What exactly is that? What part don't you get, Mr. Anderson?" She threw her hands up. "My entire life I never needed or wanted a father. He didn't want me, and I certainly don't need anything from him now!" she seethed.

"Alynna, if you think my fa – Michael Anderson didn't want you, you're dead wrong."

"Oh yeah?" she asked bitterly. "Then why did he leave my mother without saying goodbye?" Grant said nothing, so she continued. "You know, I think she may have loved him. I remember some nights she would cry herself to sleep, and she would never tell me why, but I suspected it had something to do with my father."

"I'm sorry," Grant said in a low voice. "I've had our security department put together a file on you. I know you and your mother didn't always have it easy. She worked as a waitress, correct? I can imagine it wasn't easy making ends meet, especially as a single mom."

Alynna slammed her palms on the counter. "I don't care about that! Sure, I didn't grow up in a fancy house like you, but my mother did her best and she always put food on the table and clothes on my back." She bit her lip to keep from crying. "She was sad and depressed. Where was he? Where was he when she was dying of cancer? If he left her to go back to his wife, then he should have just been straight with her instead of playing around with her feelings!"

Grant came closer to her, then put a thick file folder on the counter. "Alynna, you may not believe me, but perhaps you'll believe him."

"Who?" Alynna asked, her eyes shining bright with tears.

"Michael. Our father."

Alynna felt a lump in her throat when he said those words. Somehow, neither of them had acknowledged the fact they had shared a father and what that implied. She stared at the folder, unable to look him in the eye. Gingerly, she opened the file. The first thing she saw was a picture of an older man who looked similar to Grant. He had the same dark hair and green eyes, although his locks were liberally peppered with white hair and there more wrinkles around his mouth and brow. He was laughing and looking down at a baby wrapped in a pink cloth, while a blonde woman on a hospital bed smiled at them.

"My father's lawyers brought this to us when they heard you showed up at Fenrir and the DNA tests proved who you were," he explained.

"I don't understand," she whispered, lifting the picture up for a closer inspection.

"It's all there in the files." Grant watched as she stared disbelievingly at the photo, the rest of the papers ignored. "Let me give you a summary: Michael knew about you. In fact, he left a provision in his will for you, acknowledging you as his child with his True Mate, Amanda Chase. However, no one else knew about you," Grant stated. "He wanted to protect you, and since there hadn't been a True Mate pairing in almost two hundred years, he wanted to keep your existence a secret until a Lycan DNA test could be run." He stood by her and looked at the picture. "Alynna, check out the date on that photo."

She turned it around. "It's ... I was born that day."

"A few hours after that photo was taken, he died in a car accident," he explained.

Alynna detected a slight shake in his voice, but his face remained stoic. "I'm sorry. I mean, I didn't know ..." she stammered. She felt a knot in the pit of her stomach.

"It was a shock to all of us. I was thirteen. While your mom was pregnant, Dad had all the papers drawn up and his instructions were clear: nothing was to come out until the test results proved what he already knew. You were supposed to come in for a blood test in a few days."

For the first time in her life, Alynna was truly and utterly speechless. She looked at the other files, stuff that looked like wills and important papers. There was also a copy of her birth certificate, much like the one she had, but instead of "unknown" for "Father" it listed "Michael Dmitri Anderson." Also, it had her last name as "Anderson" and not "Chase." She held up the yellowed piece of paper and there was a note attached to it with elegant handwriting that read "amended – to be filed."

"Your middle name," Grant mentioned.

She looked up at him. "Oh god, that name?" She gave a sour face. "I never use it. Why?"

He gave her a weak smile. "Alynna Antoaneta Anderson," he said, reading the name on the certificate. "I'm glad your mom decided to keep it. It means 'priceless' in Romanian."

Turning around, Alynna let out a quiet sob and unshed tears began to flow down her cheeks. She wiped them away quickly, hoping Grant hadn't noticed them. "I can't ... I don't know ..."

"Look," Grant began. "I know this is all too much. Believe me, I'm having a difficult time myself and you ... well ..." He cleared his throat. "I'm doing this because it's what Dad would have wanted. It's the right thing to do."

She sighed. "Look, if it's a money thing, I told you, I don't want anything. I know this place isn't exactly the Ritz," she said sheepishly. "But I'm fine."

"It's not that I don't believe you," Grant stated. "But it's not just that. Don't you see, Alynna? You didn't grow up as a Lycan, nor given the same training as us. You just turned twenty-two, right? Have you ever shifted before? When you were younger?"

She shook her head.

"Alynna, all Lycans start the shift around puberty. It's usually unintentional for most of us, triggered by hormones or emotion. These types of shifts, they're dangerous because you're basically turning into an animal. Normally you do it at home, where you can be protected."

Alynna swallowed a gulp. "When I turned ... I don't remember anything. I just blacked out and then woke up hours later." She had a vision of herself as a wolf, stalking the streets of New York. *Did I hurt anyone that night?* Her heart pounded, thinking about what could have happened.

"We're all taught how to tame and take control of our wolf and how to stop shifting accidentally. Eventually, we learn how to shift back and forth at will and remember our time as a wolf." He pulled her to face him. "There are also many other things you need to be taught, to help you protect yourself and others. I can't have you running around New York knowing you could shift at any time. It's not safe for other people and you run the risk of exposing us."

Alynna gave a defeated sigh. He was right. She did not want to hurt innocent people. Plus, if she was discovered, the authorities might throw her in a lab or something and she'd end up being experimented on for the rest of her life. "So... when do I sign up for wolf lessons?" she said wryly.

Grant gave her a weak smile. "The sooner the better." His phone chirped, interrupting them. He took it out, looked at the screen for a second, then put it back into his pocket. "I have to go, but look, why don't I give you some more time? I'll have Cady contact you about what you need to do."

Alynna laughed at the name, a light bulb going off in her head. "VP of Human Relations?"

He gave her a smirk. "We call her position Liaison. She's the best, and she'll know what to do to help you transition. But," he gave her a slip of paper, "this is my personal phone number. Call me anytime for any reason. I always answer, night or day, and if I don't, it goes to a call center that will know how to contact me."

Alynna nodded, taking the paper from his fingers. "Ocean ... salt spray ... and sand ... that's how you smell to me," she said, looking up to meet his eyes.

He smiled. "That's kind of how Dad smelled to me, too. Plus I had this ... I don't know, feeling I was home." He grabbed her wrist and rubbed it against his. "This is called 'scent sharing,'" he explained. "It's very intimate; only people who are very close do it. Like family members and lovers."

She took her wrist back and put it to her nose. The smell hit her again, and this time she felt a warmth she hadn't felt in years, not since her mom died. "Thank you," she said.

"Daisies ... fresh cut, and cool, clean water. That's how you smell to me," he said, his eyes lighting up. "I was only thirteen, but I remember the day our father died clearly, the last time I saw him. Not because of what he said or what he did, but because he came home that afternoon to say hello when I came back from school. I remember smelling the same scent on him."

Alynna said nothing, and he gave her a nod before he left her apartment.

————

True to his word, Grant gave Alynna some space, allowing her time to process all the new information. She went about her days pretty much the same, working on active cases and pursuing potential clients, though the day after Grant's visit she went to her mom and Uncle Gus' graves and left them some flowers. She wasn't one to talk to the dead, but it gave her a little bit of comfort. She also knew she was being followed, but they gave her a wide berth, staying back as far as they could. Part of her was comforted they were there, though she didn't take on any dangerous cases. She didn't want to be shot with a tranquilizer again, but if it stopped her from hurting innocent people, then so be it. She also wondered who was sent to watch her. She was certain is wasn't Alex because she didn't smell a trace of his scent, which a small – *very small*, she convinced herself – part of her found disappointing.

A week after her last meeting with Grant, her phone rang from a number that wasn't on her contact list. "Alynna Chase," she answered in a professional manner.

"Alynna, it's Cady," the now familiar voice said to her. "What are you doing today? Are you free?"

"Actually, you caught me at a good time," she said. "A prospect bailed on me, and I'm kinda just hangin' around."

"Perfect! If you're not doing anything, I'll take you to lunch and out shopping, okay? See you in about thirty minutes? Bye!"

"Wait – shopping? What? Cady? Hello?" Alynna sighed. Cady was either being rude or smart. Either way, she couldn't back out now. Well, it was a good thing she was wearing her nice professional outfit – slacks, blue button down, and her best boots – so she didn't have to get all dressed up for lunch.

———

Cady put the phone down and looked at Grant, who was sitting across from her desk. "It's all set."

"Good. Take her to lunch or shopping, or whatever she wants." Grant leaned back and stretched his legs.

"I will, but you are going to spend time with her, right?" Cady asked sternly.

"Yes, I will," he chuckled. "When I have time."

"You never have time," the redhead muttered. "Should I take Alex and Patrick with me? Just in case?"

Grant put his hands together and placed them under his chin. "Yes, about that. You know who she is, Dr. Faulkner knows, and of course, Nick Vrost knows who she is. We need to keep a tight lid on this information for now, at least until we know more."

"There is the fact that Alex has seen her transform twice now." Cady seemed to read his mind. "We should inform him of who she is, so he knows and he doesn't tell anyone else."

"Right," Grant agreed.

"Well, he's right outside. Let's call him in, shall we?" Cady picked up her line and gave instructions to her assistant to let the younger Lycan in.

Alex strode in through the door a minute later. "You called for me, Ms. Gray? Primul?"

Cady motioned for him to come closer to her desk. He did but didn't sit down. He remained standing as a sign of respect to his Alpha.

"Alex, I called you in here because ..." Grant began, unsure of how to continue. "I can trust you, correct?"

"Of course, Primul. With your life."

"You're in deep with this situation with Ms. Chase, and I thank you for being discreet about it." Grant cleared his throat. "Soon everyone will know about her, but for now this information is to be kept a secret. Alynna – Ms. Chase – is my half-sister. When you met her, she didn't know. I didn't know either, until you and Mr. Vrost brought her here and she shifted in my office."

Alex's jaw tightened. "Of course, Primul. I won't tell anyone else."

"Once we've made some more adjustments, we'll be ready to announce who she is, but please keep this information to yourself for now," Grant instructed.

"Of course, Primul." He nodded in deference.

"Thank you, Alex. That's all."

"Thank you, Primul." Alex turned and headed out the door. As soon as he was out of anyone's earshot, he let out a curse. Alynna had known when they were at the diner, yet she didn't tell him.

The Alpha's sister. His mind wanted to wander, but he took a deep mental breath and cleared it. He would think about what that meant another time. His head was spinning from this new information. She probably grew up without knowing she was a Lycan, which made sense now. But what did that mean for him? He shook his head, trying to shake off the memory of key lime pie and her pretty green eyes.

CHAPTER SEVEN

Right at ten a.m. on the dot, her doorbell buzzed. Instead of opening the door, she used the intercom. "Be right down!" she quickly answered. She grabbed her purse and raced down the stairs. She didn't even have to step out to know who was waiting for her, not when her nose told her.

"Good afternoon, Ms. Chase," Alex greeted. He smiled at her, but he seemed a little more distant.

"Hello," she said, a little unnerved by his cold politeness. "Er ... thanks for picking me up."

He nodded. "No problem. Just part of the job, Miss."

She raised an eyebrow at him. "Yeah, okay, whatever." She shrugged. Why he was acting formal and distant, she didn't know.

He let her walk in front of him, toward the familiar black town car. But, before she could reach for the door, Alex stepped in front of her, opening it.

"Alynna!" Cady scooted over to make room for her. "Glad you could make it."

"I didn't exactly have a choice," she said wryly.

The redhead gave her a mischievous smile. "I've been dealing with stubborn Lycans all my life, so sometimes you just have to take the wolf by the ears. Patrick," she said to the driver as Alex slipped into the passenger seat. "Let's head to lunch first, please."

When Cady invited her for lunch, she didn't expect to go to the type of place where ladies who lunch, well ... lunched. The restaurant at Bergdorf Goodman on Fifth Avenue was the place to be seen, and when they ushered Cady into the restaurant, she thought for sure the snooty hostess would point her to the door. Her best outfit suddenly felt like last season's rags.

Sensing her unease, Cady leaned forward and put a reassuring hand on her arm. "Grant asked me to bring you here. We can go somewhere else if you want."

"No, it's fine." She turned to the menu. She hoped her eyes didn't bug out too much when she glanced at the prices.

"Order whatever you want. His treat, too," Cady said casually as she flipped through the menu.

Alynna ordered a moderately priced entrée and a salad to start. After the waiters took their menus away, she glanced around and saw Alex standing by the doorway, his back straight as a rod. "Is he ... I mean, him and Patrick. Will they be eating as well?"

"They have their scheduled breaks," Cady stated. "I don't know the details since that's Mr. Vrost's area, but they're well compensated, I assure you. Plus it's one of the more coveted positions in the clan, so it's more than just the money."

"Positions?" Alynna asked in a puzzled voice.

"Well," Cady began, "Lycan clans are mostly dynastic. Each clan has several families under it and a ruling family. Power is passed on from father to son, or whoever the Regal or Alpha chooses as heir in the family, unless there was a challenge to the rule or the presumptive heir proves to be unworthy. If you don't come from the ruling family, then the highest position available to you is Beta, or Second-in-Command."

"Like Nick Vrost?"

The redhead nodded. "Yes. As Beta, it's his job to protect the Regal. That position, however, is pretty much up for grabs by anyone in the clan, although the Alpha usually chooses someone based on who's best for the job. Security guys like Patrick and Alex are in prime position. They're close to the Alpha, and they have a chance to prove themselves and maybe even land the Beta spot should something happen to the current Beta, or they could be a head lieutenant. All the best Lycans in the clan, males and females, vie to get in once a spot in security opens. To be part of Grant's security detail is a high honor, and he gets a lot of applications because they know he and Mr. Vrost pick people based on skill and potential, not simply connections."

Alynna noticed Cady's use of Grant's first name, but not Nick's, although she said nothing. The PI in her filed that away, then continued her questions. "So, you said 'clan'. Does that mean there are more Lycans around the country?"

"Around the world actually," Cady corrected. "Most territories are divided up into clans who rule a particular city or area, though not every city has one. New York is one of the largest, oldest, and most powerful," she said rather proudly.

"Hmm ... but I thought Alex was from Chicago?"

Cady narrowed her eyes, and Alynna almost kicked herself for revealing she knew that. However, the other woman seemed to brush it off. "He's a transfer. That rarely happens, though. It's a little ... tricky. You have to get permission from your Alpha and the Alpha of where you want to transfer. Then the Lycan

High Council has to approve it. It's quite bureaucratic, almost like getting a visa to another country. I think Alex was able to do it because of legacy. One of his grandparents was from New York, and one of his grandfathers served as Beta to Grant's great-grandfather."

"Oh." Alynna took a swig of her water. All of this was a lot to absorb, kind of like learning how to do a new job. But this time, she had to learn all the intricacies of a new society.

"Well, there are lots of things for you to learn. I'm sure Grant told you."

Alynna nodded. "It seems so complicated."

"That's why we're going to have to get you up to speed. Grant has put me in charge of your lessons – history, protocol, etc. Basically whatever they teach young pups up until they're about fifteen or sixteen."

"Wow." She swallowed a gulp. "Is it even possible for me to learn?"

Cady laughed. "Don't worry. I'll give you the Cliff's notes version, okay? No tests or quizzes, but stuff you need to know and might find interesting. I want to work with your schedule, but I'm telling you, the more time you devote to this each week, then the sooner you're up to speed. We'll start with the basics."

"You mean about the stuff that makes sure I won't get into trouble, right?"

"Something like that." Cady smiled. "But really, just make sure you stay in New York State for now. Don't even venture out to New Jersey, unless you really need to. Let us know and give us time to get you permission."

"Wait. Jersey has its own clan?"

"Uh-huh. But, well, I personally don't know any of them, only that we have neutral relations. I've heard they are a ... colorful bunch. They're one of the few clans traditionally led by a Lupa."

"Okay. I hate to sound like an echo, but ... Lupa?"

"Lupa or female Alpha is the equivalent of a Regal. A female Alpha is a Lupa by her own right, but also used as an honorific title for the Alpha's wife," she explained. "Hmm ... I really need to update our records about them, actually. I don't know who the current Lupa is, which seems like an oversight since they're one of our closest neighbors." She took out her tablet and jotted down a note.

The waiter came and gave them their starters. "There's a couple of other things I need to explain to you as well, and certain things Grant has to tell you, but for now, let's enjoy our lunch shall we? There's plenty of time to learn what you need to know in the next couple of weeks."

———

"What am I supposed to do with a ball gown?" Alynna asked as she stood in front of the large mirrors in Bergdorf's plush private fitting room.

When Cady told her that she was taking her shopping, she thought it was for a new coat or maybe a couple of shirts. So far, she'd been fitted for two new suits, three cocktail dresses, some casual slacks and blouses, and three pairs of shoes that cost more than her monthly rent. And now, she was standing in a beautiful emerald green satin ball gown. Even if it had one, she didn't want to look at the price tag. The name of the designer on the label alone made her heart stop.

Cady sat in one of the white couches as she perused over all the clothes Alynna put on, saying "yes" or "no" with each look. Meanwhile, Alex stood in a corner, facing straight ahead, his features expressionless. Not that she looked at him. Well, maybe she snuck a couple of glances, hoping he'd react to some of the stuff she was wearing, but she was a little disappointed when it seemed like he wasn't even paying any attention.

"Please stay still, Miss," the young seamstress instructed as she pinned the dress to her slim frame. "I'm so sorry, but I don't want to prick you," she apologized, her eyes lowering to the ground.

Hmm ... she smelled slightly sweet to Alynna, like chocolate chip cookies with a hint of what she could only describe as nervousness. She didn't even realize the girl was a Lycan as well. Why she was uneasy, Alynna wasn't sure. "No worries." She smiled.

After she was done, she went to the dressing area behind the mirrors and took the gown off, then dressed in her street clothes. Alynna patted the girl's shoulder to put her at ease as she handed her the gown.

"Thank you. It's really lovely and you did a great job with helping. I'm really bad at this and you made some good suggestions, uh ..." She couldn't remember the girl's name, or even if she introduced herself.

"Rachel, Miss," she said, her eyes lighting up and her shoulders relaxing. "I ... I'll make sure this gets done right away." She gave her a small nod and scampered away with her dress.

"So, she's a Lycan?" Alynna asked Cady.

"You'll be surprised how many Lycans there are in New York. It helps to make sure they're in the right places," Cady explained as she looked up from her phone. After a few taps, she put it away. "That was a stunning color on you, by the way. The green really brings out your eyes. And when they see you, there'll be no doubt at all who you are."

"Now hold on," Alynna said as she yanked on her boots. "Who's 'they'? And you didn't answer my question – what ball?"

Cady sighed. "This is one of those things Grant needs to tell you."

"Tell me what? Start explaining or I'll walk out right now." She stood up with her hands on her hips.

"Well, there's the matter of your coming out ball ..."

"Wait, what? A coming out ball? I'm not exactly debutante material." She put her hands up in frustration.

Cady gave a little laugh. "Don't worry; it's not like that. This is to introduce you to Lycan society. All of New York's top Lycan families will be there, our supporters and friends, and probably prominent Alphas and Lupas. And the High Council, of course."

"Oh, so a bunch of snooty shifters get to watch me parade around in a fancy gown?" she sneered in a sardonic voice.

"Alynna, please." She motioned for the girl to sit down. Something about Cady's manner made Alynna calm down and she sat, though she crossed her arms. "I don't expect you to understand right now, but Lycans have a rich and long cultural tradition. There are protocols and customs, as well as laws to follow." She patted the young girl's hand soothingly. "I know this is confusing right now, but Grant can't hide you away now that he knows of your existence, especially when you're the first offspring of a proven True Mate pairing in over two hundred years. The Council would have his head if you weren't properly introduced. We're having enough trouble as it is researching the proper protocols because these things are usually done at a child's first birthday."

Alynna gulped. Not knowing much about Lycan society, she wondered if "have his head" was literally or figuratively. "What I don't get – and this is kind of an awkward question to ask Grant, so I need to ask you – why would they want to meet some by-blow of a billionaire and a poor waitress? Shouldn't they be shunning me or something?"

"I've only known the exact details myself for a few days, so I'll let Grant explain the intricacies. What I can tell you is Lycan society doesn't quite work like regular human society," Cady explained. "True Mate pairings trump even regular marriages, and children of such pairings are celebrated." She paused. "Although I said New York was the largest clan, that isn't saying much, really. There are maybe over two hundred Lycans in the whole of New York. Some clans have only one family branch. See, Lycans rarely produce more than one pup, maybe two at most, but it's very rare. So any offspring is cherished, no matter what the circumstances of his or her birth."

"And Grant's mom?"

Cady lowered her voice. "Grant's parents weren't in love or anything. They married for position and status and to produce an heir. They were friendly to each other, but aside from Grant, they had nothing in common. She lives in Paris now, I believe."

Alynna felt a touch of nervousness, thinking about meeting Grant's mother. Maybe that wouldn't happen, but with her luck ... "I can't wait for this to be over so I can go back to my normal life." She lay back on the couch. "Not that I mind all this." She motioned to the packages around her. "Are you sure this is okay? I don't think I spend this much in a year on rent."

The redhead smiled at her. "Don't worry. It's Grant's treat. His 'I'm sorry for having you tranquilized and chained to a bed' apology. It's not a big deal. You won't even make a dent in his bank account."

"I don't know. Those shoes looked very tempting," she laughed.

"Hmm ... he may have to re-think about getting that house in Antigua!" Cady chuckled.

They burst into fits of giggles which was, unfortunately, interrupted by the ring of Cady's phone. "Duty calls," she sighed. "Listen, I'm gonna take this call outside. Why don't you

grab your packages and we can bring you back home, okay?"
With that she left, chatting on her phone.

Alynna looked around her and stood up to get the packages
on the floor.

"Let me, Miss," Alex said as he quickly scooped up the bags
and wrapped boxes.

If his distinct scent didn't linger around all the time, Alynna
would have almost forgotten his presence. "Alex, c'mon. You
don't have to do that; I'm not an invalid." She grabbed one of the
bags from him, their hands accidentally touching. It was strange,
but there was the same weird tingling sensation where their
bare skin touched. "I'm ... uh ... maybe I should ..." she
stammered. After an awkward silence, she cleared her throat.
"How about getting another slice of pie sometime?"

"I can pick some up for you if you'd like, Miss."

Anger bubbled inside Alynna, and she grabbed the bags
from him. "What the hell is wrong with you, Alex? I thought we
were at least friendly and now you're treating me like some
piece of fine China you're afraid to drop!"

"You're the Alpha's sister," he said in an accusing tone.

"Yes, I am. And?" She stood up straight, bringing her full
height up against him, which was measly compared to his frame.

"I'm here to watch you and make sure you're safe," he said
in a low voice.

"And?"

Alex sighed. "And that's it."

Alynna looked confused. "Look, you're not some servant
and I'm not your mistress. Hey!" She grabbed his arm when he
turned away. "I thought ... I thought the other night ... don't be
like this," she pleaded.

Her words seemed to affect him, and his polite mask fell for
a moment. "I –" Alex began but was interrupted when Rachel
came back into the room.

"Ms. Chase, you forgot this!" The young seamstress handed her a garment bag.

"Thank you, Rachel." She accepted the bag from the young Lycan.

She turned back to Alex. For a moment, he had broken his cold politeness, but the mask was up again. She sighed inwardly.

"So, um ... what did you think of that gown? A little over the top, eh?" She laughed nervously, changing the subject.

Alex walked toward the door, his hands full of packages and bags. As he opened the door to leave, he turned his head. "I like pink on you better," he said before walking out. Unfortunately, Cady had chosen that moment to return.

Alynna turned bright red, her skin flushing with the memory of their encounter at Blood Moon and that skimpy pink dress. Cady shot her a suspicious look, but she quickly grabbed her bag and left the room.

———

"And so, once we're done with the meeting with Mr. Zakar, we'll have to zip uptown to dinner with the visiting Japanese delegation from Matsuki." Cady tapped her tablet as she ran through her list.

"Thank you." Grant leaned back in his chair. "Now, tell me about Alynna."

Cady relaxed as well, putting her tablet down and removing her glasses. "She's coming around, Grant. She said she'll come in on Monday afternoon to work out a schedule, something that works with her, as you requested."

"Good. Thank you, Cady. I knew I could count on you." He stared out into the distance, watching the lights turn on in the city as the sun sank on the horizon.

"Is that all or did you really want me to tell you about her?" she asked, a wry smile on her face.

He turned to look at her. "What do you mean?"

She sighed. "You know Grant, I've known you since I was a little girl. You don't have to play dumb or act all 'Alpha Lycan' with me." She crossed her arms.

Grant frowned. "It's not that. I've just never had to do this before."

"I'm sure few people have to deal with long lost sisters who show up out of nowhere. So talk to me."

"I just ... I don't know, Cady. Maybe it would have been better if we didn't find her. That's mean, I know, but still ..." he trailed off.

"Grant William Anderson." Cady stood up, hands on her hips. Few Lycans would dare take a stance in front of him, much less a human. But Cady was different. She was practically his little sister. "I know you don't believe that. She was meant to be part of this."

"I know, Cady, I know. You can sit down now and put your claws away," he said with a smirk. "What I mean is the next few months and maybe years are going to be hard on her. She doesn't know it yet, but she's going to have her life turned upside down. She thinks she can still have a 'normal' life after she learns what she needs to learn, but she won't. She can't. I wish I could spare her that."

Cady walked over to Grant, placing her hands on his shoulders. "You know you can't protect everyone, right? You can't stop destiny." He looked at her with a raised brow. "But you can make it easier on her."

"I'll try."

"There is one more thing. I'm not saying this to make it harder on you, but it has to be said." Cady walked back and sat down on the chair in front of his desk. "Err ... Lycan politics. Particularly marriage and alliances."

"Wait. I'm not giving her the sex talk, am I?"

Cady had a horrified look on her face. "Goodness no!" she exclaimed. "I'll have Dr. Faulkner give her that biology lesson," she chuckled. "I'm talking about her choice of mates. She can't marry any Joe Lycan or human off the street, right? I mean, aside from being a very attractive woman, she'll be much more important to the clan, especially if you don't have pups any time soon."

"Ah, so this is a sex talk about me then?" he teased.

She laughed. "Oh, I'm not touching that with a ten-foot pole, not with your track record, mister. But seriously, Grant. I can't be the one to tell her this," she said in a low voice. "You need to find a way to tell her these things. She was upset enough about the ball. You have to explain she's not chattel to be sold off, but she can't be making such choices lightly now. Why don't you try to get to know her this week and then take her out to dinner?"

"All right," he relented. "I'll have Jared make the reservations when I have an opening in my calendar."

"Sooner than later," Cady warned as she stood up. "I'm headed back to The Enclave. How about you?"

He shook his head. "Still finishing a few things."

Cady shrugged on her jacket and turned to leave. As she was about to grab the door to open it, she was startled as the large wooden panels opened by themselves and revealed Nick Vrost on the other side.

"Ms. Gray." He nodded curtly, stepping aside to let her by.

"Mr. Vrost," she greeted in return, passing by him. Alex was there, waiting by Jared's desk. "Hey Alex!" she called out. "Waiting for the Alpha?"

He nodded. "Yeah, got the overnight shift tonight."

"Ah, good. Let's grab a cup of coffee when you get off in the morning, okay? At the usual place?" She stopped by Jared's desk to get a folder. "I need to go over a couple of things with you."

"Sure, Cades," he said, flashing her a flirtatious smile. "It'll be a good way to end a long night."

"Alex, let's go," a chilly voice from behind barked at them.

Cady turned around and saw Nick Vrost's frowning face. She shrugged as she waved to Alex and then walked to the elevators.

CHAPTER EIGHT

Except for a few things, Alynna's life remained somewhat normal for the next week or so. She agreed to attend Cady's "lessons" for an hour or two a day for five days a week, more if she could stay longer or arrive earlier, as she was eager to get them over with. They were mostly self-study, and she spent a lot of time reading books in a little conference room at the Fenrir Headquarters. Every once in a while, Cady would come in to answer her questions. She had made it through early Lycan history in Romania starting from the rule of Michael I and ending in the first Lycan wars – there were two, plus an aborted one. Grant was super busy, stopping in once or twice during the last week to check up on her, but barely having time to stay more than five minutes.

The rest of her humdrum life seemed normal. She still went on client calls and finalized her surveillance schedule for Mr. Garson. Of course there were her new "bodyguards," although she'd warned Grant and Cady that unless she was on Fenrir property, they were to stay as far away from her as possible, especially when she was on a case or all bets were off. She hadn't quite decided yet whether she was disappointed Alex wasn't assigned to her. There was a weird, empty feeling in the pit of her stomach whenever she tried to sniff out his scent and couldn't find it.

On Friday afternoon after two hours, she finally closed the book she was reading. She sighed dramatically when she heard the door behind her open. "Are you sure this isn't some form of Lycan torture? Another chapter and I'll be your mindless slave."

There was a discreet cough and she didn't even have to turn around to know who it was. Her body practically leapt up when the familiar scent hit her nose. "Alex," she said in an embarrassed tone. "I thought you were Cady. Lycan history, you know." She laughed nervously. "How did you ever learn all of this?"

"It's something we all learn as kids, so it's pretty much ingrained. It's like learning American History, but with more magic and gore," he quipped, a slight smile on his face.

Someone cleared his throat behind Alex. "Alex, if you would," said Nick Vrost in a serious tone.

"Yes, Al Doilea." He bowed and stepped aside. Alynna remembered him calling Nick the name before, which meant "the second" in Romanian, but she wasn't quite sure when to use it. She made a mental note to ask Cady.

"Ms. Anderson," he began.

"Chase. It's Chase," she corrected, slightly annoyed. "Or Alynna."

"Ms. *Chase*," he emphasized her last name. "Mr. Anderson requests that you join him for dinner tonight. He says you are to come with us to the Red Door Spa, and they will take care of you."

"Um, where's Cady?" she asked, biting her lip. "Shouldn't she be the one to accompany me to these types of appointments?"

"Ms. Gray is busy," he explained. "But don't worry. We will

not be accompanying you into the spa. We will only take you there and pick you up to make sure to bring you to the restaurant for dinner."

"Do I get a say in this?"

He gave her a dry smile. "I'm afraid not."

"Then lead the way," she resigned, picking up her books.

"Alex will be the one to bring you there and back. Ms. Gray will have an outfit sent to the spa for you," Nick explained.

"Wow. Must be a swanky place then, eh?" She exaggerated a wiggle of her eyebrow, her poor man's Groucho Marx impression. He merely nodded. *Geez*, she thought. *Does no one around here have a sense of humor?*

"Ooookay then ... so I'll see ya around, Nicky boy," she teased. She'd only seen him crack once and made it her personal mission to see him do it again. "Let's go get me all pretty." She walked toward the elevators with Alex following behind her.

———

"Excuse me, Miss," Alex said as he opened the spa door for Alynna.

Her delicate brows knotted. "Will you stop with the 'Miss' business? It's making me nervous."

He shook his head. "I can't do that," he said. "It's protocol."

"Protocol for what?" She turned to face him.

"You're the Alpha's sister," he stated matter-of-factly.

"Yes, I am. We've had this same conversation before as I recall." She put her hand on her hip. "So what does that matter?"

"It does."

"How?"

"It just does, all right?" Alex ran his hands through his hair in frustration. "Look, there are things you don't understand yet. But you will."

"Then tell me what's wrong!" Alynna was getting frustrated and when she got too frustrated, she got angry. "One minute you're hot, the next you're cold. It's not fair, Alex. Don't make me believe one thing and then the opposite the next day."

"And what is it I'm making you believe?"

Alynna opened her mouth but closed it. Her head was spinning with all the words she wanted to say and the questions she wanted to ask. She wanted to remind him about the night at the diner, about key lime pie. Her heart clenched, screaming out for him to remember.

She balled her hands into fists. "I don't give a shit about this protocol business," she growled. "When it's just you and me, will you call me Alynna? Please?" She looked up, her eyes pleading at him.

"All right ... Alynna," he relented. "Cady wanted me to pick up a dress from Bergdorf for you since we don't have time to bring you back to your place. What dress do you want me to get?"

"Um ... does it matter? Why don't you pick one?" she said flippantly as she was ushered through the spa's building.

Alynna had never been to a spa, not even a beauty salon to get her nails done as money had always been tight growing up. By the time she was on her own, there was simply no time for such luxuries. To say she was overwhelmed at all the attention and pampering was an understatement.

The moment she stepped through the door, she was treated like a VIP. A pleasant-looking Lycan named Grace who smelled like honeysuckle ushered her into the private section of the building. She was offered tea and biscuits as she browsed through a menu book of treatments. Not quite sure which treatment to get, she gave the book back to the eager young Lycan and asked for whichever she thought was best. Looking back, she probably shouldn't have said "best" because she soon found herself bathing in a tub of goat's milk. Afterward, she was brought to a luxurious private massage room where a large Swedish woman named Agneta pounded and kneaded away all the knots in her body. After this, she was then directed to a dressing room where a hair and makeup artist did her face and hair before another team of people came in to dress her. At this point Alynna had quite enough, and she grabbed the shoes and garment bag, then politely shoved the people out of the dressing room so she could dress in peace.

Much to her chagrin, the bag contained one of the cocktail dresses she had picked out with Cady but had to send back for adjustments. She remembered she had picked a blue dress, but the bag instead contained the same dress in pink. She gave a wry smile, wondering if she should mention something to Alex as she slipped it on.

When she stepped out of the spa, Alex was already waiting for her, holding the car door open. She gave him a sideways smile as she entered the car, enjoying the way his eyes roamed and appreciated her body.

The ride to the restaurant was short, only a couple of blocks from Fifth Avenue. The building they stopped at was sleek and modern and gave no indication of what was inside, not even the name of the restaurant. Grant was already there when the severe-looking maître d' brought her to the table.

Grant made a motion to stand up, but Alynna waved him down. "Please. I feel uneasy enough in these heels," she joked. "So, uh, thanks for the invite," she said as their waiter placed a menu in front of her.

"Well, I know you've been busy and so have I, so Cady suggested we have dinner, just the two of us," he stated. "I wasn't sure what you wanted so I had my admin, Jared, book us a table here."

"What is this place?" Alynna asked, peering at the menu.

"I'm not sure. I just asked him for somewhere private and nice." He opened up the menu.

Alynna scanned the restaurant's offerings. She gulped as she realized it was mainly in French and she didn't understand half of the English translations. Shifting in her seat uncomfortably, she mumbled something and pointed to the first thing she saw when the waiter asked what she wanted.

As soon as the waiter left, Alynna and Grant sat there in uncomfortable silence, as if they were waiting for each other to speak first.

"So, nice place –"

"How are the –"

They spoke at the same time and then stopped abruptly.

"What did you –?"

"You go ahead –"

More silence. More uncomfortable shifting.

Finally, Grant cleared his throat. "Is everything going well with Cady? I mean, with the lessons and such."

Alynna shrugged. "I suppose. I just don't know why I need to know history. When am I going to learn the cool things? Like growing fangs or something?" she joked.

"Well, I agree that shifting is a big part of what you need to learn, though history is important, too. You need to learn how the clans work, about the High Council, important people and such," he said. "And I'm still not sure who can teach you the basics of controlling your Lycan side."

"Couldn't you do it?" she asked. "I mean, it sounds like you don't have formal teachers for that."

"I'm just afraid I won't be able to devote the time to it. It has to be done on a regular basis," he explained. "One of the reasons I wanted some private time with you is –"

"Your starters, sir," said their waiter as he approached. He put two plates of salad in front of them. At least Alynna thought it was salad, as she did see a couple of piles of leaves on the plate, some raisins, unidentifiable grasses, and a squirt of dressing on the side.

They ate in silence, occasionally making a comment about the weather or New York politics. Their salad plates were cleared away and the waiter came with their entrees.

"Tripes à la mode de Caen for the lady," the waiter said, setting the plate down in front of Alynna with a flourish. "And Les Escargots En Petites Tomatoes for the gentleman. Enjoy your dinner."

Alynna stared at the dish in front of her. A small bowl was filled with pieces of what looked like meat and a couple of potatoes. She looked up at Grant, who seemed to be just as puzzled as she was.

"I think this is the dish I ordered. Or at least it looks digestible, if not edible," he said with a raised brow.

She let out a laugh, which seemed to infect Grant as he struggled to keep from chuckling too loud. A couple of patrons glared at them, and Alynna cleared her throat to try to suppress the giggles.

"Hmm ... so, this is kind of going like a bad first date. What do you say we get out of here and get some real food?"

"I couldn't agree more."

———

"So, you've lived in New York all your life and never had a slice of Mama Jean's?"

Alynna put the pizza in her mouth. She was starving, and it took nearly an hour to get to Brooklyn from Manhattan.

"No, never," Grant admitted as he folded the gigantic slice in half and shoved a bit of it into his mouth. He closed his eyes and went quiet.

"Good, huh?" Alynna asked.

Grant nodded as he swallowed. "Definitely. I can't believe this place exists in Brooklyn."

"Spoken like a true Manhattanite," she joked, taking another slice.

As soon as Grant agreed to leave the awful restaurant, they asked for their food to go, much to the horror of the waiter. They jumped into the waiting town car and Alynna gave Alex directions to Mama Jean's in Brooklyn. It was a Friday night and the place was packed, so they got two large cheese pizzas to go and walked over to the nearby park. Grant and Alynna sat on a bench while Alex and Nick stood a few feet away, holding one of the pizza boxes. Alynna made Alex promise to make Nick try at least one bite.

"Seriously, how did you know about this place?" Grant asked as he finished his pizza in two more bites. He reached for another slice from the warm box between them.

"Mom used to take me here all the time," she said. "Our first apartment isn't too far away. I grew up three blocks from here." Alynna cleaned her hands with a napkin, lest she ended up accidentally wiping her greasy fingers on her dress. "The neighborhood's much nicer now ... gentrification and all that ... but at least Mama Jean's is still here."

They sat in silence, Alynna having one more piece and Grant finishing the rest of the pizza. "That was great, Alynna. Thanks. And sorry about the dinner disaster, though that was Jared's idea."

Alynna smiled. "I'm not much for fancy food, you know. If

you wanted dinner, I would have been happy with Chinese takeout at your place."

"Well, The Enclave isn't exactly welcoming to guests," he stated.

"What's an Enclave?"

"It's our community on the Upper West Side where many of the New York clan live," he explained. "It's easier to protect everyone if they are in the same place. Most work for Fenrir anyway."

"Ah, like employee housing?"

"Something like that." He cleared his throat. "Alynna, there was another reason why I wanted to have dinner with you."

"Uh-oh, here it comes," she joked. When she saw his eyes darken, she put on a serious face. "Sorry. I believe in the Band-Aid method, so just spit it out. What is it?"

"Well, you know about the ball, I suppose?"

She rolled her eyes. "Yes, my apparent 'debut'. Don't worry; I'm not gonna embarrass you. I do know which fork to use, so your friends won't think I'm a savage." She snorted. "Just don't make me curtsey in heels."

"I don't doubt that, Alynna. Believe me, this is a complicated matter." He hesitated for a moment. "I'm no good at this, so let me try to explain as best as I can. As children of the former Alpha of a Lycan clan, we have certain responsibilities."

"Like the way you take care of everyone?" she asked.

He nodded. "Yes, that's one of them. As the ruling family, we care for everyone in the clan, especially because there are so very few of us left. One of the responsibilities of an Alpha's children is to, how should I put it? Produce heirs. Strong Lycan children who will be part of the clan and add to our numbers."

"Well, you better start getting busy then," she laughed, poking him with her elbow.

Grant stared back at her with a serious face. She stopped

laughing after a couple of seconds when she saw his expression. "Oh, wait. You mean ... no. You can't be serious!" she shouted, bolting up from the bench.

"Alynna, calm down –"

"No, YOU calm down!" she exclaimed. "How can I stay calm when apparently I'm nothing more than a breeding mare?!"

"I didn't say that." Grant massaged his brow with his fingers, a headache suddenly coming on. "Look, I'm just preparing you. I'm not mated either, and right now there's nothing on the horizon for me. There's just too much damn work to be done, securing our borders, playing politics, and running a multi-billion dollar corporation. Besides, even if I do find a mate, there's no guarantee of children strong enough to take over, if at all." He stood up next to her and placed a hand on her shoulder. "If I don't have any children, Alynna, your child may one day be Alpha of the most powerful Lycan clan in the world. That is why it is important to choose the right mate."

"Mate?" she said incredulously. "It all sounds so ... clinical."

"Not at all," he stated. "I'm not going to force you to get married to the highest bidder like in the dark ages, not if you don't want to. All I'm saying is your choice of husband will be crucial, and you can't just run away to Vegas with any man who comes along. Okay?"

"I can't believe I'm having this conversation with you or anyone for that matter!"

"Look, the thing is, once the truth of your existence comes out, every unmated Lycan will come knocking on your door." He rubbed his temples with his fingers and let out a breath. "You'll be one of the most eligible female Lycans on the planet. All I'm asking is that you come to me before you start entertaining or dating any of them, or you at least let me know your choices and perhaps allow me to give you advice. As long as you do that, I'll do my best to stay out of your love life."

"And what if he is non-Lycan?" she asked, a challenging tone in her voice. "Will I be allowed to marry a human?"

"Your mother was human, and she was a True Mate to the most powerful Lycan in the world," he countered. She opened her mouth to say something, but quickly closed it. "Many Lycans marry humans, sometimes even those in powerful positions which could be for the good of the clan," he explained. "Such pairings produce non-Lycan babies who are not eligible to be heirs, but that's something we can talk about later."

"Believe me, I'm not even interested in dating right now," she confessed. "So, you're not going to force me into marriage?"

"I won't force you to marry anyone you don't want to," he assured her. "But, you can't go making rash decisions about things like this. You will be wooed, flattered, showered with gifts and praises. It will be overwhelming, plus you'll have to suppress certain instincts. Lycan sex is different. You'll have urges –"

"Oh god please!" She held her hand up toward him. "Stop right there. I'll do whatever you want, but I don't want to hear the birds and bees talk from my brother."

Grant burst out laughing and Alynna laughed along as well. They looked at each other, and Alynna felt a weird yet comforting feeling as their last word hung between them. A pleasant, ocean-spray scent filled her nose as Grant stepped closer and wrapped his hands around her upper arms.

"Alynna," he said in a low voice. "You're not something to be raffled off to the highest bidder. I won't treat you that way. However, you need to understand. You need to take all of this seriously. Your life is different now, and I'm sorry it has to be that way. But I'm not sorry you're here and that I've found you. I'm glad I have a sister."

Alynna's throat burned as she tried to suppress the tears in her eyes. She took a deep breath. "I'm ... glad, too," she said softly. "I'm doing my best. It's not easy."

Grant drew her in for a hug and Alynna had to bite her lip to keep from bawling. It was stiff and awkward at first, but Alynna reciprocated, wrapping her arms around his waist and giving a slight squeeze. Grant relaxed and eased into the hug. "I know, I know. Just please give it a chance." He released her and looked into her eyes.

She was startled for a moment as she looked at him, seeing the similarities in their features. The green eyes. The straight nose. Other little things. She knew these were things they shared and had gotten from a father she never knew. She nodded.

"Thank you, Alynna," he said.

"Yeah, yeah. Now let's get outta here before your boys see us being all mushy, okay? We wouldn't want them to think you're some kind of sentimental guy."

He smiled and said nothing, but put his arm around her shoulders when she shivered as they walked back to the car.

CHAPTER NINE

"Everything okay?" Heath Pearson asked as he entered the apartment across the street from Alynna's building.

"Yup, I think she's asleep," Alex answered as he put the binoculars down. "Lights off." He handed his partner the binoculars.

Heath waved them away. "S'okay. I know you got it." He put the package he was holding on the table. "I got dinner. Chinese good?"

The younger man nodded. "Smells great. Better than that slop you call pizza," he quipped.

"Oh, haha Westbrooke. Are we going to have this Chicago vs. New York pizza argument again?"

"Well, since you're taking second watch, I'll spare you this time," Alex joked.

"C'mon, dig in." Heath pointed a fork at the table filled with food.

"Yeah, give me a minute." He checked the monitor they had set up to check on the rear entrance of her building. All clear. Nick wanted to have a camera placed in her apartment, but the

Alpha drew the line at invading her privacy like that. Alex gritted his teeth. He was glad his Alpha had some sense. Plus, he wasn't comfortable with the idea of anyone on the security team ogling her while she lounged around at home. He took the binoculars and then looked back at the darkened windows.

"You gonna stare at the window all night? Your shift ends in twenty minutes and she's fast asleep. It's not like we'll miss anything." Heath grinned through a mouthful of chow mein.

"If I'm on the clock for another twenty minutes, then I'll wait it out," Alex said. "Besides, she's the Alpha's sister," he reminded his partner. The Beta had finally told the rest of the team who Alynna was a few days ago. "If anything happens to her, he'll have our heads." *And I wouldn't forgive myself*, he added silently.

"All right, don't be such a boy scout," Heath admonished. "You try too hard, you know?"

Alex didn't answer. Heath was a good guy overall and one of the best senior members of Fenrir's security team. But he was a New York Lycan from birth, so he didn't know what it was like for an outsider. Alex had much more to prove and so much more to lose if he didn't do things right. He adjusted the settings on the binoculars again and turned his head when he felt a presence beside him.

"Here. Get started," the older man said, pushing a plate of fried rice toward him.

"Thanks," he said, accepting the food.

"Yeah, yeah." Heath sat back down on the table. After a few minutes of silence, he spoke up. "How's New York treatin' you, kid? Ready to run back home to Chi Town?"

"Ha." Alex grinned. "It's all good. The work is challenging, the life fast. But I like it." He took a spoonful of fried rice and raised it to his lips. "And don't call it Chi Town. Only tourists say that. We all know how you New Yorkers hate tourists."

Heath burst out laughing. "You got some guts kid, bustin' my balls about New York. I can't say I understand why you'd want to leave your pack, but I kind of admire you for it."

"Yeah, thanks. It's –" Alex suddenly stopped. The hairs on the back of his neck stood up. "Shit!"

"What's wrong? Did you see someone?" Heath put his plate down and reached for his weapon. Before he could say anything, Alex held up a hand indicating silence.

"I think there's someone in there," he said, closing his eyes to try and focus his enhanced hearing. He could have sworn he heard her cry out, which was almost impossible. Lycans did have superior hearing, but not at this distance.

"Did you see anyone go in or out?" Heath asked.

"No, I mean, just the usual. Neighbors, maybe some of the tenants' guests," he recalled. The dread in the pit of his stomach grew. "Fuck this! I'm going in there!"

"Alex, you might be overreacting ..."

He knew something was wrong. There was a strange feeling in his gut. He didn't even wait for Heath to stop him as he raced out of the apartment and down the steps two at a time.

Alex ran through the empty street and went around the building. The lock on the rear entrance was old and focusing his strength, he tore it apart to let himself in. He ran up the steps, slowing down as he approached her floor. He sniffed the air. Damn. Burnt rubber and cement. There was definitely someone here. A Lycan for sure, but no one he recognized. He crossed the hallway to Alynna's door and when he realized it was open, his heart stopped. No.

He wanted to call out to her, but he bit his lip until it almost bled to keep silent. He had the element of surprise on his side. Alex walked into the living room, the smell lingering in the air. He took a deep breath and looked at her bedroom door – it was open as well. She cried out.

"Alynna!" he shouted and bolted for her room. "What's going –?"

He couldn't smell the other Lycan's scent in here, so whoever it was must have left quickly before he could get to her. There was no one in the room except Alynna. Her body was twisted in the sheets, and the room was dark except for the moonlight streaming in through her windows. He felt desire rise in him as her sweet scent seemed to call out to him.

Alynna stirred and moaned, then her eyes flew open. Before she could scream, he used his lightning speed to reach her bed and wrap his hand around her mouth.

"Shhh ... Alynna, it's me. Alex. Don't scream."

She nodded, her eyes wide with fright. Alex removed his hand. "What the heck are you doing here?" she asked.

"There was someone here," he said. "I heard you and then I came here. I scented him."

"You came here ..." she said disbelievingly. "Do you have a bug set up in here?"

He shook his head. "No, of course not. I just ... I don't know, I heard something, I think." He wasn't sure himself.

"Jesus Christ!" she cursed, sitting up in bed. "You're sure someone was in here?" He nodded. "I locked my door!"

"Picked, likely," he said.

"Fuck!" she said, running her fingers through her dark locks.

She looked terrified, something he'd never seen before. Alynna was always laughing. Or smiling. Or sometimes mad, but never afraid. Something deep inside him reached out and wanted to take it all away, to make sure she was always safe. Alex couldn't stop himself, and soon he was gathering her into his arms and pressing his lips against hers.

Alynna stayed still for a few seconds before responding to his kiss. He thought he heard himself let out a deep growl, then realized it was coming from her. She pulled him on top of her, bringing his head down on hers as she deepened the kiss. Her lovely wet tongue snaked out to tease him, and he opened his lips to let her in. She shifted her hips and he eagerly climbed on top of her, settling himself between her soft thighs.

His hands roamed down her thin tank top, cupping her breast through the fabric. She moaned as his warm hand kneaded the soft flesh. He felt the temperature spike as her scent filled his nostrils, and he struggled for control internally. He dampened down the wolf inside him, but his desire grew as he felt his cock harden as it rubbed against her hot core. He let out a moan, which only made her rock her hips up against his erection. He remembered the slickness of her pussy that night at Blood Moon, how she clenched around his fingers, and how she mewled when he touched her clit. The memory was stamped in his mind and everyday he saw her was a struggle to maintain control, especially when he scented her sweet smell. And now here she was, willing and soft and so lovely under him. He wanted her bad, and he could only control himself for so long.

Alex pulled back from her lips and grabbed both her hands, pinning them over her head. She cried out and bucked her hips up at him. He shook his head and put his finger on her lips to indicate silence, then she went still. His hand moved lower, down her stomach, until it disappeared under her sleep shorts.

He teased her at first, his fingers skimming over her clit as he moved up and down her pussy. She grew wetter at his touch, and he spread her juices all over her sweet little cunt. Her smell became overpowering, but he focused on his task. He slipped a finger inside her, making her clench involuntarily around him.

Alynna gasped aloud as he began to work her pussy, pushing in a second digit. Her hips bucked, moving against him, seeking him out.

"Alynna," he whispered as his fingers moved faster. "Let go."

"I'm scared," she cried. "I might ... the last time ... I still can't control it!"

"I'm here ... I won't let anything happen to you," he said before claiming her mouth in another kiss. She moaned against him and lifted her hips one last time. Her sweet cunt squeezed his fingers and he almost lost control himself, imagining being inside her and feeling her gripping him. Her back arched off the bed and her orgasm shot through her body, flooding her pussy while her sweet scent burst through the still air, filling his nostrils. He was rock hard, his penis straining against his pants. He had to have her now. He was going to lose control, his need driving him to tear at her clothes and his own.

"Alex, Alex!" a voice rang through the room.

Shit! Fuck. The hazy cloud of desire that filled him slowly ebbed away. He dropped his hands from her body and sat up on her bed.

"Alex, goddamnit, answer me or I'm calling Vrost!" the panicked voice said.

Alex fished the small walkie-talkie from his pocket. "Heath, I'm here," he answered. He took a deep breath, calming himself. His heart was racing still and his hands shook slightly.

"Thank God. What's going on in there?"

The young man sighed and looked at Alynna, who had scooted to the top of her bed, pulling up the covers. She had a wild yet confused look on her face.

"Heath, call Mr. Vrost. And the Regal as well. He'll want to be here."

"What's going on? What happened?"

Alex sighed. "There was someone in here. A Lycan. I can't recognize the scent, but I don't think it was a social call."

"All right. I'll let you know what they say. You know the Beta will probably want to call you directly." The radio clicked off in silence.

"What's going on?" Alynna asked.

Alex could smell the terror laced into her scent. "There was someone in here."

"What?" Her eyes went wide. "You came in here ... you saw them?"

He shook his head. "No. I don't know how...but I had this gut feeling. As soon as I came into your living room, I scented him. He was a Lycan, someone not familiar to me."

Alynna gasped. "How did they get in? I mean, I know you guys keep tabs on me, right?"

"I don't know," he said. "But I'm going to find out."

————

It turned out, not only did Nick Vrost contact him directly, but he came himself with the Alpha in tow.

"Anyone you recognize?" Grant asked as they stood in Alynna's living room.

Nick shook his head. "I'm afraid not. There's an unauthorized Lycan in New York."

"And he broke into my sister's apartment!" Grant cursed. His eyes glowed and shimmered. "How is she?" he asked, turning to Alex.

"She's scared," Alex said. "She didn't know what was going on. I believe she may have been asleep when he came in, but I must have scared the guy away."

Grant sighed. "Thank you, Alex. I owe you a great debt."

Alex bowed his head. "It's my job, Primul, to keep you and yours safe."

"Nonetheless, you have great instincts which worked in your favor," Grant said. "Where is she now?"

"I advised her to stay in her room, Primul," Alex explained. "The intruder's scent is still here. I wanted to preserve it so Mr.

Vrost would be able to scent it. With her untrained senses, I was afraid it might overwhelm her."

"Good call." Grant nodded.

"It's not safe for her to be here," Nick interrupted. "But she can't go to The Enclave yet, not with so many other Lycans unfamiliar with her and not knowing about her."

"Right," Grant agreed. "Can you fetch Cady, please, Alex? She'll know what to do. Apologize on my behalf for waking her this late."

"Perhaps I should go?" Nick suggested. "I'll call her on the way. Alex is more familiar with the situation here and he can stay and find out exactly what happened."

"All right. Just fetch her, please."

Nick gave him a curt nod and left.

"I'm going to see to Alynna. Go and grab Heath and start looking into exactly what happened."

Alex nodded. "Yes, Primul."

————

"Alynna, may I come in?"

Alynna heard the familiar voice from the other side of the room. "Give me a minute!" she said, bolting up to run to her closet. She grabbed her robe and took a deep breath, grateful Alex had opened a window. They were only together twenty minutes ago, and she wasn't sure if it was enough time to get the reek of sex out of her room. Pushing those thoughts away, she sat on her bed. "Come in!"

The door creaked open and Grant entered. "Are you all right, Alynna?" he asked in a soft voice.

"Yes, I'm fine, Grant," she assured him. "I was just spooked."

"With good reason. If Alex hadn't come in time ... it was a

good thing he was here," his voice drifted and his fists clenched at his sides.

Oh Grant, if you only knew. "Did someone really break in here? A Lycan?"

He nodded. "Yes, there were signs of a break-in and whoever it was left his scent."

"How can you be sure? What did he want?"

"I don't know, Alynna. We're going to find out."

Those words rang through her and she thought of the last time she heard those words. Alex had stood in the moonlight, gritting his teeth and his golden eyes glowing with rage. "What do I do now?"

"You're not safe here, Alynna. We're going to figure out what to do with you. Cady is on her way and she'll figure it out."

"I'm not leaving my home," she said defiantly. "You can put guards on me twenty-four hours a day, but I want to stay here."

He shook his head. "No, Alynna, I can't let you stay here. Obviously, someone outside the clan knows about you and they want to scare you. Or worse."

"How can you be sure of that?" she asked. "What if he just wanted my stuff? What if it was just break in?"

"Could be a coincidence, a Lycan breaking into your apartment, but I can't take that chance," he said. "Please don't make this difficult."

"But I don't want to go!" she protested, sounding like a petulant child. "I want to stay here and have a normal life!"

"You don't have a normal life!" he shouted at her, his anger rising.

The silence in the room was deafening. He calmed himself again. "Look, Alynna, I've been trying to give you a wide berth, but this is your safety we're talking about. Your life! If I have to choose between your freedom and your life, then I'm going to damn well lock you up in the dungeon room at The Enclave before I let anything happen to you."

Alynna was speechless, torn between her feelings of anger and this strange, familial feeling she hadn't felt in a long time. She swallowed a gulp. "I'll go," she said quietly. "For now, I'll go with you. Could you give me some privacy and let me pack?"

Grant nodded and left the room.

———

Cady arrived thirty minutes later, looking slightly disheveled but still professional in her hastily put together outfit of black slacks, a white blouse, and a blazer. She was used to three a.m. calls, and in the time since Nick woke her and during the drive to Alynna's place, she had already figured out what to do.

"I've booked her a room at the Hamilton Hotel," she informed Grant. "It's a block away from Fenrir, so we can keep an eye on her almost twenty-four/seven. I've booked the rooms across, beside, above, and below hers as well, just in case." She turned to Nick. "You can post your guys in any of the rooms and secure the others and keep them locked in case you're spread too thin. Just tell the Operations Manager, Jake Evans, whatever you need. I've already sent his number to your phone. He's not aware of Lycans, but he's an old friend of mine and will accommodate any requests."

"Thank you, Cady." Grant turned to his security team. "What did we find out about how he got in here?"

"He was hiding in one of the empty apartments, Primul," Heath explained. "The owners were on vacation and he snuck in there. Must have been there for hours, perhaps during the day when he knew there would be no surveillance."

"She'll be moved to The Enclave after the ball. We'll have to move the date as early as we can. Until then, I want around the clock surveillance at the hotel as well, but keep as many people in the dark about her identity as possible," Grant ordered. "Cady, have her entire floor bought out and have the hotel bypass access to all elevators except for those with a keycard. No housekeeping unless one of our guys are there with them, and only when Alynna's away. Even then staff will have limited access, including room service. Use the back exit or private exit only. The only people who will have access to her floor will be me, you, Nick, and Alex. Everyone else will have to get clearance from me or Nick to get through."

"Will do," Cady said as she fished out her phone from her purse and left the apartment to make another phone call.

"Why Alex?" Nick asked curiously.

Grant turned to Nick. "I want him temporarily posted to her security full time, at least until she can be moved to The Enclave," he explained. "He will take all his shifts with her. Choose only the most senior members to swap out with him when he's off duty, but only he gets direct access to her."

Nick nodded. "Of course, Primul."

"Thank you for your trust, Primul," Alex said. "I won't let you down."

He dismissed Heath and turned to Alex. "Make sure she gets to the hotel. Nick, let's head back to The Enclave and regroup in the morning."

"Would you not rather escort Ms. Chase personally to the Hamilton?" Nick asked.

"I'm not exactly her favorite person right now." He rubbed the bridge of his nose with his fingers. "She'll probably feel safer with Alex and Cady anyway."

Alex watched them leave the apartment. The Primul trusted his sister with him, but Alex wasn't sure if he could trust himself alone with her. He groaned. He'd be alone with her all the time now. It was going to be a long couple of weeks.

CHAPTER TEN

"So no one really knows why Lycans have trouble producing offspring?" Alynna asked Dr. Faulkner as they sat in his office. She liked the kindly old Lycan, and it was a good thing he was the one giving her "the talk." His office was surprisingly comfortable, with lots of knickknacks and photos from his various trips all over the world with his wife, Eileen. Though he was technically retired as Beta, he still served on the Board of Fenrir and was the clan's designated doctor. "And you can't really 'make' more Lycans by scratching or biting humans?"

He chuckled and shook his head. "Oh no, my dear. Pure fiction, I'm afraid. But to answer your first question, yes. Biologically speaking, Lycans reproduce just like humans and only do so in human form. Sperm and egg, fertilization and gestation. However, it's very difficult for the actual conception to happen. The Lycan community has done some research into it, but for the most part it's just always been the case and few people want to mess with nature. We haven't yet approved IVF to specifically produce Lycan pups, but after years of studying it, many Lycan scientists agree that it probably won't be viable."

"Why not?"

"Well," he put down his glasses and massaged his temples, "it could be the law of nature. Evolution and such. Humans are meant to be the dominant species on Earth. Having too many Lycans around might not be a good thing."

"Oh," Alynna said, her eyes dropping. She went quiet.

"My dear, are you okay?" the doctor asked, concerned.

She sighed. "Well, I never really thought about it, but it's just that ..." she hesitated. "I'm young and all, which is why I haven't decided about kids and such. But now that there's a chance I can't ..." she trailed off.

Dr. Faulkner looked at her with empathy in his eyes. "Alynna, I apologize. I didn't mean to upset you."

"Oh no. I mean, it's not your fault. Or anyone's, I suppose."

"Yes, well, I could have put it more gently or prepared you for it. Growing up as a Lycan I've heard it my whole life and for me, that's just the way it is. I had few Lycan friends as a child, and I don't recall many of them having brothers or sisters."

Alynna bit her tongue, her throat suddenly closing up. She thought of Grant and how nice it was to have dinner with him at the park and how bad things were now. She decided to at least not be so cold the next time she saw him. "I guess that makes sense. It must be easier for you then?"

"Perhaps." Alynna saw him glance briefly at his wife's smiling picture which sat right beside his desk. The look in his eyes was wistful and slightly sad. "Well, let's move on to other things. What else do we need to cover?" He glanced at his notebook where he had made a list. He cleared his throat. "So, since you'll be learning about shifting next, we should talk about that."

"Right," Alynna agreed. She wanted to write everything down, but Dr. Faulkner assured her it wasn't necessary and he'd send her books to read anyway. This session was just so she could have an actual Lycan doctor go over the basics and more importantly, answer her questions.

"So," Dr. Faulkner continued, "Lycans have the ability to shift between human and Lycan form at will. In Lycan form, you'll be able to control yourself and retain memories from your time as a wolf. You've experienced the shift twice now, and it sounds just like when a teen goes through his first couple of shifts. Uncontrollable, blackouts, throwing up afterward. Soon, that won't be the case as you learn to shift. This has to be developed, and usually it happens around puberty. The first change is usually triggered by intense emotion – anger, mostly, but that's not always the case. More likely, it's the uncontrollable hormones associated with puberty that trigger it."

"What do Lycan parents do for their kids?"

"Well, it depends. Lycan parents have to explain everything to their children from early on to prepare them. There are very few families who live outside Lycan society, so there's always support. All children must attend after-school activities that teach them about Lycan life and what happens during a shift. They are taught if they start to feel the change coming, to immediately call their parents or run home. Safety of others is the first priority here and with the measures we have in place, we have yet to have any public incidents in the last hundred years or so. Once the first shift happens, then kids go to special schools or programs, like summer camp."

"And is it easy to gain control?"

"With practice, yes. It's an instinct, but you do have to develop it. And shifting to wolf form should only be done in special circumstances, like protecting yourself or protecting other Lycans or humans – but only if there's no other choice.

You don't do it to show off or as a party trick." His voice was serious and grave as he spoke. "For hundreds of years we have kept our existence a secret because we abide by these rules."

"Then how do stories and movies of werewolves come out then?" she asked. "We have all these books and movies about them."

"Well," the old man put his glasses back on, "back in the dark ages, we couldn't quite control everyone as we do now. There were a few bad Lycans and a couple of public incidents. Perhaps a couple of writers heard of the stories and, since there are very few humans who really know about Lycans, they had to fill in the details themselves. Like werewolves only turning during the full moon or that only silver bullets can kill us, for example."

"So silver bullets can't kill us?"

"I'm afraid they can; rather, any bullet can. We're not invincible or immortal. In wolf form you'll be stronger and faster, and as a Lycan you do have a faster healing process, but any mortal wound will kill you," he said seriously. "Speaking of the full moon, there is one instance when Lycans have no control over their shifts – the Blood Moon or total lunar eclipse. It happens frequently enough that we have protocols put into place. Lycan homes have to be built with special rooms to contain the occupants during the shift, even if it's just a reinforced bathroom or closet. For example, every apartment in The Enclave has one and there are Blood Moon safe houses all over the world just in case. The problem is, when you enter the Blood Moon shift, you don't have complete control of yourself like the first few times you shift."

"And I'll know when the Blood Moon is coming?"

He nodded. "We set up alerts. Here in New York we have a system in place and as technology changes, we've adapted. We know when a Blood Moon is coming weeks and even months in advance. We'll send out reminders via email, text, and phone calls. I'm told we're even developing an app. But you must know anyone who willfully disobeys a Blood Moon warning is severely punished. For my entire life there have only been a handful of incidents where a Lycan got stuck outside during the Blood Moon, and usually it wasn't by his or her own doing."

Alynna sighed in relief. "Well, thank god for that."

"Indeed. Things have really changed with technology, but we all still abide by the old rules. Humans simply cannot know about our existence. Perhaps if in the beginning, hundreds of years ago, we learned to co-exist with them things might be different. Unfortunately, it's simply too complicated to come out now."

"I know we don't have much time." Alynna glanced at the clock on Dr. Faulkner's desk. "Can I ask one more question that's not medically or biologically related?"

Dr. Faulkner leaned back in his chair and folded his hands over his middle. "Of course. I'll do my best to answer."

"You said humans don't know about us, but how come we have people like Cady working here?"

"Ah, yes. Well, there's not many of us, so we still need reinforcements from humans. There are certain families of humans that have been our servants for generations. We don't consider or call them servants anymore, of course. Now we call them Alliance families, like Cady's. It's a special position that comes with responsibilities and perks. The Grays have been an Alliance family since the first group of Romanian wolves came to America in the seventeenth century. Cady's father, Luther Gray, was also a Human Liaison for Michael and myself as Alpha Regent, and the first few years of Grant's rule. He passed away a few years ago, and Cady was the natural replacement.

She and Grant grew up together in The Enclave. I'm sure if she was a Lycan, she'd have been first in line for Lupa."

Alynna wrinkled her nose. She couldn't imagine Cady and Grant together. They seemed more like brother and sister to her. "But didn't she want to do anything else? And what about her mother?"

"Well," Dr. Faulkner stood up. "That's rather personal, isn't it? You should ask her about that. I'm not sure it's my place."

"Of course." Alynna got to her feet. "I'm sorry for asking. I didn't mean to be so nosy."

"It's okay. You're naturally curious and you've not been around as long as us oldies." He gave her a bright smile. "But it's about that time and I need to get back home and have lunch with my wife. Just read those books and call me with questions, or we can have another session like this, okay?"

Alynna nodded. "Thank you so much Dr. Faulkner, I appreciate it." She stood up and shook his hand cordially. They exited his office, which was located one floor below the penthouse.

"I'll be on my way and leave you with your companions, dear," he said, motioning to Cady and Alex who were sitting on the plush couch in the waiting room. With that, he headed toward the elevators.

Alynna gave him one last wave and turned toward the waiting area.

"Oh stop it, Alex. You're being a tease!" Cady laughed and slapped Alex playfully in the arm.

"I'm serious, Cades." He smiled at her. "He totally did that!"

"Who did what?" Alynna asked, coming up behind them.

Cady looked up at Alynna. "Oh, hey. All done?"

"Yes. And you, are you done?" Alynna wasn't sure how the

tone in her voice changed. It seemed almost snippy. "Hope I'm not interrupting."

"Not at all. Alex here was keeping me entertained."

"I'm sure he was." Alynna could hardly keep the tone of her voice even and had to bite the inside of her cheek to keep from saying more.

"Yeah, he's always teasing me. He said Tate Miller was checking out my legs while we were performing a check on your rooms. When Nick saw him he gave him the patented Vrost 'I'm-going-to-eat-you-for-dinner' look," Cady explained.

"And then beat the living crap out of him during the next training exercise," Alex added, a twinkle in his eye.

"Right," Alynna said. "Well perhaps now that story time is over, we can get going since I'm not allowed to go anywhere without my babysitter here."

Cady's face faltered for a moment, but she seemed to brush it off. "Of course, Alynna. I didn't mean to keep Alex." She stood up, her face bright and friendly. "I know you guys have your first training session later, but how about lunch? I know this great Italian place –"

"No thanks." She cut off the other woman. "I have to go back to the hotel and change into gym clothes. I think I'd rather eat in my room."

"Oh. Next time then?" Cady gathered her purse and slipped her ever-present phone back inside. "I'm headed up to Grant's office for now. I'll see you Monday when we're back from California!" She turned and headed toward the private elevators on the other side of the room.

"Are you okay?" Alex asked quizzically.

"I'm fine," she snapped. "Let's get out of here."

"Whatever you say, Miss Chase."

———

"Do another ten laps. This time, you'll have to do it faster."

"I swear, I'm trying my best!" Alynna huffed, sweat pouring down her neck.

"Well, you're not trying hard enough." Alex crossed him arms over his chest.

"I'm not exactly out of shape, you know!" she hissed. "What you're asking me to do is hard. Why aren't we starting with the easy stuff? And what does this have to do with my shifting and controlling myself?"

They'd been in the gym at Fenrir for an hour and after some grueling stretching exercises, Alex started her off with floor exercises and then running laps. They hadn't even started with weights yet, and she was already tired.

"Your body is a tool, Alynna. What you are as a human, you are as a wolf. The only magic transformation that's happening is turning human parts into wolf parts. You still have to develop your human body so you can be a strong wolf. Since you can't learn defense techniques as a wolf, much less control your shift, for now we have to focus on you being able to get away from attackers."

"I know how to defend myself," Alynna grumbled. "You're just being mean."

"I'm not. Why would I be mean to you on purpose?" Alex asked.

"Because of what happened today."

"Oh?" Alex asked. "What happened today?" He walked closer to her.

"You ... you know what I mean," Alynna shot back. She tried to walk away from him, but his arm shot out, blocking her way. "Get your arm out of my way or I swear to god I'll –"

"You'll what, Alynna? You'll throw a tantrum? Snip at me like you did Cady?"

Alynna saw red at his words. "How dare you!"

"C'mon Alynna. Tell me what's really got your panties in a twist and why you treated Cady – a sweet and lovely person who's been nothing but kind to you – like she was your worst enemy?"

"I did not," she retorted. She was shaking with anger, her fists balling at her sides.

"Well, you're either dense or a liar." He grabbed her and pulled her closer to him. "What is it? Were you jealous?"

"What? You stupid sonofa –" she spat and pulled away. "You're insane and an idiot to think that. What would I be jealous of? You and Cady can do whatever you want; I don't give a shit!" Her vision began to swim, but she refused to lose control and prove Alex right. She was not jealous. She took a deep breath and calmed herself.

Alex watched her intently, staying silent as his eyes looked her up and down. Finally, Alynna broke the silence. "What are you looking at?"

"I'm glad to see you're learning some control." He smirked at her.

"Control? What? Wait, were you messing with me?"

He didn't say anything and turned away from her, walking to one of the benches. She stomped over to him. "Seriously, Alex, what the hell is going on?"

He tossed her a towel and a bottle of water. "Here. Sit down and take a break. You deserve it."

She caught the towel and bottle effortlessly. "Fine, but you have to tell me what that was about."

Alex wiped the sweat off his face, then tossed the used towel to the side. "You're starting to take control of your wolf side. I saw you – your eyes were blazing, your body started shifting – but you controlled it instead of letting it control you. I say that was a good first lesson."

"Lesson?" Alynna's face suddenly changed. "You jerk!" She

tossed the towel at him, smacking him right in the chest. "You did all of this on purpose! Making me do these stupid exercises, running me around, making me –" She stopped suddenly.

"Jealous?" he said in a teasing voice, giving her a wry smile.

"Asshole!" she answered, this time chucking her bottle at him. He didn't anticipate it and the bottle bounced right off his shoulder. She turned around and walked away.

"Hey, we're not done yet," Alex called out.

"I know!" she said, turning around just as she reached the middle of the room where the training mats were. "You said I didn't know how to defend myself. Why don't you come over here and start the real training, huh?" she challenged.

He smiled again and walked over to her. "All right, fine. If that's what you want, Ms. Chase."

She guffawed. "At least you're using the right name. Now let's get on with it."

"Fine. Now, the key to defending yourself is to first try and disable your attacker. You'll have to hit him –"

"Or her," she countered, giving him a sweet smile.

"Or her," he continued, "in the right places. Sensitive areas, like the nose, the neck, the stomach, and, uh," he faltered.

"The babymaker?" she continued.

"Right. And the foot. So, if someone comes at you without any weapons and tries to reach for you, look for the nearest sensitive spot you can reach with your hands or feet."

"Sure," she said. "So why don't we give it a try? Go ahead and try to grab me."

"Are you sure?" he asked. "I'll go slow for now, just to give you some time to prepare. Hopefully, once we do this regularly, you'll get faster."

"Well, if you stop yapping, maybe we'll get to do this more than once," Alynna said wryly.

"Haha. Now try to reach out to me. Try to hit me hard, but

don't worry, I can take it." Alex stalked toward her, extending his arms as if to grab her. He lunged at her, closing his arms to try and catch her, but came up empty. He wasn't quite sure what happened next, but all of a sudden he found himself on the floor staring up into Alynna's face.

"How was that?" she asked sweetly as she stood above him.

"Something you care to tell me?" Alex asked as he slowly got up.

"I've been going to self-defense classes since I was fifteen," Alynna declared proudly. "You and my brother and Nick seem to forget I'm also a private investigator. Things can get sticky for me – ahhh!" Alynna cried out in surprise as Alex turned the tables on her, sweeping her legs so she landed flat on her behind. Alex grabbed her arm and rolled her under him.

"Still need to learn a few more things," he whispered into her ear as he leaned down.

Alynna felt dizzy, his earthy scent enveloping her, her skin tingling where it touched him. Memories from the night he was in her bed flooded her mind and a low moan escaped her mouth. "Don't ..."

Alex pressed his body down lower to hers, his semi-hard cock pressing against her stomach. "Don't what?" he teased, his lips ghosting over the shell of her ear.

"Don't start what you can't finish," she answered, pushing her body up against his.

He let out a low growl and moved his head, trailing his lips along her jaw until they reached her mouth. He captured her lips in a searing kiss, making her moan softly and open her mouth to him.

Alynna couldn't stop herself. The desire crept up from somewhere deep inside her, spreading through her as his fingers roamed her body. Large, warm hands cupped her breasts through her sports bra.

"Alynna ..." he moaned as he tore his mouth from hers.

"Shhh," she whispered, not wanting him to say anything that could ruin the moment. Her body was burning up, the warmth and wetness between her legs driving her crazy. It was like she couldn't control herself and she had to have him now.

"This isn't ... I mean, not here."

"Yes, here," she said insistently.

"I want it to be slow and sure."

"We can do that later," she cooed. "But, please ... I need you. Inside me. Fuck me, fast and hard," she growled, reaching up to his neck as she gave him a playful nip with her teeth.

He snarled, then grabbed her wrists and pinned them over her head. His mouth came down savagely on hers, lips crashing, his tongue invading her mouth. She opened up to him, letting his tongue dance along her teeth and clash with hers. Alynna reached to tug his tank top off, practically ripping it from him so she could touch the hard muscles on his chest and stomach.

Alex countered by whipping her bra top off, freeing her breasts, then taking a nipple deep inside his mouth. She whimpered and he shoved her shorts down to her knees. Alynna kicked her shorts away, spreading her legs to wrap them around Alex, rubbing her naked pussy against his erection. He let out another growl and reached down to pull his shorts off.

He cupped her face and looked down at her. "I want you, but Alynna ... I don't have any protection."

"I've been taking the pill since I was eighteen," she said in a strained voice. "Please ... just ..."

Alex touched his forehead to hers and let out a breath. Grabbing his shaft, he pointed the tip of his cock against the slick folds of her pussy. Slowly he began to fill her, inch-by-inch, moving into her tight passage.

Alynna moaned, her body tensing as he entered her. She

gasped when he met a bit of resistance, but she was too far into a passionate haze to protest.

Beads of sweat dropped from Alex's forehead, but it was like he was possessed as he continued to push into her. When he felt the barrier, he became lucid for a moment. "Alynna ... you've never ..." He pulled out of her.

She shook her head. "Not technically, no," she said in a small voice. "Do you ... are you mad?"

Alex leaned down and kissed her, gently this time. "No, I'm not mad, babydoll." He sighed and relaxed. Slowly, he began to fill her again. Alynna tensed, waiting for the pain. "Look at me," he said, tipping her chin up. She nodded.

He let out a breath and pushed into her. When she let out a gasp of pain, he immediately captured her mouth in a kiss. She whimpered against him as he broke the last barrier, fully seating himself inside her.

The pain subsided, and Alynna relaxed. She sighed into him, arching her back as pleasure began to spread through her again. Alex grunted, bracing himself as he drew out of her. She gasped when he moved back in again, his hand snaking between her legs. He found her clit, stroking it roughly with the pad of his thumb, which drove her nuts. Alynna clawed at him, pushing up against him as he began to move.

"Alex," she whispered, feeling him build his movements as they found their stride. Rolling her head back, she closed her eyes, breathing in his scent and feeling him fill her up. His cock was deep inside her, stretching her as she thrust her hips up to meet his. Each thrust pushed him further, and he began to move faster as he kept playing with her hardened clit.

"Alex!" she cried out, her face twisting in pleasure. Her pussy tightened around his cock and her body shook, her hips arching off the floor. She moaned his name over and over, and he nearly lost it. Her body collapsed back on the floor and he didn't waste any time, grabbing her right leg and placing it over his shoulder. In this position, he was able to thrust deeper inside her. Alynna gasped as his cock filled her and he started fucking her harder. There was no more pain or discomfort, only pure pleasure. She screamed his name as her orgasm began to build and he pounded her into the floor. It was enough to push him over the edge and his hips jerked, her name stuttering from his lips as he spilled his cum deep inside her.

They were both breathing heavily as Alex eased her leg down, rubbing her inner thigh in a soothing manner. His semi-hard cock slipped out of her, and he collapsed beside her on the floor. He gathered her against his side, pressing their bodies together. Alynna curled up against him, resting her head against the crook of his arm, and closed her eyes. It seemed an eternity before either of them spoke.

Alex shifted his arm. "I think you need to get up."

"Oh. Right." She mentally squared her shoulders and sat up. "I should get going," she said, crawling over the nearest pile of clothing she thought might be hers. It was her shorts, and she stood up to wiggle into them.

"Alynna." Alex immediately got to his feet and stood behind her. Ignoring him, she focused on finding her bra top and not on the lump building in her throat.

"Alynna," he called again, this time grabbing her arm and spinning her around.

"What?" she snapped.

"What I meant was," he tugged her closer to him, "you should get up because my arm was falling asleep."

"Oh."

Reading the confusion in her face, Alex continued. "And we should get back to your room. I have my entire shift with you this weekend." He wrapped his arms around her, pulling her against him as he kissed her square on the mouth.

"Wha – oohhmm ..." she moaned into his kiss. She pulled back and blinked up at him.

"Unless you'd rather have Heath guarding your floor?" he asked.

She smirked up at him and gave him a playful smack on the chest. "Let's go."

CHAPTER ELEVEN

After getting dressed in street clothes, Alex and Alynna went straight to the hotel. When they reached her floor, she nodded at Tate Miller and went straight to her room.

"Everything okay?" Miller asked, handing Alex the elevator keycards.

"Sure, everything's good. You?"

"Yup, just me here for the last six hours," the younger man said, rubbing the back of his head. "You okay with taking the weekend shift? Kinda sucks you're stuck babysitting when you could be out hanging with us at Blood Moon. We could ask Mr. Vrost if we could at least switch out with you Saturday night. I'm sure Heath or one of the other guys wouldn't mind."

"Nah, I'm good," Alex said. "Besides, Mr. Vrost already has the schedule set up and he's in California with the Alpha and Ms. Gray. He wouldn't like things changing when he's out of town."

"Right." Miller nodded, gathering his things from his station next to the elevator. "See ya Monday, buddy."

"Have a good weekend." Alex watched the other man go,

sighing with relief internally when the elevator doors closed and the numbers on the top started ticking down. He turned around, whistling as he reached the middle suite, swiping the keycard to let himself in.

He stepped on a piece of fabric on the floor as soon as he entered the suite. Picking it up, he recognized it as the top Alynna was wearing. Her sweet scent filled his nostrils as he brought the shirt to his nose, and his eyes followed the trail of discarded clothes to the master bedroom and eventually to the bathroom.

"Alynna?" he called out as he opened the door. The bathroom was massive, with a large tub in one corner and a glass shower in the other. The shower was running, the hot water steaming up the door, but he could make out Alynna's delicious naked form through the frosted glass. Desire pooled in his belly again and he stalked across the room, taking off each piece of his clothing until he reached the shower.

"Glad you could make it," she said in a low voice, smiling up at him. She was fully naked and wet, black tendrils of hair curling around her shoulders and breasts while suds clung to her nipples and stomach. The rainfall showerhead trickled to a stop as she shut it off.

Alex said nothing as he pushed her up against the wall, trapping her body with his. She let out a small moan as his muscled chest pressed against her wet breasts. He grabbed her buttocks and pulled her to him, so she could feel his semi-hard cock against her belly. She gasped and pulled his head down for a kiss. His lips searched hers, gently and slowly, tasting her. Alex pulled away and she let out a small cry of disappointment. He trailed his lips to her jawline, down to her neck. When he reached her breasts, he took a nipple in his mouth and lashed his tongue around the hard bud. She sighed contentedly, and he continued to lave attention on her breasts. After a while he moved lower, licking a path to her belly.

"What are you ... oh!" she cried out when his lips reached her pussy. She was already wet, and his tongue easily parted her lips. Her hands fisted in his hair, pushing him deeper.

"God, yes!" Alynna panted as his tongue and lips continued to explore. He traced his tongue along her seam, licking up and down, while his hand found her clit. He rubbed against it, stimulating her until she was squirming and wriggling in his grasp. She began to push her hips forward, wanting more of him. He complied, his tongue spearing into her core, licking up her delicious juices.

"I can't ... oh ... oh!" she moaned as pleasure began to wash over her. She screamed his name as her orgasm hit her, her body shaking and shuddering as he continued to tease her pussy with his tongue.

When the waves subsided, she slumped back against the wet tiles. Alex moved up, kissed her again, making her taste her own juices. She opened her mouth and accepted him, their tongues dancing together.

"Are you sore at all?" Alex asked quietly.

"I'm good. Please Alex, I need you again," she sighed against his mouth. He grunted and nodded, lifting her up by the waist and wrapping her legs around him. He impaled her on his stiff cock, letting her warm, wet pussy envelope him. He moaned, feeling her tight cunt squeeze around his shaft as he lowered her down on his cock.

"Alex!" she cried out as she began to move her hips. Using the leverage of the wall, he pushed up into her, drilling her against the wet tiles.

Alex buried his nose in her hair, inhaling her sweet feminine floral scent. "Fuck, fuck," he whispered. Alex began to move faster, his breathing coming in heavier gasps. "Moan for me, Alynna."

"Alex!" she said again, letting his name drag on her lips. She gasped and clutched at his shoulders. He fucked her hard and each time he moved inside her, she moaned. Alex clutched her ass, then slowed down his thrusts. "Damn!" she cursed. God, he needed her so bad. It was all he could think about, the primal need to fuck and fill her with his seed.

He shifted his hips a little, and Alynna gasped out loud. The change in angle made her body shudder. "Yes! Oh god, I need you so bad, Alex. Please!"

He continued to fuck her against the wall, sometimes going faster until she was at the edge of orgasm, then slowing down. It was maddening, frustrating, and Alynna wanted more. "Fuck! Please, baby, I need it!" she cried out. He complied. One. Two. Three. Four hard thrusts, and her body began to spiral in pleasure. She closed her eyes, the orgasm hitting her so hard she saw white behind her eyelids.

Alynna sagged against him, her body limp. It was a good thing Alex was strong or they would have toppled over. "Fuck, you look so hot, Alex," she babbled, then pressed her lips to his neck. He let out a primal growl and thrust up against her. Surprised by his reaction, she goaded him further by grazing her bare teeth against his neck.

Alex let out a low, guttural sound. She continued, pressing a gentle kiss to the spot below his ear before licking it. She drew the flesh into her mouth, suckling him while shoving her hands into his hair. This made Alex shove her back against the wall and begin to fuck her faster.

"Keep doing that ..."

Alynna pulled his head back using the hand buried in his scalp, then sucked harder. Her teeth bit down, nearly drawing blood. "Fuck, Alynna!" he said in a low voice. "I'm c-c-coming!" he stuttered.

"Please!" she moaned.

His cock started twitching inside her and flooding her with his hot cum. She came again, a small shudder going through her body.

Alex leaned into her, letting go of her ass and thighs. Slowly, Alynna lowered her legs, her feet reaching the solid ground. Alex groaned as he rested his forehead on the wall behind her. "God, Alynna ... you're going to be the death of me."

"Wouldn't that be a headline?" Alynna said, suppressing a giggle. She bit her lip when he lowered his mouth to her neck, licking a sensitive spot. "Hmm," she moaned.

He pulled away and reached behind them to turn the shower back on, letting the hot water pour over them. "Let's finish this shower, shall we?"

"Well, excuse me. I wasn't the one who interrupted your shower, now was I?" she teased. He laughed, grabbing the soap on the shelf, and lathered himself up.

The shower took longer than necessary much to Alynna's delight. Alex took pleasure in making sure she was thoroughly clean, as well as soaping up her breasts and nipples. When they were finally done, he wrapped her up in a big fluffy towel and carried her back to the room. He laid her on the bed, opened up the towel, and then shook his hair all over her, making her wet all over again. He declared it was his fault and proceeded to lick her dry, much to her satisfaction. It wasn't long before he was hard again, and he proceeded to fuck her into the mattress. After another two orgasms, Alynna crept up to his side and fell asleep in his arms.

———

"I'm hungry," she declared, her face buried in his neck. Alynna had been awake for a few minutes when she felt the pangs of hunger.

"What?" he asked sleepily, opening one eye. "Give me a minute, baby, I just need some time to recover."

"For food, you nitwit!" she said, playfully swatting him on the head. "Could you please, please call room service?"

He gave a fake pained sound. "All this time I thought you wanted me for my body."

"Yes, but I also want you for your mad room service ordering skills," she quipped, smacking him with a pillow.

"All right, all right," he grumbled as he stood up and walked over to the desk.

"I hate to watch you go, but I love to watch you leave," she laughed. He turned around and gave her a thumbs up before picking up the phone.

"What do you want?" he asked.

"Umm, let's see ..." Alynna thought for a moment. She was famished for some reason. *I guess sex does burn a lot of calories,* she thought. "A large pizza. Pepperoni and mushroom. And a cheeseburger with extra cheese and extra bacon. French fries and onion rings. And some of those chocolate chip cookies."

He stared at her, a strange look on his face.

"What?" she asked. "I'm hungry!" As if on cue, her stomach growled loudly.

He laughed and she dove into the covers in embarrassment. "Anything else?"

"A strawberry milkshake," she said from under the sheet.

Alex repeated the order into the phone, confirmed the time of delivery, and began to gather his discarded clothing.

Alynna settled back into the bed, looking up at the ceiling. *Dear Lord, was this happening?* She didn't feel guilty or anything. In fact, it was like ... relief. Since meeting Alex, it was like she was a wound up coil, tense and ready to break. And now ... she wasn't sure what was going to happen, and she didn't want to think about the consequences yet.

"You know, I can practically hear you thinking over here," Alex said. He came closer and plopped down on the bed next to her. She crawled up to him, settling herself in his arms. He sighed and lay back on the pillows, stroking her hair.

"Alynna, can we talk about –"

"Shhhhh," she said, closing her eyes tight. "Let's not talk about anything outside this room." She looked up at him with a pleading look in her eyes. "For now?"

He nodded. "I was just going to ask why you didn't tell me it was your first time."

"Would you have stopped?" she asked defensively, sitting up to look him straight in the eyes.

"No," he answered with little hesitation.

His words and honesty surprised her. She sighed and settled back into his arms. "I wasn't saving myself for anyone, or for marriage. It just didn't happen for me. I didn't have any time for dating, not with my mom dying, working with Uncle Gus, and then suddenly having to fend for myself when he died. There were more important things to do."

"But you're on birth control."

She sighed. "Did you grow up with both your parents?"

He nodded.

"Then maybe you don't understand what it's like to grow up with a single parent. I'm not blaming you or trying to make you feel guilty. We don't choose our circumstances." She collected her thoughts for a moment, then continued. "My mom was awesome. She did everything she could to support me, and I was never hungry. We always had a roof over our heads. My clothes weren't always new, but they didn't have any holes and they were always clean. But you know, I got teased a lot by other kids growing up because we were poor and because I didn't have a dad. I just ..." she hesitated, trying to compose herself. "I just wouldn't want anyone else to go through that and so as soon as I could, I got on the pill and vowed I'd never get pregnant without being sure the dad would stick around. I'm sorry, that sounds selfish."

He shook his head and placed a kiss on her forehead. "Not selfish at all."

"Yeah well, joke's on me." She let out a laugh. "Turns out that's not even a problem anymore, right? Since there's very little chance I'd get pregnant anyway."

Alex gave her a sad smile. "It's not like it's never going to happen. It's just rare. And you could be one of the few that could have a pup or two."

Before she could answer, a ringing sound interrupted them. Her heart beat wildly, thinking it was the doorbell. Only Grant, Nick, and Cady had access to the floor and she dreaded thinking they were on the other side of the door.

"Phone," Alex piped up as he picked up her discarded purse.

Sighing in relief, Alynna opened her bag and pulled out her phone. It was Cady.

"Hey, Alynna," the other woman greeted. "Just checking up on you. Are you settled for the evening?"

"Yeah, sure. I mean, yes, I am." She cursed internally. She hoped her voice didn't sound too suspicious.

"Are you okay? You seem anxious?" Concern tinged the other woman's voice.

"Yeah, uh, just watching this movie ... a suspense thriller," she lied.

"Oh, okay. I hope it's a good one," she said cheerfully. Alynna felt guilty at Cady's friendly tone, and Alex's words from earlier today came back to haunt her. She would have to find a way to make up for her snippiness.

"Yeah, it is. By the way, is Grant there?"

"Grant?" the other woman seemed surprised. "Yeah, he's here. We're just settling into his office."

"Can I talk to him?"

"Of course," she said. The line went quiet for moment.

"Hello?" There was a hesitation in Grant's voice.

"Hello, Grant," she greeted. "How's California?"

"It's nice," he replied. "Sunny and warm. And everyone's perky and polite."

"Can't wait to get back to New York, huh?" she joked weakly.

Grant chuckled. "You bet." There was a pause. "Is everything okay? Is anything the matter?"

"Naw," she said. "I just wanted to say hi, that's all. I was thinking if you liked that pizza place we could go to this shawarma place right down the street. It's awesome. If you like wraps and stuff."

"I would love to," Grant said warmly. "Just name the day."

"Great!" Alynna chirped. "I'll swing by your office Monday and check in with you. I won't keep you any longer. Goodbye Grant, have fun in California. Get me a t-shirt or something."

Grant chuckled. "'Bye, Alynna," he said right before she pressed the end button on her screen. She sighed and put the phone away.

"Finally done freezing out your brother?" Alex asked.

"Yeah, well, I couldn't ignore him forever," she said. "Now," she tugged at Alex's arm and pulled him into bed, "come and distract me while we wait for the food."

———

"So," Alynna said as she sat cross-legged beside Alex on the enormous couch. She balanced a plate piled with food expertly on her lap. "Tell me about the Chicago clan."

"Well," Alex thought for a moment as he took a bite of pizza. "The Chicago clan's not much different from most other clans in the world. There's less than a hundred Lycans living in the city and the suburbs. There's no one place where the Lycans live, but we do have to check in with the clan. The current Alpha is in the construction business, and they work on a lot of Fenrir's projects."

"What was it like growing up?" Alynna asked as she sipped from her milkshake glass.

"We lived away from central clan life. My parents wanted a 'normal' life – my mom's a retired schoolteacher and my dad was a Fire Chief, also retired. I was gonna be a fireman like him, but I wanted to be entrenched in clan life. Being a Lycan was important to me, and I wanted to serve our kind."

"And New York?"

Alex paused, thinking if he should answer. "Well, the Chicago clan's pretty small. I trained and worked with the Alpha's security team, but they were a close-knit group. My family didn't have the right connections for me to move up, seeing as we were second-generation. When I got a chance to relocate to New York, I took it."

"I see," Alynna contemplated his answer. "Sounds like a nice life."

"You could grow to like it," he said. "Being part of a clan is special. Like you'll always have a family. The clan will accept you, but you have to accept the clan and who you are." Alynna remained silent, so he continued. "How are you coping with it? The Lycan thing? I mean, I'm just curious because all the Lycans I grew up with knew what we were from the beginning."

"Some days it's like 'is this really happening'? And other

days I just kind of go with it, you know? What else can I do, right?" She pushed the empty plate aside. "Ugh, the food here is amazing! If I don't move out of here soon, you'll have to roll me out the door."

"Wow. Are you finally full?" he teased.

"Oh haha. You finished off the other half of that pizza!" Her eyes glanced over at the warm chocolate chip cookies in the basket. The chocolate – it smelled incredible. Damn her heightened senses. She grabbed one and nibbled on it. "Hmm." She munched on the cookie, closing her eyes.

"Better than sex?" Alex asked.

She opened one eye and looked at him. "Almost."

He laughed and took the last cookie from the basket. "I don't know. These are pretty good. Hey!" he protested when she hopped on his lap and grabbed the cookie from him. She planted a long, deep kiss on his lips.

"So ... still want that cookie?" she challenged, holding the treat away from him.

He answered by rolling her under him on the couch, his hands roaming all over her body.

———

They didn't leave the hotel room all weekend, ordering room service and watching movies in between having sex on every possible surface in the suite. Alex did leave once to head uptown to Elsie's for some key lime pie. Alynna greedily opened the box when he brought it into the suite, and they ate it whole with two spoons. By Sunday night, Alynna was exhausted and she ached in places she didn't know could ache. She felt wonderful and for the first time in many weeks, she was satisfied – and it wasn't just because of the fantastic sex. She laid awake sometime after midnight, Alex spooning her from behind, thinking about this weekend. As agreed, neither brought up the subject of what would happen after they both left the suite, but she fell asleep dreading what was to come.

It was around six a.m. when she felt the bed shift. Alex got up and began to gather his discarded clothes. Someone would come in around six-thirty to relieve him. He would have to be right at his post when that person came. Alynna closed her eyes, pretending to be asleep. She thought she felt him hover over her for a second before he headed toward the door. The lock clicked, the door swung open, and then closed with a soft thud. She bit her lip and forced herself to go back to sleep.

CHAPTER TWELVE

"Come in," Cady called from her desk. She tapped a few keys on her keyboard, then looked toward the door. Alynna stood there, holding two large cups of coffee. "Hey, Alynna. What's up?"

"Oh, you know. Just passing by. I thought I'd bring you a little something." Alynna held up a cup. "Large peppermint mocha with extra whip cream and peppermint drizzle on top?"

The redhead's eyes lit up. "How did you know?"

"A little birdie told me," Alynna answered, placing the cup on Cady's desk. Alex had mentioned this little peace offering might help smooth things over, or at least score some points with Cady. Still, Cady seemed warm and inviting, as if she had forgotten Alynna's small tantrum on Friday.

Cady closed her eyes as she took a sip of the coffee and made a satisfied sound. "Hmm ... how did you even find a place that stocked peppermint at this time of year?"

"Oh. I tracked a place down near my apartment. The owner likes me. He owes me a favor, and he gladly took out what he had in stock." Alynna sat down.

"Oh, you're such a sweetheart." Cady closed her eyes,

savoring the minty, chocolatey drink. A soft ping from her computer indicated new emails and she looked at her screen with a slight scowl on her face.

"Is Grant working you too hard?" Alynna asked.

Cady laughed. "I'm afraid *I* work me too hard."

"What are you doing?" she asked, sitting on the chair in front of Cady's desk.

"Well, first and foremost, I have to make sure Grant's calendar is organized, then schedule all his travel arrangements, prepare reports, summaries ..."

"Wow. Sounds important." Alynna's eyes scanned the redhead's immaculately organized desk.

"More like boring." Cady smiled wryly. "And sometimes frustrating."

"Is he difficult to work for?"

"Oh, no." Cady shook her head. "It's this company that's tough."

"What about Lycan stuff? Doesn't he have you do that, too?"

"Yes, but most of the time stuff like that goes to Nick's desk."

"Oh yeah? Like what?"

Cady paused and took a sip of coffee. "Most of the time disputes or problems concerning Lycans are handled by the normal authorities, although if they're Fenrir employees we can let our lawyers handle them. I'm told there used to be some sort of Lycan protection authority, but with numbers dwindling they simply couldn't handle it or there wasn't really much work to do."

"Do Lycans get into trouble?" Alynna wondered aloud.

"Well ..." Cady's delicate brows wrinkled. "There are a few things I wish we could handle privately. And I know Nick can't get to all of them, since his main function is to protect Grant and be his eyes and ears on all Lycan matters."

"What would you wish we could handle privately?"

"Last year there was a Lycan who went missing," Cady began. "He was married to a human, and they had a young son on the way. She knew about him being a Lycan, so she went to Grant. Grant helped as much as he could and Nick made a few phone calls, but in the end he had to let the police handle it."

"What happened?"

Cady frowned. "Turns out he was depressed and was off his meds. He had been wandering the streets and then, well, they found him in the river."

Alynna gasped. "Why didn't Grant or Nick do anything?"

"They tried. I mean, they did as much as they could. But they couldn't tell the police about him being a Lycan and unless he did something to endanger Lycan society, they aren't allowed to meddle in investigations."

"But that's no excuse!" Alynna was outraged. "I thought we were a family."

"I know," Cady said quietly. "It's not fair. Of course, we helped the widow and her son. They won't want for anything for the rest of their lives, and she has a job here at Fenrir, as well as her child when he grows up. But you have to remember, there are rules in place, rules that protect all of Lycan society. Nick gets requests like these about a dozen times a year, and so do all Alphas."

"Wow, I didn't know," Alynna said quietly. "I guess I've got a lot to learn."

"Don't worry, there's no test or anything. Just get through the basics and don't get in trouble." Cady tapped a couple of keys on her computer, then turned back to Alynna. "How are you getting along? How's the hotel? Hope you weren't too lonely?"

Alynna mentally crossed her fingers. "It's fine. I caught up on some TV shows and movies I haven't watched."

"You know you can ask Jake or his staff for just about anything. They'll even pick up anything in your apartment if you need it."

"Nah, I'm good. I hope Grant doesn't blow his top when he sees the room service bill," Alynna joked.

"I'm sure he'll be happy you have the appetite of two Lycans," Cady remarked.

Alynna had to bite her lip from blurting out the truth, but instead changed the subject. "Speaking of Grant, is he free right now?"

Cady looked at her computer screen. "Yes, he should be free. I think he's in there with Nick, but I'm sure you can pop in. I'll join you in five as well; I think Grant wanted to go over this week's schedule with you."

"Great!" Alynna stood up. "Thanks. I'll go see him now."

She left Cady's office and headed down the hall to Grant's. "Good morning, Jared," she greeted the young Lycan.

"Good morning, Ms. Chase," Jared greeted back. "The Alpha said you can go right in."

"Thank you." She headed for the doors to Grant's office, but was caught by surprise when they swung open.

"Hey, watch it – oh!" she gasped when she looked up into a familiar pair of hazel eyes. Alex's familiar scent wrapped around her like a blanket, making her feel fuzzy and warm. "Alex, what are you doing here? I thought you'd be at home or ... something."

"Ms. Chase," he greeted, his voice flat. "The Beta asked me to come in for a meeting today, but I stopped by to deliver some reports to the Alpha." He gave her a nod and turned around to walk toward Nick's office.

Alynna looked after him quizzically, but brushed it off as she walked toward Grant's desk.

———

Alex counted to ten before he looked back and saw the door to the Primul's office swing closed. He let out the breath he was holding. Alynna's scent seemed to linger in the air, even with her gone from his sight. He looked at the time. He had to get out of the lobby. The Beta's office should be a welcome relief as he was pretty sure Alynna had never been in there. Her scent was driving him mad with desire and want, the memories from the weekend flooding his mind. He allowed guilt to flow through him instead, as if that was much better than the lust he felt when he was around Alynna.

God, he was a fool, thinking he had a right to touch her, to be with her. She was the Alpha's sister, a True Mate offspring. She didn't realize it yet, but there were things expected of her, things he didn't even want to say or think out loud. He shouldn't expect or want more than what they had during the weekend. He had to get out and clear his head.

"Alex," Nick called as he opened his office door. "I thought you'd want to get some rest after your forty-eight hour shift."

The younger man stood up, giving the second-in-command a slight head bow. "I needed to come and talk to you, Mr. Vrost. In private."

Nick motioned for him to come into his office.

"I'll be quick," Alex said, shaking his head when the other man offered him a seat. "I think I'd like to go back to Chicago for two days at least, to check up on a few things."

Nick raised a brow. "Now? We need you, Alex. The Alpha trusts you to guard his sister."

"Yes, but this concerns her troubles," he explained. "We know the intruder from the other day was definitely not from New York. We should expand our search, and you know I can ask the Chicago clan for help."

Nick paused for a moment. "While I think that's a good plan overall, we'll have to run it by the Alpha. However, I think discretion would be the best course of action. I'm going to talk to him about it, but I'm going to suggest a more subtle approach. You'll need to inform Craig Masterson of course, although that's a mere formality," he said, referring to Chicago's Alpha. "Perhaps you could say you were going to visit family and make some discreet inquiries to some contacts?"

Alex nodded. "Of course, Mr. Vrost."

"I'll let Grant know as soon as he gets out of his meeting with Alynna and give you a call. Now go back to The Enclave and get some rest."

This was for the best, Alex told himself. Stay away from Alynna and clear his head for a few days. He just hoped that he could get her out of his system.

———

"Really, Grant?" Alynna snorted as she read the front of the shirt. The white t-shirt had a graphic of a smiling sun on the front and read: "My family went to California and all I got was this lousy t-shirt."

"Hey, you asked for a t-shirt. You didn't specify what kind," Grant said, amusement in his eyes.

"He picked it out," Cady quipped. "I kinda like it."

Alynna let out a laugh. "I'll treasure it forever." She stood up to leave, as she had already taken a lot of their time. She wanted to set up another dinner date with Grant and chat about his trip to California. "Well, I'll see you tonight then. I'm sure you'll enjoy the shawarma place I picked out."

On her way out of the office she nearly bumped into Nick Vrost. "Hey Nicky-boy," she greeted, giving him an affectionate slap on the shoulder. "Whoa. Work out much, buddy?"

He gave her a smirk. "Just a little," he retorted before heading into Grant's office. She chuckled and stepped out. "'Bye Jared." She waved to the young Lycan.

She saw Alex waiting by the elevator, jamming the buttons angrily as if willing it to come faster. She knew she wouldn't see him again until tomorrow, but she had this weird feeling *she had* to be alone with him somehow. He seemed distant but also agitated, and she couldn't imagine waiting another second to talk to him.

The elevator dinged and the doors opened. Alex stepped inside and Alynna nearly tripped trying to get in just behind him.

"Hey!" she said breathlessly. The doors closed and the elevator began to descend.

Alex acknowledged her presence with a nod, but remained silent. Alynna huffed, sensing something was wrong.

"Meeting went okay?" she asked.

"Yup," he said.

Something was definitely wrong. Alynna slammed her palm against the emergency button on the panel sending the car to a screeching halt.

"Alynna, what the hell?!" Alex braced himself on one of the walls. "What's going on?"

"Why don't *you* tell me what's going on?" Alynna accused, poking his chest with a finger. "What's wrong? Why are you acting like this?"

Alex stepped back. "Alynna, there might be cameras in here," he warned.

"I don't give a fuck about cameras!" she said, raising her voice. "But I think you should tell me why you're acting so weird. I don't think we'll have much privacy until you take your shift with me tomorrow."

"You're right. We need to talk," he said, squaring his

shoulders. "And I won't be taking my shift with you tomorrow. I'm going home for a few days."

"When were you going to tell me this?" she asked incredulously. Alex said nothing, shifting his weight from one foot to the other. "Oh, you weren't going to tell me at all!" she shouted, throwing her hands up at him. "I suppose I was going to find out from Nick or Cady!"

"It wasn't my intention –"

"What was your intention?" she interrupted, anger flowing through her.

"I'll be gone two days," he explained.

"And then what?" she asked.

He couldn't say anything, but he also couldn't look her in the eyes. The silence seemed to stretch on forever. "Look, Alynna," he began. "This, you and me ... let's not pretend it's more than what it is."

Alynna's felt her stomach drop, like the elevator had jerked in mid-motion once more. She cleared her throat to get rid of the lump slowly forming there. "And what is that?"

"Listen, we had some fun, right?" Alex let out a forced laugh. "I can't ... it wasn't going to go anywhere, and I'm not a relationship kind of guy." He paused. "This just isn't working out. We both have our own thing going on."

She stared at him, not saying anything. When she finally had the sense to open her mouth, the elevator jerked back to life.

"This past weekend was great." He moved closer, touching her cheek. Her eyes flinched, but she remained still. "But you know we both should be free to do what we want, right? We never said we would be exclusive or anything."

Before she could respond, the elevator stopped, opening on the next floor. "Right," she said, then shrugged away from him. "I'll see you around then."

———

"Alynna? Alynna?" Grant asked as he sat across from her at the shawarma restaurant later that night. "Are you okay?"

"Huh?" she asked, whipping her head back to Grant. "Yeah, I'm fine. Just a lot on my mind, you know." Truth was, she felt numb. Her conversation with Alex played in her head over and over again. She still couldn't figure it out. Sure, they never talked about commitment, but she at least hoped he'd wait twenty-four hours before dropping her like a hot potato. Still, she couldn't help but wonder if there was something else. What she felt that weekend ... she didn't know what it was, but it had to be real, right? Maybe he just needed some space.

"Have you been feeling okay? Safe?" he asked, concern in his eyes.

"Yes, I'm good." She gave a small laugh and grabbed some fries off his plate. "Just restless, you know?"

He put down his sandwich. "I know this isn't the best situation, but what can I do to help?"

Alynna swallowed her food and took a swig of water. "Well, I know you're not going to let me go back and live at my place, but will you let me at least get back to my cases? I've been holding off my current clients, telling them I've been handling a personal emergency. I can only do it for so long."

Grant thought for a moment. "I suppose it wouldn't hurt to let you at least wrap them up. If there's nothing that will put you in danger ..."

"Of course not!" Alynna perked up. "I just need to meet with two of them and finish up one more round of surveillance on another. You can even have your lackeys follow me, as long as they don't give me away."

He laughed. "They'll keep a respectable distance," he

promised. "But you also need to be in contact with them at all times."

She nodded. "I promise I'll be good! My clients need some closure and so do I."

Grant looked at her. "Closure?"

She nodded. "I've had a lot of time to think about things. I can keep fighting it, fighting you for the rest of my life, or just accept it and adjust to what my life is now."

Grant had a hopeful look on his face. "Alynna, I'm happy to hear that," he said, raising his bottle of beer at her. She grabbed her own and clinked it with his. "Now I've been giving it some thought. Once you're moved into The Enclave, there are a couple of spots here at Fenrir you'd be perfect for. You could also go to college, if you want. Cady suggested you could work at one of our security subsidiaries, right here in New York. Or I could assign you as a consultant for a couple of government contracts –"

"Hold on there!" she laughed. "I appreciate the offer, but I've got a lot on my plate right now. I need to think about it."

"Sorry," he apologized. "I was a little over enthusiastic." He gave her a genuine smile. "But I'm glad you're finally open to integrating into Lycan society."

"I can't imagine myself getting to that point anytime soon, but I'm trying," she said.

"That's all I ask," Grant replied. "I'm sorry I've been so heavy handed with you."

"You're only trying to protect me," she conceded. "I just don't like having decisions made for me. By you, or this psycho who may be stalking me."

"I don't want to see anything happen to you," Grant said with a protective growl.

"Nothing will happen to me," she said confidently. "Not with you around." Grant snapped his head up at her and stared at her. "Wow, I guess I finally know how to make you speechless!" she joked.

"Here, have some more food. You're getting too skinny!" He laughed and tossed a fry at her head.

She laughed as she opened her mouth and caught the flying fry.

CHAPTER THIRTEEN

In the next two days Alynna met with her last two clients and finished surveillance on the third, with Miller shadowing her and even helping her by posing as her dinner companion. She typed up her last report and then printed it for her meeting the next day. She also called back a couple of people who left messages on her machine and contacted them. Since she didn't know what was going to happen the next couple of months, she had to turn down the offers. She couldn't, in good conscience, accept new clients when she couldn't give them her full attention.

While it hurt to turn away any business since it paid her bills, she didn't need to worry about those, either. The apartment was hers in full after Gus passed away, but she still had her normal bills, including those that piled up from when her mom and Gus got sick. However, when she checked her mailbox, she didn't find them waiting for her this month. She thought there was something wrong, but when she called the bank, the only thing they would tell her was that all accounts were paid in full and closed. She didn't need to know more though – who else would pay for those bills? She stormed into

Grant's office, demanding to let her pay him back. He said she didn't have to. The money came from her personal trust from their dad. As executor, Grant's last act was to pay off all her bills in case she tried to return the money or get rid of it. Alynna was speechless, especially after seeing all those zeroes in the bank statement Grant handed to her.

"Is this ... are you sure?" she asked, her eyes widening. "There has to be some mistake. You've already paid off my mom and Uncles Gus' hospital bills with this?"

He nodded, his face serious. "Plus taxes on your apartment for the year."

"But what do I do with all this?"

Grant shrugged. "It's your money Alynna, you can do what you want. Spend it. Give it away. The choice is yours."

She was shaking, her mind still reeling. "I don't know."

"Why don't you consult with one of my financial advisers?" he suggested. "Most of the money is invested, and I wouldn't suggest liquidating everything. The interest alone can keep you comfortable."

"I don't want ... I mean, this is too much!" she protested.

He laughed. "Then talk to Cady. I'm sure she knows some charities that can help you get rid of your burden. But really," he said, coming over to her and putting her hands in his. "Dad wanted you to have it, so you don't have to worry about anything. I'm only sorry it was too late to help you and your mom."

Unshed tears shone in Alynna's eyes. "It's not that. Mom ... it was stage four when they found it. No amount of money could have helped her and as you can see from those bills, we spent a lot." She straightened her shoulders. "Thank you Grant, and I guess Dad, too. I promise, I won't blow it on hookers and blow!"

He laughed. "It'd be a hell of a lot of hookers and blow."

Alynna left Grant's office in a daze. The last week had been an emotional roller coaster ride, and she just needed some time alone. She asked Miller to take her back to the hotel, where she spent the night watching movies and ordering food from room service. Miller could hardly keep a straight face when the poor waiter nearly tripped carrying the trays into her room. She also contemplated what she wanted to do next. She enjoyed her job, somehow it made her feel close to her roots on her mom's side, but it seemed almost impossible to go back to the way things were. She put down a few ideas on paper and thought about running them by Grant and Cady when she had a chance.

The next day, Alynna prepared for possibly her last client meeting with Tom Garson. She put on her nicest suit and her sensible heels, then cursed when she realized she was running late. "Ugh," she said aloud. She was looking forward to this one and didn't want to keep him waiting. She jerked the door to her suite open, hoping whoever was on her guard duty wasn't going to make her even later.

"You," she said in a breathless voice when those familiar hazel eyes locked with hers. Alex's scent once again enveloped her. All this time she avoided thoughts of him, and she was a little startled to find him waiting for her. She didn't make any decision about him, but she did decide she wasn't going to be a pushover. They could talk things over like adults. But that could wait. She straightened her jacket. "Good morning, Alex," she greeted.

He gave her a cool nod. "Ms. Chase."

"How do I look?" She twirled, showing off her outfit.

Alynna felt his eyes rake over her hungrily. A small part of her celebrated at the thought. "Very professional," he said.

"Thanks. Let's head to the coffee shop by my house, okay?"

"Whatever you want, Ms. Chase."

———

"So, what you're trying to say is that I was wrong?" Tom Garson asked.

Alynna nodded. "Yes, Mr. Garson. I'm happy to say you are indeed very wrong."

A smile lit up his face. "I was just ... I was worried!"

"I totally understand. But that man she was 'seeing' turned out to be a headhunter for the biggest law firm in town. He wants her to join the firm, and sources tell me there's a big compensation package that comes with the offer and a possibility of moving up to partner in eighteen months or so."

"Wow!" he exclaimed, pride in his eyes. "It's what Lydia's always wanted. She had to put a hold on her career when our son came along, but she's worked hard to get back up there." He looked at the report again. "Thank you, Ms. Chase! I'm happy to know."

She nodded. "No problem, Mr. Garson. To tell you the truth, I rarely get happy endings like this."

Tom Garson stood up. "I should get going, Ms. Chase. Thank you again." They shook hands and he left.

Alynna gathered her things, but before she could even lift her laptop bag, Alex was by her elbow, taking the heavy briefcase from her. "Allow me, please," he said.

She didn't protest, handing her bag over to him and picking up her to-go cup. "Thank you," she said as she stood up and waved goodbye to the coffee shop owner. They walked together in silence, leaving the cool climate of the shop.

"I don't suppose you could let me walk back to the Hamilton?" she asked. It was such a gorgeous late summer day, and the sun was out but not stifling.

"I'm afraid not, Ms. Chase," he said coolly.

The name on his lips irritated Alynna, but she strived to

keep calm. "How about we both take a walk instead? Maybe have someone else pick up the car later?"

Alynna could see the hesitation in his face, but she looked him straight in the eyes as if daring him to say no. "I suppose that's fine. I can get the car once you're safe inside."

"Cool," she said. "Let's go."

They walked back toward Lexington Avenue where the Hamilton was located. The silence between them seemed almost unbearable, heavy and thick, and Alynna regretted not taking the car. "So, I suppose you heard everything during my client meeting?" she asked as they crossed Fifth Avenue.

"I couldn't help it," he said. "I was only a table away. But I'm well compensated and with the ironclad NDAs I signed, I won't be blabbing to the tabloids about your clients."

She laughed. "Not that there's anything to blab about. 'Woman Faithful to Her Husband! Will Aliens Land Tomorrow?'" She gestured in the air, as if placing the headline on an invisible newspaper.

"I suppose it's a surprise for someone in your line of work?" he asked without looking at her.

"My line of work?" she said, her voice rising slightly. She paused. "Yes, actually it is. Human nature is predictable. We all want what we can't have. And when we do have something good, we want more." The words were out of her mouth before she could stop herself. *Talk about word vomit.* "Anyway, all's well that ends well."

"It doesn't bother you?" he asked nonchalantly.

"Doesn't what bother me? That Mr. Garson is going home to his wife and I've saved a marriage instead of breaking one up?"

"That Mr. Garson didn't trust his wife enough. That he lied to her, had her followed, and now is lying to her again, pretending everything is okay."

"Everything *is* okay. I don't presume to meddle in what clients do with the information I gather for them," she said. "Besides, it's a simple misunderstanding. Sure, he was a little insecure. Who wouldn't be?"

"Because she's a high-powered attorney who makes six figures and he's just a public schoolteacher?"

Alynna stopped, his words jarring her. "What's that supposed to mean?"

He stood beside her, never making eye contact. "Maybe he shouldn't have been reaching so high."

She was confused. "I don't see how that's relevant."

He shrugged. "Forget it."

Alynna felt anger rise in her, and she stepped in front of him. "And what should he do? Should he divorce her instead, leave her and settle down with someone 'at his level'? What good would that do? What about her and what she wants?"

Alex stared down at her. "Perhaps we should talk about something else."

"Oh no, you're not getting out of this easily, not when you started it," she huffed. "So you think it was all his fault for marrying someone out of his league? Someone rich and powerful? Forgetting the fact he supports her and it doesn't seem to matter to him. That was never the issue in the first place!"

"And what was the issue?" he shouted. "That he couldn't trust her and deep down inside maybe he knew he wasn't worthy of her?"

"How could you even make such presumptions?" she yelled back. "You know nothing about their relationship!"

"Neither do you!"

"I know more than you!" She threw her coffee cup down in anger, the black liquid staining the pavement and splashing her shoes.

They stared each other down for a few seconds before he squared his shoulders. "Why don't we call a cab?" he said, changing the subject.

"Yes, why don't we?" she mocked. Alynna crossed her arms and watched him hail a cab on the street. She crawled into the back of a yellow cab, scooting over to the edge so she could be as far away from him as possible. He slammed the door closed and gave the cabbie directions.

Alynna fumed silently throughout the short cab ride. *God, what a jerk. What did I ever see in him?* She thought they could at least act like adults and talk about what was bothering him. It was obvious to her he'd rather behave like a child.

As soon as the cab stopped in front of the hotel, Alynna stepped out and ran toward the elevator, not caring that she left him stuck with the fare or that she wasn't supposed to be out of his sight. He could go to hell.

CHAPTER FOURTEEN

Alynna was bored. She spent the rest of the afternoon ordering more movies and a massive ice cream sundae from room service. She tried to swig a small bottle of whiskey from the minibar, but the smell made her gag. *Well, I wasn't much of a drinker anyway*, she thought. The sun had set long ago and she was making her way through a violent action flick, as well as a double bacon cheeseburger and cheese fries. Checking her watch, she saw it was nine p.m. "Ugh." She pushed her plate aside. At least her security detail had changed a couple of hours ago and she didn't need to see Alex's stupid face. She buried her face in her hands. She was stuck with him for the near future, at least until they found the psycho stalking her.

She hopped up from her couch. "Pathetic," she said aloud, looking at the dirty dishes and her pajamas. "Screw this!" She grabbed her phone and checked her messages and contacts. No one except clients, Grant, and Cady. With her finger hovering the screen, she tapped on that last contact.

"Alynna," greeted the cheery voice on the other end. "What's going on? Everything okay?"

"Yeah, I'm good. Listen, are you busy? Can you come over please?" she asked.

"I was just wrapping up work. Did you need something? Perhaps Heath could get it for you?" Cady answered with concern in her voice.

"Actually, I'd prefer it if you came over. It's a girl thing, and I'm too embarrassed to ask Grant, Nick, or Heath." She crossed her fingers mentally, telling herself this would be the only time she'd take advantage of the redhead's sweet nature.

"Oh, of course, don't worry about it!" Cady exclaimed. "Did you want me to pick something up for you?"

"No, just come over and I can explain what I need."

"Okay, I'm headed down the elevators now. I should be there in ten."

"Thanks Cady!" she chirped. "You're a lifesaver."

"Anything for you, sweetie."

———

"When I said 'anything for you', this wasn't what I meant!" Cady shouted over the din at Blood Moon.

"I needed to get out of that hotel and have a girl's night! Who else can I bring that won't get me in trouble with Grant?" Alynna nodded her thanks to Sean the bartender when he put their drinks in front of her. She took her cola and pushed a glass of vodka tonic toward the redhead. "C'mon Cady, live a little!"

When Cady arrived at the hotel, Alynna was already dressed to go out. She put on a short, black body-fitting dress and some makeup. She convinced Cady to go out with her, and the redhead agreed but only on the condition that they went to one place – Blood Moon. Alynna didn't care and agreed, dragging Heath with them. He, however, chose to keep a low profile, standing against the wall about ten feet away where he could see all the exits and entrances.

Cady grabbed the drink and took a swig. "I don't see you drinking! I thought this was a girl's night!"

"Ugh, no. I must be getting a cold or something because whiskey, vodka, and beer seem to be making me nauseous." She grabbed a nacho from their plate and scooped up extra cheese onto the chip before popping it in her mouth.

"You're certainly not sick! That's your second plate." Cady took another piece of nacho for herself and then took another sip of her vodka as Sean refilled her glass. "Whoa. A little heavy handed there, Sean?"

The handsome bartender winked at her. "Alynna said you needed to relax!"

"Alynna!" Cady exclaimed. "That was my third drink!"

Alynna laughed. "C'mon, you needed to loosen up as much as I did. You know, I've never thanked you for helping me all those times."

"You're very welcome," Cady crooned. "Wow, it's getting hot in here, isn't it?"

"Not as hot as you ladies," a voice said from behind. Cady turned to see a guy standing right behind them at the bar. He gave them a big smile, his eyes lingering on the redhead.

Alynna rolled her eyes. This guy wasn't the first to approach them, but he was the first non-Lycan to do so. She could literally smell them a mile away. Cady had gone to the bathroom, and she was sitting there alone. Two Lycans came up to her and asked if they could buy her a drink, but when Cady came back they seemed to recognize who she was and apologized, practically slinking away from them.

"Hi, I'm Joseph," he said, putting his hand out. Joseph was handsome with short, dark hair. He wore a tight-fitting t-shirt that showed off his well-muscled shoulders and arms. Alynna fanned herself mentally.

"Alynna." She shook his hand. "And my friend here is Cady."

"That's a pretty name, very unusual," Joseph remarked. "What are you ladies drinking? Can I buy you another one?"

Cady tried to protest, but Alynna answered for her. "She's having a vodka tonic and just a Coke for me." Joseph nodded thanks and signaled to Sean.

"So, where are you ladies from?" he asked as he paid for the drinks.

For the next hour Joseph stayed with them, and Alynna was happy to see her friend having a good time. Unlike most guys she'd met at bars in Manhattan, Joseph seemed nice. He was from Brooklyn and recently started working as a foreman at a construction site in a major shopping development downtown. He had heard from other people at work that Blood Moon was one of the hottest clubs in New York, so he thought he'd check it out.

"And are you liking it?" Alynna asked.

Joseph gave Cady one of many meaningful glances. "I am so far."

Alynna stifled a laugh. If he only knew he was in a Lycan club, he might change his mind. It wasn't like they were unwelcoming to non-Lycans, but there definitely were very few human regulars at Blood Moon. "Excuse me," Alynna said. "Gotta go to the ladies!" She left, hoping to give her friend – and *her* new friend – some time alone.

Alynna took her time taking care of nature's call and fixing her makeup. As she was exiting the bathroom, she nearly fell back as someone bumped into her – a tall, leggy blonde who gave her a slight sneer.

"Excuse me," Alynna said. The blonde's scent tickled her nose. It was a strong, flowery perfume on top of a sugary, sickly fragrance that made her stomach roil. The blonde looked down at her and flipped her hair, walking away without another word. Alynna shrugged. Lycan or human, some girls were just born bitches.

She began to walk back to the bar, and she smiled at the sight that greeted her. Joseph and Cady were definitely getting very cozy. *You go girl*, she said to herself, giving Cady a mental high five. Joseph was hot and seemed like a really nice guy. *At least someone would be getting some tonight*, she thought.

"Alynna!" Cady called out as she came near to them. "Guess who I found lurking here?"

The guy beside Cady and Joseph turned around. Alynna stopped, her heart jumping into her throat. *Of course. Just my luck.* "Hello Alex," she greeted weakly. She really wished she could have a drink right now.

Alex gave her a nod. He leaned back against the bar, taking a sip of his beer.

"Sorry to keep you waiting babe!" a perky voice chirped. Alynna turned around. It was the haughty blonde Lycan from the bathroom. "Had to go powder my nose!" The tall, sleek blonde snaked her arm around Alex's neck and pushed her body against his possessively. Alex said nothing, though he put a hand around her waist. She ignored the rest of them, focusing her gaze up at Alex instead.

"A glass of red, please," Alynna said to Sean. Fuck this sickness, she needed alcohol now. Something seethed and raged inside of her, and she struggled to keep it under wraps. She didn't know what it was, but it made her want to claw the other woman's eyes out and rip her hair out of her scalp. She had to calm down.

"How was your trip to Chicago, Alex?" Cady asked, breaking the silence.

"It was good. Thanks for asking, Cady."

The blonde seemed to perk up when she heard the name. She finally looked away from Alex, her head turning toward Cady. "Oh my! You're the Alpha's ..." She cleared her throat. "I'm Jenna," she said, her eyes directed at Cady. "I work down on the twentieth floor. Ms. Gray, it's finally nice to meet you," she crooned, her voice sweet as sugar.

"Oh, uh," Cady mumbled, a little embarrassed. "Yes, nice to meet you Jenna!"

"Alex told me he worked closely with you. And the Alpha, of course." She looked up at Alex, her eyes devouring him. Alynna gagged mentally, then swallowed half the glass of wine Sean put in front of her. It wasn't as bad as hard liquor, but drinking it quickly before she could smell or taste it helped.

"This is Joseph." Cady nodded towards the man beside her. "And uh, Alynna."

"Yup, still here," Alynna snarked. "The reports about my disappearance have been greatly exaggerated." She downed the rest of the glass and motioned to Sean for another.

Jenna looked down at her as if she wanted her to disappear. Her eyes flashed recognition for a second, taking a shallow breath as if to sniff out her scent. "Alynna. I've never seen you around here before." She looked at Joseph for a brief moment, assessing if he was human or Lycan. "Did you transfer or are you just visiting?"

Alynna laughed. "I guess a little bit of both." She winked at Cady. No one was supposed to know about her existence yet, at least not before the ball.

"She's a consultant for Fenrir," Cady explained. "Brought in by the team to help with a special project."

"Oh, how nice," she said, then turned back to fawning over Alex.

Sean returned with another beer for Alex and Alynna's wine. "Why don't we move over there?" Jenna suggested. "It's getting a little crowded over here," she said, her eyes flickering to Alynna briefly.

Alex picked up his beer. "Cady, Joseph." He turned around. "Alynna."

Alynna gave a noncommittal sound, instead taking another sip of her second glass of wine. "Jerk," she said under her breath. When both Alex and Jenna were out of sight, she breathed a sigh.

"Are you all right?" Joseph asked. "You should slow down maybe. That's your second glass in ten minutes."

"I'll be fine," she said, sipping her wine. "I had a lot of food."

Cady looked at her with concern in her eyes. "Are you sure?"

"Yeah, I'm good."

"Maybe you'd like to come out for a smoke." Joseph took some cigarettes out of his pocket. "Or fresh air for you girls, if you don't smoke."

"No, you guys go," Alynna said, motioning to Cady. "I'm gonna stay here for a bit."

Cady hopped off the stool and followed Joseph out of the bar. Alynna did her best to stop herself from looking across the room, but it was like her eyes were drawn toward Alex and Jenna. They were talking, or at least Jenna was, with her whispering and giggling into his ear while his hand rubbed her lower back.

Alynna watched them for another minute, her blood boiling, as the tall, svelte Lycan tugged at his arm, signaling for them to leave. Alex drank the rest of his drink, then followed Jenna as she led him toward the exit.

She threw her head back and took the rest of the wine in one gulp. As soon as she put the glass down, she instantly regretted it. "Oh fuck!" The world began to spin and she held onto the counter for support.

"Alynna, are you okay?" Sean asked. Alynna looked at him, his voice seemed to be drowned out by the loud thrumming in her brain.

"I ... I ..." She felt nauseous. "I need ..." She spun around, placing her hands over her mouth to stop herself from vomiting all over the floor. She ran across the room, bumping into other patrons. She didn't care and pushed past them as fast as she could. She barely made it to the last stall as she lost her dinner and drinks right into the ceramic bowl.

She knelt on the floor, her stomach rolling as it emptied its contents. Finally, when she was dry heaving into the bowl, she stood up weakly and wiped her mouth with some toilet paper.

"Ms. Chase! Ms. Chase!" a voice outside said with alarm.

Heath! she thought. She almost forgot about him. Damn. "I'm okay! No worries."

"Are you sure?"

She turned on the sink and scooped up some water to wash out the acidic taste in her mouth. "Mmm-hmm!" She spit out the water, then wet some more tissues to wipe up her face. *What a mess*, she thought as she looked at herself. "I just want to go home," she said softly, closing her eyes.

"Maybe you shouldn't have left."

Alynna nearly jumped out of her skin. She turned and saw Nick Vrost standing in the doorway. "I'm not a prisoner; I can go where I want and Heath was with me. And so was Cady."

A brief, inscrutable look passed on his face. "Cady? I wasn't told she was here."

"Do you know whenever I pee, too?" Alynna asked sarcastically as she threw the wet tissues into the trashcan.

"I review the report logs every few hours," Nick said nonchalantly. "I saw you had left to go to Blood Moon, and I was concerned as you didn't mention anything."

"I can go where I want," she said petulantly. "As long as I have my security with me."

"And Cady?"

"Oh shit." Alynna said the words before she could stop them. Cady was probably somewhere making out with Joseph and with Nick's weird vibe around Cady, she wasn't sure how he'd react to that.

Nick suddenly came up to her, grabbing her arm firmly. "Is she okay? Has she been hurt?" His eyes literally glowed at her, his face a mask of restrained concern.

"Geez Nicky boy, tone down the whole protective Lycan thing, all right?" She jerked her arm back. "I'm pretty sure she's fine. She might be a little tipsy, but she's okay."

Nick straightened his posture, smoothing down his jacket. "I think it's time we go home. And maybe we can find Ms. Gray and take her home, too."

I bet you want to take her home, she said to herself. She hoped they wouldn't run into Joseph and Cady in some compromising position, as she wasn't sure what Nick's reaction would be. She followed him out of the bathroom and Nick nodded to Heath, who was keeping guard.

As they were walking toward the door, she breathed a sigh of relief when she saw Cady enter the bar. That relief was short-lived however, when she saw Joseph following closely behind her. The handsome man grabbed her hand and whispered something in her ear that made her blush prettily.

"Ms. Gray," Nick said as they approached the couple.

Cady's eyes grew wide at the sight of Nick Vrost. "Mr. Vrost! What are you ...? I mean ..." She slurred her words slightly, unable to complete the rest of her sentence.

"I was passing by and I saw Ms. Chase," Nick said coolly, his eyes raking over her appearance. Cady's usually immaculate hair was mussed and her lips were pink and swollen, her lipstick practically gone. She blushed heatedly at Nick's appraisal. "She was sick. In the bathroom." His voice was cold and accusing.

"Alynna!" Cady exclaimed, going to the younger girl's side. "Are you all right? You should have told me! Let's get you home."

"Perhaps you should go home as well, Ms. Gray," Nick observed. "Don't you have the early meeting tomorrow?"

Cady shot him back an angry look. "Mr. Vrost, I –"

"You should stay," Alynna said, glancing at Joseph, who seemed confused at what was happening. "Fenrir doesn't own you," she said, emphasizing 'own'. "You can do what you want on your off time without having bullheaded men push you around."

The redhead looked torn, glancing at Joseph and then Alynna while Nick continued to give her a steely stare. "Will you wait for me? I'll settle my bill with Sean and be right out." The younger woman nodded, then walked outside, Nick and Heath hot on her heels.

As soon as they were outside, Alynna breathed the fresh, cool air into her lungs. She was already feeling better, getting out of the hot, stuffy bar. Cady didn't take too long and soon joined them.

"Glad you could join us, Ms. Gray," Nick said icily.

"Mr. Vrost, I assure you Alynna was in no danger at any point. Heath was with her the entire time," Cady explained.

"And you? Were you with her the whole night or just with your friend?" he sneered.

Cady was obviously stung at the acidity dripping from his voice. Alynna had just about had enough. "Whoa, Nicky-boy. Calm yo tits, will ya?" she said, poking him in the chest. Nick whipped his head toward her with a steely gaze. "So I threw up in the bathroom. I just drank a little too much wine, and I think the cheese on those nachos was old or something. Cady's not to blame, it's all me."

The redhead looked at her gratefully and cleared her throat. "Thank you, Alynna. I didn't mean to leave her and she was fine when I, uh, went out for some fresh air," Cady explained. "Now, maybe you should go and get some rest? I'll take you home."

"No," Nick interjected. "Heath will take her home. Ms. Gray, you can ride with me back to The Enclave."

"I can take a cab," Cady said brusquely.

"I insist," Nick said, grabbing her arm. He clearly was not taking no for an answer.

"Cady ..." Alynna began.

"I'll be fine, Alynna," Cady said, straightening her shoulders. "Mr. Vrost and I are headed to the same place anyway."

"Fine, but if he ..." Alynna wasn't sure. Nick had murder in his eyes, but she doubted it was for the lovely redhead. Rather it was directed to her handsome companion from earlier. *Hmmm ... this was definitely interesting.* Too bad Joseph seemed to have disappeared.

"All right." She looked at Heath. "Let's go back to The Hamilton." Alynna walked by Nick, giving him the stink eye as Heath trailed behind her.

———

Cady watched Heath and Alynna walk away. Letting out a breath, she turned around. "Well, I suppose we should get going."

"You're not going to stay with your boyfriend?" Nick's tone was cutting.

"He's not ... I mean I just met him and we ... ugh!" She turned around and began walking in the opposite direction. She was not in the mood to duke it out with Nick Vrost tonight.

Cady was surprised if not confused by his actions. Yes, she and Nick sometimes clashed on certain issues, especially when it came to Grant, but he had never been mean to her. She sighed. Nick was usually indifferent to Cady, not exactly ignoring her, but always keeping a respectable distance. She was confused as to why he'd been acting so strange for the past few weeks.

"Taxi!" she called out to a passing yellow cab. It stopped a few feet from her and she chased it.

"Ms. Gray!" Nick called out. "I have a car; we don't need a cab."

"*You* don't need a cab," she sneered. "I do." She grabbed the door and yanked it open.

Nick slammed his palm on the door and shut it. "Stop."

"I'm not one of your Lycan employees, Mr. Vrost," she said icily.

"No, you are not," he replied in a frustrated voice. He ran his fingers through his hair. "Look, stop being ridiculous and just come with me. There's no need to waste money on a cab when I have a car and we're headed the same way."

"Hey lady," the cab driver called from inside. "Are you comin' or not?"

Cady sighed, too tired to argue. "Sorry." She shrugged. The cab drove off and Cady stared after it, wondering if she would regret her choice.

"Let's go," she said, walking toward the parking lot at Blood Moon. Nick followed beside her, not saying a word.

Cady walked over to his sleek black Mercedes and to her surprise, Nick opened the door for her. She stepped in, settling herself into the passenger seat. Nick walked to the driver's side, climbing in smoothly.

Cady opened her mouth, but suddenly froze when Nick leaned over to the passenger side, his body practically covering hers. The spicy smell of his cologne filled her nostrils, a scent that wasn't unpleasant. The scent seemed familiar, yet not. She felt a slight shiver as the warmth of his body seemed to radiate and overwhelm her. She could have sworn she felt the lightest touch of his breath and lips over her neck.

"Mr. Vrost, what are you –"

A loud click interrupted her, and she felt the seatbelt tighten across her lap and chest.

"Don't want you to get hurt now, do we?" Nick asked as leaned back into his seat and started the engine.

Cady wrinkled her nose. "I – thank you, Mr. Vrost. As I was saying earlier, there's no need for your concern. Alynna wasn't in trouble."

"And you would know because you were with her the whole time?" Nick's voice dripped with accusation.

"It's not my job to keep an eye on Alynna; that's why we have security on her," Cady countered. "I was there with her as a friend. After office hours. She was lonely and going stir-crazy trapped in that hotel room. She wanted company and to get out."

Nick kept his eyes on the road. "And you let her leave?"

"She's not a prisoner. Grant said so himself," Cady stated.

The Lycan remained silent, but Cady could feel the tension radiating off him. It filled the car, making the air between them thick enough to cut with a knife. Mercifully, they soon pulled into The Enclave's private garage.

She unbuckled her seat belt and grabbed the door handle to let herself out.

"Ms. Gray ..." Nick called, his voice low and hoarse.

Cady froze, her fingers remaining still. She turned her head. "What is it?" she asked impatiently.

Nick's ice blue eyes stared back at her. For a moment she thought he looked almost hesitant, very un-Nick. He was always sure of himself with each gesture and movement efficient and well-executed.

"Good night."

She nodded without a word and stepped out of the car, then through the glass doors toward the elevators

———

Alex took a deep breath as they exited Blood Moon, the cool evening air clearing his senses. A vice-like grip constricted his chest when he thought of Alynna. *What the hell was I thinking bringing Jenna here?*

Jenna had been flirting with him mercilessly ever since he transferred to New York, and he had always rebuffed her advances. As he was walking out of Fenrir that night, Jenna cornered him in the elevator, begging him to come for a drink. She said some regular at Blood Moon had been stalking her for the last couple of weeks, and she asked if he could do her a solid and pretend to be her date to send a message to the guy. She also offered to pay for his drinks. He could hardly turn away such a request, especially when all he had to do was stand there and drink free beer.

He had expected Alynna to be holed up at the hotel, not out and about with Cady. He immediately regretted his decision as soon as he saw her. Of course, Jenna kept up appearances, although the mysterious stalker hadn't shown up. After a few beers, he couldn't stand being there, being around Alynna and not being able to talk to her or touch her. It was a good thing Jenna said she wanted to leave Blood Moon right away, and he was eager to get home and try to get some sleep.

They split a cab and arrived at the front door of the main building at the center of The Enclave. He opened the door for her, greeted the security guard at the front desk, and headed to the elevators, pressing the "up" button.

"So, Alex," Jenna drawled in a low voice. "Thanks for keeping me company tonight."

"Uh, sure." He shrugged. "Too bad that guy didn't show up." He looked at the numbers on the floor display above the elevator door as they began to descend.

"Yeah, too bad." Jenna put her hand on his arm, giving his bicep a light squeeze. "So, how about a nightcap at my place?"

Alex shook his head. "Sorry. I need to get some sleep. I've got an early day."

Jenna pouted. "Just one drink, please?" She batted her eyelashes and moved closer, brushing the curve of her breasts against his arm.

Alex mentally recoiled at her touch. "I'm on duty with the Alpha tomorrow," he lied. "Have to be on full alert."

Jenna sighed. "All right, well …" She was interrupted by the ding of the elevator. The doors opened and she stepped inside. "Are you coming?"

He shook his head. "Actually, you go ahead. I need to talk to Chris." He motioned to the guard. "Something the Alpha wanted me to check for him."

The blonde shrugged. "Well, okay. Goodnight then. If you change your mind, you know where I am." She saucily gave him a wink.

Alex let out a deep breath as soon as the elevator doors closed. He watched the numbers go up, and then stop at Jenna's floor before he pressed the up button again. When the doors dinged and opened, he gave a last wave to the guard and headed into the mercifully empty elevator.

CHAPTER FIFTEEN

Alynna collapsed on the grass, sweat pouring down her forehead, neck, and back. She grabbed her water bottle, taking a swig of the clean, cool liquid. It was the fifth day in a row she'd been up at the crack of dawn to go jogging in Central Park. Her bodyguard of the day, Patrick, didn't have any problems keeping up. He was physically fit, being a Lycan and a member of Grant's security team, though she could tell he wasn't exactly expecting to run a couple of miles at the start of his shift.

"Are you all right, Ms. Chase?" he asked as he offered her his hand,

She took it and let him help her up. "Never better, Patrick, never better," she huffed. "I think it's time to go back."

Unable to do little else with her time, exercise became Alynna's way of letting off steam. After the night at Blood Moon, she wanted nothing more than to drive herself to exhaustion, so she could stop lying awake in bed wondering about Alex and that bimbo Jenna. They left together that night, and she couldn't erase the image in her head of them in bed. It only enraged her, and she could almost feel the wolf inside her growling and snapping, wanting to be let out so she could rip the other Lycan's throat to shreds. By keeping herself occupied, she was able to stop from thinking those thoughts, especially when she collapsed in bed after a long day.

They walked back to the hotel, which was only a few blocks away from where they had ended up. As soon as she got to her room, she showered, dressed, and her breakfast of pancakes and extra bacon, plus a pot of coffee, was waiting for her on a room service cart next to the desk and her laptop.

For the next hour she answered emails, mostly from Cady, Grant, and a few more inquiries from people looking to hire a PI. She didn't want to ignore any of them since they could be referrals from previous clients, but she couldn't take them on right now. While she wasn't shutting down one hundred percent, she couldn't leave them hanging, so she referred them to other PIs she knew and trusted.

Stretching her hands over her head, she looked at the clock. Eight a.m. Seeing as she had thrown herself into her Lycan "studies" full time, she met with Dr. Faulkner almost every day. She was learning a whole lot about Lycans, though there was very limited scientific information available. The afternoons she spent with Cady, learning about customs and etiquette, as well as information about the families and clans who would be coming to the ball. Thank god Cady was taking care of the party arrangements, as she frankly didn't know how to pick the right silverware or centerpieces for such an occasion. In between those activities she would usually grab a quick bite to eat at the company cafeteria, or any of the cafés in the building, but today Grant had invited her to have lunch in his office.

At least for now wolf lessons had stopped. Apparently, Grant had assigned Alex to another important task, and between twenty-four hour shifts with her and the preparations for the ball, the security team was spread thin. No one else could be tasked to help her. Alynna was relieved. As far as she could tell from her lessons, there wasn't any real need for her to learn to shift back and forth. As long as she could control it in public places, she was fine. Grant said he would make time after the ball to help her, but he needed a few weeks to clear his schedule. He also encouraged her to use the gym at Fenrir and close it down if necessary, should she want a safe place to shift, but Alynna had yet to take him up on that offer.

Alynna left the hotel room with Patrick trailing right behind her. They walked in silence, headed toward Fenrir, as they did every morning for the past week.

After her Lycan lessons with Dr. Faulkner, she went straight up to Grant's office. As she stepped out of the library, she stiffened slightly, as something familiar took over her senses. It was as if Alex's scent and his presence were teasing her, and she knew he had just been there. She sighed when she looked around and didn't see the Lycan, then walked to Grant's office.

Jared smiled as he stood up to greet her. "Ms. Chase! Mr. Anderson is expecting you."

"Thanks, Jared." She smiled back. "And how many times do I have to tell you, it's Alynna."

The young Lycan laughed nervously. "As many times as you want, but I can't call you that." He lowered his voice. "At least not when the Alpha is around." As Grant's trusted admin and the only other Lycan working on the floor, he knew who she really was.

She winked at him. "I've got your back, Jared. No worries."

He gave her a thumbs up as she entered the office.

The smell of fresh-baked dough, tomatoes, and mozzarella filled Alynna's nose and made her mouth water and stomach grumble. "You didn't!" she said in an excited voice.

Grant smiled at his sister and stood up from behind his desk. "I did."

Alynna practically skipped to the pile of white and red boxes set on the bar top off to the side of Grant's office. "Mama Jean's!" She ripped open the top box on one of the two stacks and took a deep breath. "Oh my god, Grant."

"You approve?" he asked with a twinkle in his eye.

She nodded. "I think I may need a few moments alone," she joked, hopping on one of the bar chairs. "By the way, did you buy all their pizzas for the day?" The double stack totaled about a dozen pizzas.

Grant laughed and sat beside her. "I heard you'd been eating a lot; I didn't want to be left hungry."

She gave him a playful punch on the shoulder. "You said I could order anything from room service!"

Grant picked up a piece and motioned for her to get one, not that Alynna needed any more encouragement. "I'm kidding, I'm kidding! Besides, it's probably your Lycan metabolism kicking in. I remember when I was growing up, the staff at home could hardly keep the fridge stocked when I was around."

"Hmm ..." Alynna moaned as she took a bite of the pizza. "I think I'll need one box for me," she said happily. "And maybe one to take back to the hotel?"

"Whatever you want, Alynna," Grant said before taking a big bite from his slice.

They continued their small talk, Grant asking Alynna about her plans and what she did over the last week. Alynna was also curious what exactly a billionaire Alpha did with his time, so she let him tell her about his day, which didn't sound fun. In fact, it sounded quite boring and tedious to her.

Alynna put away an impressive seven slices, the same as Grant, and after they finished eating, he motioned for her to sit down on the comfy couch. "I'll ask Jared to bring us some coffee." He called for Jared on the intercom.

They sat in silence for a few minutes after Jared left them.

Finally, Grant cleared his throat. "Alynna," he began. The Alpha's face was a mask of seriousness.

Alynna looked at him, puzzled. "Grant, what is it?"

He let out a breath. "I know I don't know you that well yet, but something's wrong. It's as if something's happened to you. You still laugh and put on a front, but you almost seem ... deflated." He gave her a concerned look. "I know this isn't the ideal situation right now, but I promise after the ball and everything's settled, we'll find a place for you where you can be yourself."

Alynna stared at him. Part of her wanted to brush it off and tell him he was imagining things. He didn't need to know about Alex. But it was like a wave of emotions passed through her all at once when she saw the look of genuine concern and worry on his face. In a move very unlike her, Alynna burst into tears.

Grant was visibly taken aback at the surge of emotion from Alynna. He pulled her into a hug, rubbing her back as he whispered soothing words to her.

Finally, Alynna pulled away, wiping her face with a tissue from the box Grant handed her.

"Do you want to ... I mean, I'm sure I can ask Cady if we could send out a message to the clans or something ..." Grant wasn't sure if that was possible, but he would do his best to find out alternatives to putting Alynna through all this pressure.

"No!" Alynna protested. "I know this is important to you and if I'm honest, it's not that, okay? I ... I ... ugh!" She stood up and walked over the window, leaning her head against the cool glass. She took a deep breath. "If you really want to know, promise me you won't get mad."

"Alynna," Grant started.

"Promise!"

He sighed. "All right, I promise."

"And promise you won't do anything hasty."

"Now you've got me worried." Grant crossed his arms over his chest.

She turned around. "Grant, please."

He gave another sigh. "All right, all right. I promise I won't get mad and I won't do anything hasty."

Alynna felt her heart beating wildly in her chest, but she took a deep breath. "It's ... I was ... this is silly! I don't even know why I'm acting this way! He's just a stupid man, and I won't act like a fool over this." She balled her hands into fists. "I swear it's over. I'm over it."

Grant looked at her with a confused look on his face. "Alynna, what's wrong? What are you rambling about?"

She sighed. "I slept with Alex. And now it's awkward between us."

"I'm going to kill him." Grant launched to his feet.

"Grant!" she admonished. "You said you wouldn't do anything hasty!"

"I won't!" he growled. "I'm going to kill him slowly and deliberately. Nothing will be hasty about it."

Alynna could feel the waves of anger radiating from Grant, his eyes glowing with barely contained fury. She hadn't seen Grant's wolf before, but if she didn't do something fast, she would probably be in for quite a show.

"Jesus Christ, Grant!" She stalked up to him and put her hands on her hips. "Stop it with this Lycan Alpha shit!"

"You're my sister! He's my employee!" he shouted.

"And so what? So, maybe it wasn't professional, but this isn't the fifteenth century! I'm not a princess in a tower, and he's not your vassal. We are consenting adults."

"But –"

"No buts!" She put her hands up to stop him. "You wanted to know and I told you. It wasn't easy to admit I lost my head over a charming face. I gave into my needs, but you wanted to know."

Grant ran his fingers through his hair. "Christ, Alynna." He sat down, his shoulders slumping in defeat. "You're right. You are both adults, although Alex should have known better seeing as you're new to being a Lycan."

"As much as you might want to think I'm an innocent in this, I'm not. I wanted him; I was the one who seduced him," she admitted. "And if it blows up in my face, then I'm to blame in all this."

"What happened?" Grant asked. "Do you want to tell me?"

"Ugh!" She sat down next to him, putting her palm on her forehead. "I won't go into details ..."

"Thanks," Grant groaned.

"Eww, no!" She playfully threw one of her balled up tissues at him. "Oh, Grant. You're going to think me naive and a fool."

"I won't," Grant said quietly. "I promise."

"I just wanted ... I mean, I thought I could handle it, you know? No strings attached, just se –, uh, a roll in the hay. He didn't promise me a relationship or anything if I went to bed with him, you have to believe that. I went into this with my eyes open. But then, afterward, it got awkward and I think I scared him off. I thought he felt something, but I misread him. He said he didn't think we should see each other anymore. He said he wasn't a relationship kind of guy, and it wasn't working out. Then, that night at Blood Moon, he was with some ... hussy and I almost lost control."

"Alynna, are you in love with him?"

"No!" she denied. "I mean, I can't explain it. I was drawn to him from the beginning, like I couldn't help it. Maybe it was the Lycan biology. I had never felt something like that. It was pure physical attraction."

"Alynna," he began, "this is probably confusing for you. Yes,

Lycan biology and urges are quite different from normal human ones. You were never taught about this, never warned about it. But, aside from that ... what can I say? Perhaps Alex – and it's hard for me to say this as your brother – but sometimes men just want sex. If you were willing and agreed to the no-strings thing, then he assumed you'd be on the same level." He paused. "Your feelings changed, but that's not your fault."

"I'm not ... I swear, I'm just ..."

"Your pride was hurt?" Grant finished. "I'm not an expert in relationships, but maybe that's part of it."

"True." She nodded weakly.

"Yes, I still want to kill him," he said with an edge to his voice. "Not because he's my employee and you're the sister of an Alpha, but because you're *my* sister and you're hurting. I don't want you to feel like this."

She sighed. "I'll get over it. He's just a pretty face. Plenty of fish in the sea and all that."

"That's my girl." Grant gave her a tight hug. "Just don't rush into anything, okay?"

Alynna nodded. "Don't treat Alex differently," she pleaded. "Don't punish him and have his hard work go down the toilet because I'm being a stupid girly-girl who can't handle a one night stand." She sniffed. "He really is devoted to you, and you can't punish him for one mistake."

"You are not stupid." Grant put his hands on her shoulders. "You're a person with feelings and emotions. As for Alex, while I still want to wring his neck for sleeping with you and hurting you, as you said, it's not the dark ages. I'm not selling off your virtue to the highest bidder. He is a good worker and as long as he stays professional, he'll have a place here. I'll do my best not to let my personal feelings interfere. But, I'm still your brother. He's been going back and forth from here and Chicago, taking care of a few other matters. I'll have Nick arrange his schedule so you don't have to see him too much, at least for now. Until I see you're okay."

She nodded and stood up. "I'll get over it and act like an adult around him. Thank you. I should go ... you probably have more stuff to do." She gathered her things and walked to the door.

"And Alynna?" Grant called after her. She turned around.

"You're not a mistake. If anything, Alex is making the mistake for not seeing what a great girl you are."

She smiled weakly at him. "Thanks, Grant. I'll see you tomorrow."

———

As promised, Grant did not let his personal feelings interfere with Alex and his duties. He did tell Nick that the younger Lycan should be rotated out of Alynna's and his personal detail, but his second in command didn't question the decision.

Alynna was just glad that she didn't have to face him again, at least until the ball. Unfortunately, security would be tight and all teams (plus the non-Lycan ones they had hired) would be on duty. Grant warned her that Alex, of course, would be working that night, but other than that, she didn't have to see him.

The days seemed to rush by her, and there were so many things to do before the big event. Soon, there were only two more weeks until the ball. She had to have her dress altered a couple of times, as her body seemed to change shape with all the exercising she was doing, plus the stress. Cady, thankfully, had been taking care of all the details, but did consult her on a few things.

"Did you want to do a formal entrance from the top of stairs?" Cady asked, as they sat down in her office one afternoon. The two women agreed to sit down for a few hours and just get all the planning out of the way. *This must be what planning a wedding feels like*, Alynna thought.

"Good god, no!" she sputtered, choking on the tea she had been sipping on. She cleared her throat. "That's not necessary, is it?"

Cady shook her head. "No, but that means...you'll have to be introduced to the guests. The alternative to the formal entrance is a receiving line. Grant can introduce you to the people on the line."

She sighed. "That's better than being on display like a zoo animal, I guess."

Cady frowned. "Alynna, you're not—"

"I know, I know," Alynna interrupted in an exasperated voice. "So, how many people are coming to this thing?"

Cady looked at her computer screen. "About 500 people."

Alynna almost choked again. "Five—what?"

"You won't be introduced to all of them," Cady explained. "Only to the Alphas and Lupas. We have about a 95% RSVP for now. The rest are members of the ruling families, Alliance families, and a very select group of humans who know about us. We like to keep friends in high places after all. It's not required attendance for everyone, as long as they get the message that you're one of the clan and Grant's sister, that's really all we care about. However, the Lycan High Council will be there and you will be presented to them at the beginning of the evening. Privately, in the ante room."

"What do I have to know for that?"

"Nothing really, just the pledge to honor your clan and abide by the rules, but that's like, two or three sentences. And also, everyone's names and background information. There are only five of them and you have the files, right?"

Alynna nodded. She was a PI, after all, and she studied the

files like she was getting to know a client. Thank god she had a practically flawless memory and knew the files forwards and backwards.

"Then that's it. I can give you a list of all the Alphas and Lupas, but Grant will be introducing you to everyone important. If you forget their names, no one will mind, you're the sister of the Alpha of New York, after all. But like any social situation...there will be some cliques and people will talk."

"Like high school, huh?" Alynna said wryly.

The redhead grinned at her. "Yeah, like high school. You're more likely to be metaphorically stabbed in the back than have your throat ripped out by fangs." She clucked her tongue. "Honestly...these women. And the men can be worse!"

Alynna giggled. "Aren't you...I mean...why? Why did you choose this life, Cady?" she finally asked the burning question that had been on her mind.

Cady paused and wrinkled her brow. "I...honestly? I owe the Lycans. For everything I have, my life. Michael left me a generous trust that allowed me to go to school and live anywhere I wanted, no strings attached. I went to Sorbonne and Oxford, but, well..." she sighed. "New York is my home. Fenrir is my home. I chose to be here."

"Wow, I...I don't know what to say." In truth, Alynna felt awe, envy, and respect at the same time. That Cady had this feeling of family and belonging growing up, but also that she didn't have to stay with the New York clan. She could have done anything with her life but chose to come back instead.

Cady shrugged and then gave Alynna a small smile. "I've thought about it, you know. I get offers all the time from CEOs all over the world, asking me to work with them. Offering triple what I make now. But, I don't know...it just doesn't feel right, being anywhere else." She took her glasses off and sighed. "Anyway, let's not get sidetracked. I mean, not if we want all the details hammered out by the time you leave here."

"And get some real dinner!" Alynna's stomach growled in agreement.

Cady laughed, opened her top desk drawer and handed her two candy bars. "Here, you bottomless pit. This should tide you over."

Alynna tore open the snack. "I swear, I gotta stop exercising so much. It's making me hungry all the damn time!"

"Well, let's continue then," Cady turned back to her screen.

"Wait, can I ask one more thing?"

"Sure."

"A personal thing?"

Cady raised an eyebrow at her and took a sip of her tea. "Yes...?"

"I'm just curious...you and Grant. You never...you know? Dr. Faulkner said that you could've been great Lupa material, if you were Lycan."

This time, it was Cady who almost choked on her drink. "Good lord, no!" she took a napkin and wiped her chin. "That would be like...well he's like a brother to me. We grew up together. That would be just..."

"Weird?" Alynna finished for her. "Gross?"

"Yes," Cady wrinkled her nose delicately. "And definitely yes."

Alynna wanted to ask if there was any other man or a certain handsome, tall, albeit humorless, blonde Lycan on her radar, but she wanted to get out of there sooner than later. Besides, that sounded like a talk that would go better over a drink or six.

"So, let's proceed. Any preference in terms of music?

CHAPTER SIXTEEN

"Alynna? May I come in?"

Alynna had been staring at herself in the mirror for the last twenty minutes. She couldn't quite believe her reflection. Cady had a team of hair and makeup artists working on her, adding just the right amount of cosmetics to emphasize her features and sweep her dark hair up into an elegant updo. Then, once they were done, Rachel, the Lycan seamstress from Bergdorf Goodman, helped her into the dress she and Cady had chosen. Alynna felt the green gown she had tried on a few weeks ago was just too much, so they looked at other dresses. When Rachel came into the changing room with the last dress, Cady and Alynna knew they found the one.

It was an elegant light champagne-colored ball gown with a full tulle skirt that seemed to float around her. The top was off the shoulder, showing her pale, delicate neck. The tight bodice hugged her curves, and it was made of a fine silky material that felt divine on her naked skin. It was simple and understated, but when she put it on the first time both she and Cady knew it was the dress for her.

She looked like Cinderella going to the ball, but all she

wanted to do was turn into a pumpkin. *Just one night*, she thought. *Get through this one night and get on with my life.*

"Yes, please come in," she called from her room in the suite she shared with Grant. She didn't even have to guess who it was. Her keen senses recognized her brother's scent. He entered her room, dressed in a gorgeous tuxedo that fit him perfectly. Clean-shaven and dressed to the nines, Grant Anderson looked very handsome and exuded power and confidence. Alynna swallowed a gulp, wishing she had some of the same confidence.

"You look beautiful," he complimented her, pride shining in his eyes. "Stunning. Gorgeous. Ama –"

"All right, all right," she giggled, holding up a hand.

He came closer and drew her into a loose hug, not wanting to crush her gown or muss her hair. "Nervous?"

She nodded.

"Don't be. You'll be great. There's nothing to it."

Alynna pulled away from Grant. "I hate being the center of attention." She scowled at her reflection in the mirror.

"It'll be over soon. I promise you won't have to be the center of attention again, except at your wedding."

Alynna made a face and stuck her tongue out. "Eww, no. If, and that's a big if, I do get married, I'm eloping."

Grant laughed. "Well, I'm not a fan of these shindigs, so I'll make you a deal. *I'll* drive you to the courthouse myself if it means not having to do this again."

"In the Maserati?"

"In the Maserati."

Alynna gave him a thumbs up and then smoothed her ball gown. "I still have some time before meeting the Council, right?"

"Yes, an hour, but uh," Grant cleared his throat, "there's someone ... somebody I want you to meet. And I'd really appreciate it if you would let me introduce you to her."

Alynna's eyebrow shot up. "Who is it?"

"My mother."

Alynna's heart jumped in her throat and she paled. "Grant. I'm ..."

"Please, Alynna?" he implored.

With the look on Grant's face, how could she say no? "Of course. Please tell her I would love to meet her. Where is she? Should I go down?"

He shook his head. "No, she's here. Just outside. Let me call her in."

"Oh no, no." She smoothed her ball gown of imaginary wrinkles again. "I mean, I should go out and meet her, right?"

Grant nodded and put his hand on her lower back, guiding her out the room.

Alynna was wringing her hands, trying to figure out what she was going to say to her father's wife. She held her breath as they walked out into the main room.

"Mother," Grant called to the trio standing by the large French doors that led to the balcony.

A tall elegant blonde woman who was softly speaking to Cady in French turned her head toward them. She was dressed in a long red gown that hugged her slim figure. Her beautiful face broke out into a smile when her eyes landed on Alynna.

"Mother, may I present Alynna Chase, my sister. Alynna, this is Callista Mayfair, my mother."

"H – how do you do, ma'am?" Alynna greeted, bowing her head.

"Oh my dear! I've waited so long to meet you, ever since Grant told me the news," Callista exclaimed, her voice light and cheery. Her cornflower blue eyes sparkled as she leaned over and gave Alynna a kiss on each cheek. Alynna breathed in the scent of jasmine flowers. "Please, call me Callista." She looked at the handsome older Lycan beside her. "Jean-Luc, doesn't she look like Michael? It's incredible, absolutely incredible!"

"*Oui, ma-chere.*" The man nodded in agreement.

"Oh, sorry, this is Jean-Luc Allonse, my husband. He's second cousin to the Alpha of Paris, and we are officially part of his delegation tonight."

The older man with snowy white hair wearing a white tuxedo bowed his head and then kissed Alynna's hand. He smelled of cedar wood. "Very lovely to meet you my dear," he said in a thick French accent. He gave her a warm smile. "We've heard so much about you."

"I, uh, thank you." Alynna was slightly flustered at the attention and warm reception from Grant's mother and stepfather. "I hope you had a nice flight?"

"It was comfortable enough. I do get tired from the time difference, but the jet makes traveling quite pleasant these days." She looked at Alynna from head to toe appraisingly. "*Magnifique!* Cady, this is a wonderful dress."

"Alynna and I picked it out together." The redhead smiled from behind Callista, giving Alynna a small wink.

"Ah, such good taste!" the older woman exclaimed. "But ..." She motioned to one of the tall men wearing a dark suit standing by the door. Alynna didn't recognize any of them, so they were probably part of Jean-Luc's team. The Lycan handed Callista a small briefcase. Turning to Alynna, she opened the case.

Alynna's eyes went wide as saucers. "Holy shi – I mean, oh wow!"

Sitting on top of rich black velvet inside the case was a beautiful emerald and diamond necklace. The large green stone in the middle was the size of her palm, and flawless diamonds surrounded it. She gasped when Callista picked it up and motioned for her to turn around. "Ma'am ... I ... no ..."

"Callista, please," she corrected.

"Ma' ... Callista ... I couldn't!" She shook her head.

"Nonsense, my dear." She handed the case to Grant and took the necklace out. "You must wear this."

"What if I lose your necklace? Or it gets stolen?" The necklace must cost more than her apartment.

"Well, first of all, I know for a fact you'll have eyes on you all evening, so no one would dare try to take it, and second, this is not my necklace anymore. It's yours."

Alynna was taken aback. "E – excuse me?"

"What my mother means," Grant interrupted before Alynna could protest, "is the necklace is part of the Anderson family collection. The jewelry belongs to the family and all the women get to wear anything from the vault." He looked at the necklace. "This was grandma's favorite piece, right, Mother? A gift from my grandfather?"

Callista nodded. "When you told me she had your father's eyes, I knew she had your grandmother's, too. I knew this would be perfect." She turned to Alynna. "Would you please, my dear?"

Alynna turned around, letting the older woman drape the piece around her neck. "There you go," she said, giving her shoulder an affectionate pat. "Wonderful, perfect!" she exclaimed as Alynna turned back around.

The necklace felt heavy around her neck and shoulders, but it wasn't just the jewels. The weight of it all – family, brother, father, grandmother ... for years she had wondered about them and now she couldn't quite grasp everything.

"Are you all right, my dear?" Callista asked with a concerned look on her face.

"Yes, ma'am - I mean, Callista," she stammered, then took a deep breath. "Thank you."

Callista smiled. "That's it. Take deep breaths."

Alynna nodded. "I really appreciate this. It's very generous of you."

"You'll do great. Now," she turned to her husband, "I don't want to break further protocol, as technically Gaultier, the Alpha of the Paris clan, has to meet you first."

"Don't worry. I'm sure my cousin will not begrudge you the company of your son, *ma chere*," Jean-Luc said.

"In any case, I'll let you relax, my dear. Have a glass of champagne before you meet the stuffed shirts of the Council." With that, she gave Alynna a kiss on both cheeks.

"I'll walk you out, Mother." Grant nodded to Alynna before guiding the couple out of the suite.

Alynna let out a breath. "Wow," she said to Cady. "That was *not* what I expected."

Cady laughed. "What did you expect?"

"I dunno ... maybe a cold matriarch type? I didn't think she'd be so ..."

"Cheerful? Young?" Cady quipped.

"Warm and friendly." Alynna touched the jewels at her neck. "I thought ... I don't know. I thought she'd see me as some sort of outsider or interloper, and she'd be indifferent toward me at best."

Cady walked over, smoothing down her own sapphire blue gown. "Callista Mayfair is certainly one of a kind."

"Wasn't Grant's parents' marriage arranged or something?" Alynna asked.

"Sort of. Michael and Callista were friends before they got married, or so my dad told me. She's the daughter of another high-ranking family from Philadelphia. With few options for mates and as Lycans with notable positions, everyone assumed they would be married and produce an heir. They weren't very romantic or affectionate, at least not in public, but they held a deep respect for each other," Cady explained.

"That seems weird." Alynna's brows knitted in confusion.

"Yeah well, don't ask me. I'm just the help." Cady shrugged her shoulders.

"Cady!" Alynna admonished.

"I'm joking, Alynna, I'm joking!" Cady said defensively. "It's complicated and I don't really understand it myself. But, I suppose if the human race was dying out, I'd do my part to help, too."

"Cady." Alynna dropped her voice. "You don't mean ... are Lycans dying out?"

She shrugged her shoulders. "I don't have the exact numbers, but there have been rumors swirling around. Lycan births have dropped in the last two decades. Not enough that the High Council has taken action, but from what I've heard, they are certainly monitoring it. Anyway," Cady straightened her shoulders, "do you want a glass of champagne or something before you go meet the Council?"

"Ugh." Alynna made a disgusted face. Just thinking about alcohol made her nauseous. "Hey, you think you can sneak me one of those petite fours from the kitchen instead?"

———

The presentation to the High Council seemed almost anticlimactic. Grant introduced her to the five members, all high-ranking Lycans who were never chosen as Alpha for their clans. They came from various corners of the world – Europe, Africa, the Middle East, Asia, and South America. The youngest member was Rodrigo Baeles from Brazil, a lively and affable man in his late forties who welcomed her warmly. The other members, Oded Khan from Iran, Jun Park from Korea, and Adama Amuyaga from Ghana, also greeted her cordially. The oldest member and unofficial leader, Lljuffa Suitdottir from

Sweden, was cool toward her and said nothing, but gave her a nod. The older lady regarded her with a curious eye, but then all of them were probably intrigued and maybe slightly wary of the young outsider who had seemed to infiltrate their close-knit society.

Despite the scrutiny, Alynna managed to remember their names, how to call each one, to kiss their rings to show her allegiance, and to recite the words pledging her fealty to the clan, to follow her Alpha and the High Council, and to never reveal her true nature to anyone.

Afterward, they broke out the champagne, and Baeles spoke a few words to formally welcome her into the fold. Then, it was time for the receiving line.

The New York clan had rented out the Grand Ballroom at the Waldorf Astoria for this occasion. The ballroom was decorated in green and silver, Fenrir's colors. The staff at the hotel was told very little of what was happening, in addition to being strictly instructed not to stare or watch any of the guests. Everyone from the waiters to the dishwashers was given background checks, and all of their phones were locked up while they were working the event. Though Lycans themselves were very discreet, the clan couldn't take any chances of a coat check person overhearing the wrong things, or a waiter taking pictures and posting them online.

"Ready to collapse yet?" Cady whispered from behind Alynna. She handed her a glass of water.

The young woman took the water and sipped as much as she could, letting the cool liquid quench her parched throat. "Oh my god, how many more?"

"Ten more pairs, then that's it."

Alynna took a deep breath. She asked Grant to give her a one minute break every two or three introductions. Surprisingly, he and Nick Vrost were quite adept at delaying the guests and keeping them occupied while Alynna took a breather.

"Wow, they are quite smooth, aren't they?" She motioned to the Alpha and Beta as they shook hands and made small talk with the people in line.

"You'd never know it considering Mr. Vrost says about ten words a day," Cady chuckled.

"So, he's not working tonight?"

"Oh, he is," Cady answered. "But he's working as Beta, right beside Grant. His job is to stick by the Alpha and entertain guests, be his proxy in case he's busy doing something else."

"Wow. I thought his only job was to stand there and look scary," Alynna giggled.

Cady let out a loud laugh which prompted both men to look over to them. Nick gave them a wry smile and motioned with his head, calling Alynna over to them.

"All right, duty calls," Cady said, giving Alynna a gentle push.

"Right." Alynna walked over to the two men. Nick looked particularly handsome in his black tux, though there was an edge of danger to him, like a caged animal. She could tell he was enjoying this as much as she was, but this was probably one of those things he had to endure if he wanted such a prominent position.

"Great job tonight, Ms. Chase," he said as she walked by.

"You too, Nicky-boy. You clean up well." She gave him a wink only he could see, and he responded with a smirk.

Alynna took her place next to Grant, who was talking to two other men.

"Ah, here she is. Liam, may I present Alynna Chase. Alynna, this is Liam Henney, Alpha of San Francisco and his Beta and cousin, Takeda Matsumoto."

The taller of the two men turned to her, his handsome face

breaking into a smile. Dark hair swept across his brow and electric blue eyes sparkled as he greeted her. "Very lovely to meet you, Ms. Chase," he said, taking the hand she offered and giving it a firm shake. Liam was perhaps the youngest Alpha she had seen tonight, younger than Grant and maybe only a few years older than herself.

"Alpha," she nodded. "Thank you for coming all the way here to join us tonight."

"The pleasure's all mine. And on behalf of my clan, I would like to say we are overjoyed you have found your family and your pack."

"Thank you," she replied. Cady explained the welcoming words were a modified version of the traditional welcome for newborns. Usually Alphas would have to say or write to the parents: "We are overjoyed a new life has joined your family and your pack." But, since she wasn't exactly a newborn, they had to change the greeting.

Alynna shook hands with his Beta, a shorter Japanese man who was dressed in a traditional formal kimono and hakama in dark blue. "Ms. Chase, I am overjoyed you have found your family and your pack," he said in an accented tone, though his English had a slight British affectation.

"Thank you, Matsumoto-san." She gave him a slight bow. "I hope your trip here was pleasant."

"It was, Ms. Chase," he replied.

"It's been a while since we came to New York," Liam interjected. "I do miss this lovely city."

"But I heard San Francisco is beautiful as well," Alynna said. She was getting the hang of this small talk. "I would love to visit ... uh, I mean, you know, if you would allow me." She blushed, thinking it was too forward inviting herself into another clan's territory. Okay, so maybe she needed some practice with the Lycan small talk.

Liam grinned. "Of course, Ms. Chase. You and your brother are always welcome in San Francisco. But do let me know if you're planning a trip, as I would love to show you all the best places."

His electric blue eyes seemed to pierce right into her, making her blush even more and her stomach flip flop. Sure, there were a lot of handsome Lycans in the room and few of them hid their obvious interest in her, but there was something different and more sincere about Liam.

"Of course," she replied, staring back at him.

She must have stared a little too long, as a light cough jolted her out of her trance. "Alpha, we mustn't keep the line, Ms. Chase has more guests," Takeda politely declared, nodding toward the line of guests.

"Of course, my apologies." He bowed. "Ms. Chase, I hope to see you later."

"Uh-huh ..." was all Alynna could say.

The two men left and walked toward the ballroom, though they stopped when they passed by another couple standing by the doors.

"Hmm ..."

Alynna looked up at Grant who was staring at her with a contemplative look on his face. "What?"

"Nothing," her brother answered, though the start of a smile was tugging at his lips.

"Grant Horace Anderson!" she mocked.

"That's not my middle name," he quipped, touching her chin lightly with his finger.

"It should be since it sounds like the name of the town busybody."

"Oh yeah, well I'm not the one who's *still* blushing and has a bit of drool on her chin!"

Alynna gasped and touched her chin. Finding it dry, she nudged him lightly on the shin with her foot.

"Ouch," he joked.

Alynna glared up at him and he countered with a smile. "As far as prospects go, Liam isn't a bad choice."

"Excuse me?" she asked in an incredulous voice.

"He's only twenty-nine, and he's been an Alpha for about six months now. He's definitely under pressure to choose a Lupa and produce an heir, though I heard his mom's your typical Tiger Mom. The current Tokyo Alpha's aunt, I think. But, they're good connections – you'll not only be connected to another clan in the country, but also in another continent."

"Whoa there, cowboy," Alynna said. "Drop the keys to the Maserati; you're not driving to the courthouse anytime soon." Alynna looked down the hallway and watched Liam and Takeda walk into the ballroom. To her surprise, just before they turned the corner, Liam looked back and gave her a slow smile and a wink before they walked into the main room.

Alynna felt her stomach flip flop again and her cheeks grow hot. She never really dated or had high school crushes, but now she understood why those girls acted silly around cute guys.

"Shall I warm up the Maserati? Just make sure you bring enough quarters for the meters. I hear those meter maids are tough down in City Hall," Grant said, looking at her with his knowing smile.

The urge to punch him in the shoulder was almost too hard to resist. "Let's get this show on the road."

They turned back to the receiving line and made quick work of the remaining guests. Finally, they reached the end of the line where a short, balding man and a tall, willowy blonde in a slinky white gown were waiting.

"Grayson, this is Alynna Chase, my sister. Alynna, this is

Grayson Charles, Alpha of Connecticut and his companion, Ms. Vanessa Bennet."

"How do you do? Thank you for accepting our invitation, Alpha."

The older man grabbed her hands and rubbed his sweaty palms against hers. His eyes raked over her, lingering a little too long on her breasts. She almost gagged at the sensation of his damp palms and his perusal but kept her smile. "Ms. Chase, on behalf of my clan, I would like to say we are overjoyed you have found your family and your pack."

"Er, thank you, Alpha," she said. She looked toward the woman who accompanied him, and she seemed to be a little too preoccupied talking to Grant. She was definitely invading his personal space, sidling up to him and giving him little touches here and there while giggling at whatever he said. *Oh brother*, she thought. Finally, Grayson Charles loudly cleared his throat, catching her attention. He gave her a disapproving look as she turned to Alynna.

"Ms. Chase," Vanessa said in a sweet voice. "So lovely and an honor to meet you!" She grabbed her hand and shook it enthusiastically. "Our Lupa, Caroline, sends her regards and deepest regrets for not being able to make it."

"She's due any day now," Grayson interrupted.

"An heir," Grant said. "I didn't know, Grayson. Congratulations. I wish your family health and your wife a safe delivery."

"Thank you," the older man said, though he seemed distracted staring at Alynna's "charms." "Uh, yes, well maybe in a month you'll be coming up to Connecticut for another welcoming ceremony."

"Looking forward to it," Grant said dryly. "Anyway, I do apologize, seeing as we're done with the receiving line, I need to prepare to welcome everyone. Alynna." He offered his arm to his sister.

"Yes, let's go," Alynna said a little too quickly, wanting to get away from Grayson Charles and his greedy, roving eyes. "'Bye! I mean, see you ..." She let out a sigh of relief as Grant led her into the ante room. She was looking forward to kicking off her shoes for a bit until she had to go out into the den of literal wolves.

CHAPTER SEVENTEEN

After a quick fifteen minute break, Alynna was on her feet again. She accompanied Grant to the small stage set up at the front of the four story ballroom. Thank god she didn't have to say anything, at least not until the end of the night. Also, she was glad it was a semi-public space so Grant was quite vague in his welcoming remarks. Frankly, she had seen all kinds of reactions and comments about her being the "True Mate" offspring, from disbelief, to excitement, to intense scrutiny, as if she'd sprout wings or horns at any moment.

"And so, I'd like to formally begin tonight's festivities. Please enjoy the music, the dancing, the food, and the champagne!" He raised his glass to the audience, and everyone did the same. He motioned to the orchestra as he took Alynna by the arm and led her down to the ballroom floor.

"I'm glad we don't have to do a dance or something," she remarked.

"Afraid you'd get your toes stepped on?" Grant laughed.

"Have you seen *my* feet? They're as graceful as hooves!" she giggled. Grant had really loosened up around her and it was hard to imagine this was the man who was threatening her in his office just weeks ago. Despite all her reservations about being part of the Lycan world, knowing Grant was one of the things she was grateful for.

They walked around the ballroom, stopping and talking to some of the people she had met. Many of the delegation members who were not part of the receiving line were clamoring to be introduced to her. Soon her head was spinning again from all the new faces and names she was trying to remember.

"... and so I was hoping we could talk about that deal in Panama, Don Alvarez," Grant said. Sensing her distress, Grant had grabbed the first group he saw, brought them to a quiet alcove, and kept Alynna next to the wall, where his intimidating frame effectively blocked her from prying eyes and well-wishers. She sighed with relief, giving her brother a grateful squeeze on the arm and tried not to fall asleep as he and the businessmen from Panama talked about cement prices and last year's banana crops.

"I think we can do something about that, Alpha." The head of the group nodded.

"That would be great, Don Alvarez. I'll have –"

Alynna looked up at Grant as she felt him freeze beside her. His eyes narrowed and the muscles in his arm tensed.

"Alpha? Are you all right?" Don Alvarez asked politely.

"Grant?" Alynna rubbed his arm, trying to catch his attention.

"What? Oh, my apologies. I thought I heard my assistant call for me." He smiled. "Keen senses, you know?"

"Of course!" The group of human businessmen laughed.

Alynna's eyebrows shot up. She didn't hear anything, and she could have sworn she saw Cady run to the ladies room just five minutes before.

Grant gave the Panamanians a nod and excused himself and

Alynna, citing Lycan business. He gently pulled Alynna away, his eyes scanning the room intently.

"Grant, what's wrong?" she asked nervously. "Is there ... is someone here?"

"Yes. I mean ... no, I don't think so. Didn't you smell that? That scent?"

"What scent?" She was surrounded by about three hundred Lycans from around the world, so she had her fill of scents. She was so glad she practiced tuning them out weeks ago.

"It was ... I don't know. Weird. Like I couldn't ignore it."

"Did you recognize it?"

"Sort of. I mean, that's the weird thing. I only know it's pleasant, but I can't quite name what it is. Like ... smelling cookies or the rain for the first time." Grant's eyes went glassy for a moment, and he shook his head. "Sorry. I don't mean to alarm you. It's a weird feeling. The hairs on the back of my neck just went straight up, but not in a bad way. Are you sure you didn't smell cookies?" He wrinkled his nose, as if trying to catch the scent again.

"Well, don't ask me. I've only been a Lycan for a couple of weeks," Alynna joked. Then, she nudged his side and nodded across the room where Vanessa was talking to a group of Lycans from Italy. She laughed and tossed her head back, swatting the Italian Lycan who had his arm around her waist. "Maybe it's the dreaded feeling of having someone devour you with their eyes."

As if on cue, Vanessa turned to them, giving Grant a sweet smile. She disentangled herself from the Italian and began to stalk toward them. "Speaking of which ..."

Grant groaned inwardly.

"Oops, I feel Mother Nature calling," Alynna cackled.

"Please Alynna, don't –"

"Throw you to the wolves?" She grinned. "I'll be back ... maybe!"

She sprinted as fast as she could away from him and made her way to the bathroom. Maybe Cady was there and she could finally talk to someone she knew.

The bathroom was practically empty except for a woman in a green gown who had just exited one of the stalls. Alynna realized she actually did have to answer Mother Nature's call. Thank god the stalls were extra wide to accommodate fluffy ball gowns like the one she was wearing.

As she was fixing her skirt inside the stall, she heard the bathroom doors creak open and a group of girls entered, laughing and chatting.

"Can you believe it?" one of the voices said. "True Mate indeed! How can they be sure she's a True Mate offspring? I thought that was a myth!"

"Yeah, how can they be sure she wasn't just born on the wrong side of the blanket?"

Giggling followed, and Alynna bit her lip and balled her hands into fists.

"Well, this certainly does change things, girls," a voice she hadn't heard yet say. "Grant Anderson will be even harder to catch now that he doesn't *have* to produce the next heir of the New York Clan."

"Humph. That little thing? Produce the heir of the New York clan?" another said haughtily. "I heard she was raised in Brooklyn and her mom was a waitress!"

The anger bubbling in her was ready to erupt. They could insult the clan, insult her, but *not* her mother. She grabbed the door handle of the stall, ready to show her metaphorical and possibly physical claws, but before she could open the door, another voice boomed through the bathroom.

"Oh, shut the fuck up," the voice said. "Just who the hell are you girls, anyway? How could you judge that poor girl without even meeting her?"

"Excuse me," said the haughty voice. "Do I know you? We're having a private conversation here."

"Well, this isn't exactly a private place," the other woman countered. "So what if her mother's a waitress? Raising a child by herself without the help of a husband or a clan? That doesn't even make you half the woman she is."

"How dare you!"

"You wanna take this outside, beanpole?"

"Lorraine, let's go. It's not worth it. Besides, I saw Liam Henney by the bar just before we came in here. You know him? That hot young Alpha from San Francisco? I'm sure he'd enjoy our company."

Alynna heard the door creak open again, and the bathroom went silent. Then, she heard a string of curses that would make a sailor blush. She pushed the door open and took a deep breath.

The woman in green Alynna had seen earlier was sitting in one of the chairs, checking her makeup, muttering to herself. She walked up to her, catching the other woman's attention when she appeared in the reflection behind her.

The woman jumped up in surprise. "*Cazzo madre de dio!*" The woman turned and put her hand on her chest. "You do *not* sneak up on a Lycan like that!"

"I'm sorry!" Alynna quickly apologized. "I didn't mean to ... it's just that ..."

The woman let out a breath. "It's okay. Ugh, I swear, I hate going to these things! I wasn't even supposed to be here, you know? I have more important things to do." She checked her cherry red lipstick in the mirror. "But my Ma and Nonna, god bless their souls, they'd be rolling in their graves if I didn't come."

Alynna stared at the woman – no, Lycan, definitely. *Hmm ... cookies or fresh baked goods*, she thought as she scented the Lycan. She was dressed in a gorgeous silk gown in a blue-green shade along with white gloves that came up to her elbows. The woman was a little shorter than her with generous curves that filled her beautiful dress. Her face was gorgeous – dusky olive skin, thick lashes, high cheekbones, full red lips, almost like a petite, younger Monica Bellucci. Her dark, thick curly hair was piled on top of her head, and when she turned to look at her, Alynna was taken aback by her eyes. One was a stark green color and the other a bright blue. "Oh my! I mean, I'm sorry to stare, it's just ..."

The other woman smiled. "Yeah, yeah, I know. The eyes. I have heterochromia. It runs in the family. All of us Lycans have it, but not the humans for some reason." She put her hands on her hips. "Anything I can do for you, honey? Did you need a tampon or something?"

"No. I ..." She didn't recognize the woman, which meant she wasn't at the receiving line. She definitely would have remembered those eyes. "I wanted to say thank you."

The woman looked at her quizzically. "Thank you? For what?"

"For what you said to those women about me ... and my mother."

"Your mom?" Her eyes widened. "Oh *figlio di puttana!* You're her! It's you, I mean!" Her face went red. "Oh my god, I'm so sorry ..."

Alynna laughed. "Don't be, please don't!" She sat down. "I would have torn their throats out if you hadn't said anything first. Then where would we be?"

"I'll tell ya, honey. I'd be right beside you, getting in my own hits." The other woman chuckled. "Girls like that ... they think their shit don't stink, you know? They think they're better because they're from this or that clan, or someone's daughter, or wife, or whatever. Don't listen to them. They're just jealous."

"I wouldn't know why," Alynna said, slumping down on the couch in the corner. She kicked her shoes off and sighed.

The other woman joined her and slipped her own shoes off. "You probably have heard it all, the whole clan thing and how privileged you are and how people will be vying for your attention, and I get it. It's a lot of responsibility."

Alynna nodded.

"But you can't let that or what others have to say get to you, you know? My Nonna always said, '*Esse nufesso qui dice male di macaruni.*'"

"Sounds like good stuff," Alynna sighed. "What does it mean?"

"Who speaks badly of macaroni is a fool."

Alynna laughed out loud.

"Yeah, Nonna was getting senile by the end." They both erupted into peals of laughter.

"Thank you ..." Alynna realized she didn't know the girl's name.

"Frankie. I'm Frankie."

"Nice to meet you. I'm Alynna."

"I know who you are. Don't you go by another name? A nickname?" Alynna shook her head. "A middle name?"

"Eww, no," Alynna said. She now knew the meaning of her middle name, but she still remembered how she got teased for it.

"It can't be worse than mine."

"What is it?"

"I won't tell if you won't tell me yours!" Frankie laughed.

"Is it Horace?"

"No!" Both girls went into a fit of giggles.

"Oh, Alynna," Frankie sobered. "What I wouldn't do to see those girl's reactions when they realize you heard what they said. Because you know those catty bitches would never say that to your face."

"Oh, really? Would you now?"

———

"Who's that with Alynna?" Grant asked Cady as his eyes followed the two women exiting the bathroom. They were walking arm-in-arm, whispering to each other. His sister laughed and then quickly covered her mouth as they walked by two members of the High Council. Alynna blocked Grant's view as he tried to make out the face of the woman wearing a green dress.

Cady turned around. "Who?" She saw the twosome, but they walked so fast they were a blur to her. "Hmm ... I don't know. Must be part of some delegation. It's nice that she found a friend."

Grant's brow wrinkled. "Make sure you find out who she is," he said, his brow furrowing. "I want to know everyone who approaches her tonight when she's alone."

"She's hardly alone, Grant." Cady took a sip of her champagne. "You have eyes trained on her every move. I swear you would have bugged the bathrooms if laws didn't prohibit it."

"Looks like they're making their way toward Liam Henney," Nick quipped as he came up behind Grant and Cady.

"Liam Henney?" Cady asked, a delicate brow raising. "That's the Alpha from San Francisco, right? The new one? His father died ..."

"Six months ago," Grant finished. He had been at the funeral of course, and he remembered the younger man who seemed to have the weight of the world on his shoulders. Now, he stood in a circle surrounded by gorgeous young woman, smiling and laughing. He was glad Liam seemed to be having a good time. As another Alpha who had responsibility thrust at him unexpectedly, he could relate.

"And now our little bird is flying the nest," Nick observed as Alynna tapped Liam on the shoulder to catch his attention.

"What?" Cady looked confused. "Liam and Alynna?"

Nick stifled a laugh. "Did you actually *miss* something, Ms. Gray?"

Cady gave him a smirk. "Contrary to popular belief, I can't be everywhere at the same time."

"Who is ... ugh, Alynna, get out of the way ..." Grant was muttering, weaving his head left and right as he tried to get a better view of Alynna's mystery companion.

"Grant, are you all right?" Nick asked. Grant had looked distracted for the last thirty minutes or so, and the Beta could sense his Alpha's unease. "Do you think that the man who tried to hurt Alynna is here?"

"I haven't scented him." Grant's shoulders tensed, but it made him focus. "But with so many Lycans here, it would be easy to hide."

"That's why I have Alex and Heath roving around. They were able to catch the scent that night, so they know what to look for."

"What is going on there?" Cady's brows knitted, her eyes glued to Alynna, her companion, and Liam Henney.

"I should go check it out," Grant said, handing his glass of champagne to a passing waiter as he stalked toward the group across the ballroom.

Left alone with Nick, Cady wasn't sure if she should make a hasty retreat or stand her ground.

Finally, he said the first words. "You look lovely, Ms. Gray," Nick noted.

"Um, thanks," she said. She had picked out a simple, floor-length sapphire blue gown; nothing flashy or fancy, after all, she wasn't the center of attention at this party. "You too. Look nice. I mean, you ..."

"Clean up nice?" he asked wryly, with an almost bitter tone.

"That's not ... I mean, your tuxedo fits well." She mentally slapped her palm to her head. "Um, I have to go and check on the canapes ... or something." With that, she left Nick standing there, staring after her.

———

"Excuse me." Alynna tapped Liam Henney on his broad shoulder.

The taller man turned around and smiled when he realized who it was. "Ms. Chase," he said warmly.

"Alynna, please," she said, giving him her best smile.

"Then please, call me Liam." His eyes twinkled.

"Liam," a voice behind him said. "Who's your little friend?"

"Oh yes, sorry." Liam took Alynna by the arm and guided her around to their group. "If you haven't met her yet, ladies, this is our guest of honor, Ms. Alynna Chase."

"Hello," she greeted.

The women – all three of them – gasped and then started fawning over her.

"Oh my! Of course! It's nice to meet you!" Their ringleader, a tall, slim brunette extended her hand. "I'm Lorraine Johnson. From Texas. My uncle Gus is Alpha. Oh, I love your dress! And that necklace!"

This must be beanpole, Alynna thought. *Geez. Lorraine must have at least six inches over Frankie.* She couldn't believe the petite brunette wanted to take her on. "Nice to meet you, Lorraine. Have you met my friend, Frankie?"

Alynna drew Frankie forward. "Hello, ladies," she smirked.

Lorraine visibly paled. "N ... nice to meet you, Frankie," she said nervously.

"Likewise," Frankie answered. Alynna could almost hear her follow it with "bitch" in her head.

Lorraine introduced the rest of her friends whose names Alynna couldn't recall because she kept calling them Twiddledum and Twiddledumber in her head.

"Liam was just telling us about growing up in San Francisco," Lorraine cooed.

"It's beautiful if you love nature," Liam said. "Lots of places to go hiking, swimming, running, biking. And the food is phenomenal!"

"I don't know." Lorraine's red lips curved into a flirtatious smile. "He's never tried Texas barbecue, so I said he had to come visit sometime."

"Where did you grow up, Alynna?" Frankie asked sweetly.

"In Brooklyn," Alynna said, her eyes darting towards Lorraine. She didn't think the Texan could get any paler, but more blood seemed to drain out of her face. "My mother was a waitress. And I have to tell you, there're some really good restaurants down there. I used to come with her to work sometimes, and they'd give me staff meals."

"My mother made me work in a restaurant kitchen when I was sixteen!" Liam interjected.

"Really?!" Frankie said. "But you were the heir to the San Francisco clan!"

He shook his head. "She didn't care. She said, 'If you're going to be Alpha someday, you're going to learn what it's like to put in a hard day's work.' She sent me to work at one of her friend's restaurants in the Mission district. Every day I would come home and collapse on the couch, but I stuck it out for three years every summer. Learned how to make a mean *arroz con pollo*."

Alynna looked at Frankie, who seemed to be reveling in all that was happening. She sipped her champagne and kept glancing over at Lorraine, Twiddledum, and Twiddledumber as they struggled to keep their composure. She smirked at them, but it only made Lorraine's face turn red in anger.

"What are you looking at you little ..." Lorraine began, but Twiddledum – or was it Twiddledumber? – put her hand on her shoulder.

"Well, now! I think Lorraine's had a little too much to drink." Her friend took the glass from her hand. "I think we'll go and ... powder our nose and get some fresh air. It was nice to meet you, Alynna, Frankie. 'Bye Liam!" The girls quickly made their exit.

Alynna and Frankie looked at each other and then burst into laughter.

"Did I do something wrong?" Liam asked, a confused look on his face.

"Oh no, sweetie," Frankie laughed. "You did everything right!"

Alynna giggled some more. "I'm sorry Liam, private joke. I'll explain more if you want."

A ringing interrupted them. "Oh crap!" Frankie cursed, digging her phone from her purse. She looked at the screen. "Sorry, I gotta take this, hon. Family business. But if I have to go, I'll come find you first, okay?"

Alynna nodded and watched her new friend's retreating back.

"Interesting friend you got there," Liam commented.

"Yeah," Alynna said fondly. "She's nice."

"Unlike the brainless brigade?"

"Liam!" Alynna sounded rather shocked. She could see the glint of intelligence in the Alpha's eyes. Alynna realized Liam was being polite and humoring the ditzy Lycans but was in no way interested in Lorraine or her friends.

"Too bad." Alynna gave a fake sigh. "Lorraine and Liam. I

was already picturing the monogrammed pillows, towels, maybe the gate to your mansion ..."

Liam laughed, making his boyish face even more handsome. "L and L. It would save a lot on printing costs."

"Alynna, Liam," Grant said as he approached the laughing duo. "Glad to see you're both having a good time."

"I am now." Liam glanced down at Alynna.

"Good. I wanted to ask who's your ..." He looked around, his brows knitting. "Friend?"

"Oh, Lorraine and her cohorts?" Alynna said. "Don't worry, they've decided to call it a night."

"No, not them. I mean the other –"

"Grant!" Someone from behind called, then slapped him on the shoulder. "You are a difficult man to find! And your lovely sister is here, too! Please, I've been dying to be introduced to her." An older man and his companion stood beside Grant, looking at him expectantly.

Here we go again, Alynna thought. She put on her best smile as Grant introduced her to the couple. "Nice to meet you..."

CHAPTER EIGHTEEN

After about three more introductions, Alynna was able to get away from the crowd thanks to Liam. He discretely guided her away as Grant was making small talk, placing his hand on the small of her back. A little while later, she found herself with him on one of the balconies off the side of ballroom, the view of the Manhattan skyline behind them.

"So, you're really a private investigator?" Liam asked.

"Yes, I am," Alynna laughed. She leaned against the stone balustrade and breathed in the fresh air.

"So tell me ..."

"You want sordid stories?"

"Not about your clients. I mean ... not about you, or er ..." He smiled sheepishly and rubbed the back of his head with his palm. Alynna thought it was adorable.

"Okay, well, it's not a sordid story ..." she began, "but I can tell you about this time I was trapped in a client's pantry for almost twenty hours."

"Really?" His eyes lit up and Alynna felt her stomach doing flip flops again.

"Really! He had me come over to try and catch his wife cheating on him. He said I should come during the day and install the cameras. So, I went in around two p.m. and started doing my thing," she paused. "Then, I heard the door open. It was the wife and her lover, who decided to have a little afternoon delight."

"No."

"Yes!" she shrieked. "I run to the closest door I could find – the kitchen pantry. I thought, hey, it can't be that bad. They'll have a quickie in the bedroom, then head back to work and I can finish my job."

"But?"

"Well, afternoon delight turned into evening delight. At six p.m. lover boy says goodbye, and the wife goes about her business, cleaning up and whatnot. Husband comes home thirty minutes later, and they decide to stay in and order dinner."

"What? But why didn't you call the husband?"

"That's the thing! It was just my luck my phone battery was running out. Believe me, to this day I carry two extra batteries."

"What happened? Why didn't you sneak away while they were watching TV or eating dinner?" Liam looked genuinely interested and looked at her with those beautiful eyes, hanging on her every word.

"Well, the problem was their apartment was one of those fancy loft places that had an open floor plan. Everything was out in the open. I couldn't get away unless I was Spiderman and could crawl outside the building."

"So you stayed there all night?" She nodded. "At least you were in the pantry and there was food!"

Alynna burst out laughing, and she could hardly continue as tears streaked down her cheeks. "They ... never ... cooked. There ... was ... nothing ... but Campbell's Chunky Chicken soup in the pantry!"

Liam laughed. "And you ate it?"

Alynna nodded. "Five cans total. I didn't get out until eight a.m. the next day when they left."

"Oh my god," Liam guffawed. "Holy sh ... you must hate that soup now!"

"No," Alynna laughed again. "I actually crave it sometimes! Especially when I need a laugh."

Both of them howled with laughter until Alynna couldn't breathe. She let out a sigh. "I can't believe I told you that story!" She turned around and covered her burning cheeks.

"No, no," Liam protested. "To tell you the truth I haven't laughed like that in a long time."

She turned back around. "Your dad?" Alynna covered her cheeks again. "Sorry! I don't mean ..."

"Don't worry about it. Really, it's okay. I ..." He touched her cheek with his fingertip, tracing a line down her jaw.

Alynna's heart slammed into her chest. Oh lord, he was going to kiss her. She moved a fraction of an inch closer ...

"Shit!" Liam cursed softly as a ringing sound pierced the quiet night. He sighed and then stepped back, taking his phone from his pocket. "I have to take this. Sorry."

Trying to hide her disappointment, Alynna nodded, shooing him so he could step away and conduct his phone call.

He spoke on the phone for a minute and Alynna could make out some English words mixed in with Japanese. Finally, he slipped the phone in his pocket and turned back to her, his face a mask of disappointment.

"I'm sorry, Alynna. I have to go back to San Francisco."

"You're leaving?" she asked, trying not to sound too whiney. "Now?"

He nodded. "It's a family matter. I'm sorry. I had, I mean, I was having a good time. Thank you for sharing your story."

"I'm glad you had a good time," she said softly. Now came

the awkward part. "Thanks for coming and all that. I guess ... I'll see you around."

He smiled at her. "Definitely." He gave her a curt nod and then walked toward the double doors leading to the balcony.

"Crap!" she said to no one in particular. *Oh god, what happened?* It was a strange feeling. Liam was funny and nice and handsome, plus he was an Alpha. Grant would approve if they started dating. She couldn't think of that. Not right now. Not when she was still so broken up over Alex. "Oh crap," she said again. She vowed she wouldn't think of him, even say his name tonight. And for the most part, all the hubbub over the ball made it easy to not think of Alex. But now ... she knew he was watching her all night. She could feel his eyes on her and once in a while, his scent seemed to call to her like a siren song. Of course he was watching her, it was his job.

Her thoughts were interrupted by the sound of the balcony door clicking open and then closing.

"Liam?" she called out. It was dark, and she could just make out the tall shadow standing by the doors.

"Sorry to disappoint you. It's not Liam."

Alynna froze at the sound of the familiar voice as the masculine scent filled her nose. "Alex," she said softly. "What are you doing here?"

"My job." He walked toward her. "I'm working tonight." He looked dangerously handsome in his formal attire with his hair slicked back.

"Oh, have a glass of champagne on me at the end of your shift then," she said in a bitter tone. She grabbed her skirt and tried to pass by him, but stopped when she felt his warm hand grasp her upper arm. Shivers went down her spine, and his touch sent light tingles across her bare skin. "Alex, I have to get back. Please let go of me."

"Did he leave you too soon?" he sneered. "Off to party somewhere else?"

Anger began to rise in her. "Don't say anything you might regret later," she warned.

"I'll say what I want to say."

"Not to me!" She tried to wrestle away from his grasp. "You gave up that right weeks ago." *When you decided I wasn't what you wanted,* she wanted to add. "So, where's Jenna?"

"At home." He shrugged. "People like her don't get invited to things like this. You know that."

"Is that your way of saying she knows her place?" she asked, venom dripping from her words. God, she hated the tall, lithe blonde.

He said nothing, but pulled her closer instead. The more she struggled, the more his grip tightened. He hauled her back, spinning her around to trap her between the balustrade and his warm, hard body. She froze. "His scent is all over you," he said distastefully as his nose nuzzled her neck.

"Alex ..." she sighed. "We can't ..." But she made no motion to stop him.

"I hate it," he sneered. "I hate watching you from afar, watching him fawn all over you, leaving his scent on you." Alex growled possessively and ran his fingers across her collarbone. His hand moved higher, rubbing his wrists along her neck, covering her with his delicious scent. "If I had my way, I'd toss you in the shower to get rid of it, but this will have to do for now." His masculine, male scent enveloped her, filling her senses and her very core. A rush of wetness flooded her pussy, and she purred lightly at the sensation.

"Please ..."

"Please what?"

"Kiss me," she said, unable to stop herself. She wrapped her arms around his neck and pull him down.

He didn't need further encouragement. He crashed his lips against hers in a needy, searing kiss.

Alynna wasn't sure what was happening, only that she wanted – no, needed – Alex. It was as if her body was dying of thirst and Alex was her oasis.

His lips roughly moved against hers, and she whimpered into his mouth. His delicious scent filled her nose and she breathed in deeply, savoring it. His hands roamed lower, down the bodice of her dress, and then pulled up her voluminous skirts.

"Tell me to stop," he rasped into her ear.

"Don't stop," she growled, pressing her breasts up against his chest. She bit at his lip and pulled her body tighter against his.

There was a deep rumbling sound from somewhere in his chest, and she felt him grab her lacy panties, ripping them off with little difficulty. His lips moved lower, lingering over the tops of her breasts, and she gasped when she heard him unzip his pants and lift her onto the balustrade.

He was hard and ready, and when he pushed his cock into her, she bit his shoulder to keep from screaming out. Alex gripped her tighter, one hand snaking around her waist and the other over her shoulder to slam her down on his cock as he pounded up into her wet and willing pussy.

She squeezed him tight with her inner muscles, welcoming him into her warmth. The pleasure spread over her body, making her toes curl and her nipples ache as they rubbed against the silk of her gown. Alynna thrust her fingers into his hair, wrapping them around the strands and pulling on them as an orgasm ripped through her body.

As she came down, he slowed and slipped out of her. She whimpered in protest, but he spun her around, lifted up her skirts again, and then swiftly entered her from behind. Alynna yelped in surprise but was quickly overwhelmed with pleasure.

Alex pulled her against him, pulling her back up to his chest as he slammed his cock into her. He wasn't thinking and didn't care about who could catch them. The only thing he cared about was fucking Alynna, making her come again, and spilling his cum into her.

Alynna gripped the balcony railing tight as she pushed back against him, savoring the feeling of his cock in her again. God, she missed this, feeling his body, having his scent envelope her. He continued to fuck her deep and hard, and soon she felt another orgasm coming.

"Alex ... please ... yes ... don't stop ..." she murmured incoherently. He picked up his pace, fucking into her hard as her body shuddered.

It wasn't long before Alex grunted loudly, then slammed hard into her. She could feel his hot seed fill her up, the excess running down between her thighs in a sticky mess. He slowed down, grabbing her tight as he finished his orgasm. He grunted and held his breath as his cock slipped out of her and he let her go.

Alynna gasped and pulled away from him, her knuckles going white from gripping the railing tight. The cold air made her shiver.

"Alynna ..." Alex began, his voice broken and gravelly.

She bit her lip, trying not to let the tears spill down her cheeks. She sucked in air into her lungs. "Alex, I –"

She heard the balcony door click, and when she turned around, Alex was gone.

"Fucking hell!" she cursed loudly. What the fuck just happened? One moment she was enjoying Liam's company, and then she was having sex with Alex. Alex! Who came out of nowhere, acting like some jealous lover! He was the one who was sleeping with that bimbo Jenna and god knew who else. And she was waiting at home for him while he was fucking another woman behind her back.

Suddenly, she heard the door click open again. Alynna froze, hoping it wasn't Cady or worse, Grant.

"Alynna, are you okay? What happened?" Frankie's pretty face was lit up by the moonlight, her luminous mismatched eyes seemed to glow. "You ... *madre de dio!*" She gave the air a delicate sniff, her eyes scanning the younger woman up and down. "Did you and Liam get it on out here? Jesus Christ on a cracker, I think *I* need a cigarette!"

"No!" Alynna protested, but knew it was hopeless. She reeked of sex, and even if Frankie couldn't smell it, she knew she looked disheveled. "I mean ... it's complicated. I'll explain another time, I promise."

Frankie tsked as she approached Alynna. "Okay, well, we need to do something. Christ, Alynna, what were you thinking?"

"I wasn't." Alynna frowned. "Oh crap, I need to go out there and say thank you in like fifteen minutes."

"Okay, okay, don't panic. I'll take care of it." Frankie bit her lip. "Stay here."

Frankie had quickly sprung into action to help her get ready. She grabbed a passing waiter, shoved a hundred-dollar bill into his hand, and ordered him to go clear out the ladies' room nearby and then get them. Soon, they made their way to the bathroom, where a "closed for cleaning" sign blocked the door.

Frankie grabbed every type of perfume and lotion in the room, spraying Alynna liberally after wiping her down with damp towels. She helped the younger woman fix her hair and gave her a swipe of her own cherry red lipstick. "Bombshell red for good luck," she said, giving the tube a kiss and tucking it back into her clutch.

The bruises on Alynna's arms, however, were harder to hide, so Frankie stripped off her own white gloves and gave them to Alynna. They were barely long enough to cover the bruises, but they would do.

"You look great, sweetie." Frankie gave her a small kiss on the cheek. "Now, go get 'em!"

Alynna rushed out the bathroom and found Cady, who immediately ushered her to the front to make her speech. She also passed by Grant and Nick, and she gave a silent thanks to Frankie as they didn't seem to notice anything was wrong.

"I'm deeply humbled by your presence here," Alynna recited the words she and Cady had written together the previous week. She was standing midway up the grand staircase, with everyone in the ballroom looking up at her. "I would like to thank those who traveled from near and far just to be here tonight. I wish your family and your clan health, wealth, and happiness."

Alynna sighed with relief. She scanned her audience, trying to find Frankie, but once again, her newfound friend had seemingly vanished.

She raised her glass and then took a small sip of her champagne. Everyone in the room followed suit. "Thank you and please continue to enjoy the evening!"

Everyone clapped, and Alynna made her way to the bottom of the stairs. She greeted everyone, tried her best to recall their names, and slowly made her way to Grant and Cady, who were standing off to the side by the ante room. She stumbled slightly, but regained her footing quickly. "Too much champagne," she laughed at the older Lycan who had come forward to introduce himself. She suddenly felt tired, her limbs feeling loose and achy.

"How'd I do?" she joked when she reached her brother and Cady.

"You did great!" Cady said, embracing the younger woman.

"I'm proud of you, Alynna." Grant beamed at her.

"Thank you," she said breathlessly. "Cady did all the work though, and ..." She stopped talking as if she forgot something.

"Yes, Alynna?" Cady asked, her eyes narrowed. "Are you okay? Your pupils ..."

"Huh?" she asked. Alynna suddenly felt loopy, as if she was drunk.

"Alynna." Grant tipped her head up. "Are you okay?"

Oh shit, oh shit, Alynna thought to herself. Did Grant smell Alex on her? He was giving her a serious look.

"I'm sorry, Grant I –" But before she could continue, the floor underneath her gave way and her vision went to black.

"Alynna!"

———

"Grant?" Dr. Faulkner called out as he entered the waiting room where Grant, Cady, and Nick were sitting. Alex stood off to the side, guarding the door to the medical center located inside The Enclave where they rushed Alynna after she remained unresponsive. They were all still in their formal wear, though Grant and Nick had long ago removed their ties and jackets. Cady was barefoot, stretched out on the couch with Nick's coat draped over her as she napped.

"Dr. Faulkner." Grant shot up to his feet and stalked over to the older man. "Is she up? Can I see her? What happened?"

The older man shook his head. "Alynna will be fine." Tension lifted from the room. "She's resting now; I don't want her disturbed. You can see her in a few hours."

"No, I want to know –"

"Please Grant," Dr. Faulkner implored. "Sit down. I'll tell you what we know, but you can't disturb her now, okay?"

Grant nodded and sat back down on the chair he had been occupying for hours. Outside the sky was pink as the sun slowly began to rise over Manhattan. "Doc, tell us what happened."

The older man sighed and sat down on the couch next to Cady, who was now wide awake. "Well, I can confirm she was definitely poisoned with a strain of nightshade, aka belladonna."

The redhead gasped. "Belladonna? That poison is deadly to Lycans! Were you able to administer an antidote?"

"See, that's it." Dr. Faulkner's brows knitted in confusion. "We had the antidote on route from one of the hospitals in the area. But by the time it got here, she hardly needed it."

"What do you mean?" Grant asked. "She's going to be fine, you said?"

"Yes, she's tired, but healthy. She'll wake up feeling like she ran a marathon. She almost coded on us, but then ... her vitals became steady. She was sweating and vomiting for a while, as if her body was flushing out the poison."

"Is that normal?" Cady asked.

He shook his head. "No. Not to humans or Lycans. Our bodies don't just reject poison for no reason." Before anyone else could ask, he continued. "And no, I don't know why her body reacted like that or have any other explanation. I'm going to run some more tests of course, to make sure she's okay. We have the antidote on standby."

Grant rubbed his temples with his fingers. "Is it because she's a True Mate offspring?"

"Could be. That's the only thing different about her. Maybe she has antibodies that reject belladonna. Belladonna was traditionally used by witches to kill Lycans back in the day. It could also be that someone in your family line survived such a poisoning and developed this antibody. I can't know for sure, and I'm not sure I'll be able to find out without serious testing and research."

"Thank you, Dr. Faulkner," Grant said. "If you say she needs a few hours rest, then we should all go home. I'll be back before lunch time, but call me if anything changes." He turned to Nick and Cady. "Get some rest, but first thing tomorrow, I want all security tapes reviewed and all staff interviewed."

"Yes, Primul," Nick said, nodding. "I've had my team confiscate all the tapes from tonight and last night as well, just in case. I'll be overseeing the interviews myself in the morning."

"Do you think it was Alynna's friend in green that did this?" Cady asked.

"I don't know." Grant's eyes turned hard as steel. "But if she is, then there will be hell to pay."

Alex said nothing while he sat in the corner, but he agreed with his Alpha silently.

CHAPTER NINETEEN

"Grant, I need one more thing," Alynna said as she pushed the tray away. She had been up since nine that morning but couldn't find the strength to get out of bed. It was lunch time and as Grant promised, he showed up just in time for Alynna's first meal since the night before.

"What is it? Do you need more pillows? Some soup? Water?"

"No." She shook her head. "I need you to stop acting like a mother hen and give me some room. I swear if you invade any more of my personal space, we'd be breaking the laws of physics!" Since he showed up, Grant had done nothing but hover over her, offering her food, pillows, and blankets.

"Sorry!" he said, putting his hands up. "I just want you to be comfortable."

"I am comfortable," she sighed, motioning for him to come and sit on her bed. He sat down beside her and, to his surprise, she cuddled up to his side, throwing an arm across his chest and squeezing him tight. "I'm fine. I'll be fine. And thanks for getting all those flowers out of here. I was starting to think I'd died and woken up in floral hell."

Unfortunately, about a dozen other Lycans had seen Alynna collapse at the ball. They rushed her to the ante room and blocked anyone from seeing her, but it was too late. Cady came out of the room and announced to everyone that Alynna had fainted from exhaustion and she lacked sleep, so she was going to retire for the evening. They were able to discreetly rush her out of the hotel to the waiting unmarked van in the service entrance.

"Cady!" she greeted as soon as she saw the pretty redhead enter the door. She was followed by Nick and to her surprise, Alex. She said nothing, but nodded to them.

"Alynna!" Cady rushed to her side. "Oh my lord, how are you feeling? Do you need anything?"

She shook her head. "Like I was telling Mr. Florence Nightingale here, I'm perfectly all right. Just tired and achy."

"Good," Cady sighed with relief. "Are you feeling okay to talk? I can call Dr. Faulkner or we could re-schedule."

"I'm good." Alynna nodded. "But, if you're going to ask me about last night ... my memory's a little foggy."

"That's okay," Grant said, giving her a kiss on the forehead. "Just tell us as much as you can."

"Where should I start?" she asked.

"When did you begin feeling woozy?" Nick asked, stepping forward.

"Hmm ..." she paused. "After the speech, I guess? People were kind of crushing against me, and I felt hot and overwhelmed."

"How about before you went up to say thank you? What did you do?"

Alynna swallowed a gulp and it took all her concentration not to look at Alex. "My memory's a little bit hazy ..."

"Alex was the last person on the team to see you just before you went up to speak," Cady explained. "He says he saw you on the balcony and checked up on you?"

She nodded and mentally sighed with relief. "Yes ... I had gone out there with Liam for some fresh air. We were there alone maybe thirty minutes? Then he got a phone call and had to leave."

"Liam Henney?" Cady looked up at Grant.

"Did he give you anything to drink or eat?" Grant inquired.

"No ... and no! It couldn't have been him," Alynna said defensively. "Doesn't poison act quickly? I would have collapsed on the balcony and ..." she drifted off.

"And what?" Nick asked. "What else happened?" He looked at Alex. "You said you saw Ms. Chase after the Alpha had left?

"Yes, Al Doilea," Alex said coolly. "I went out, checked in on her, and left." Alex's face was a stoic mask, his lie expertly told.

"Um ..." Alynna scrambled. "After that my friend found me ..." *Oh dear. Frankie. Was it Frankie?*

"Who?" Grant's voice took on a forceful tone. "Was it that woman in green you were talking to with Liam and the Texas delegation?"

She nodded. "She had to take a phone call, and I didn't see her after that. Then you came and introduced us to more people, then Liam and I went to the balcony. After he left and, uh, Alex came to check on me, she came out."

"Did you see this woman?" Grant turned to Alex. "After you left?"

The Lycan shook his head. "No, Primul, forgive me. I did not."

"We need to find her and interrogate her," Grant said.

"No!" Alynna protested. "I mean, she couldn't have poisoned me. She didn't hand me anything to eat or drink."

"Who was she?" Cady asked soothingly, patting the younger woman's arm.

"I don't know. She's a Lycan for sure. She said she didn't RSVP, but she changed her mind last minute."

"Her name?"

"Uh ... she didn't say," Alynna lied. An idea formed in her head. She would find Frankie first and get to the bottom of this. She was sick and tired of living in fear. "Really guys, it can't be her. She's so nice and kind, and she defended me and my mom from those catty bitches."

"We can't rule out anyone," Nick explained. "Not yet. If you can remember anything more about her, we can at least eliminate her from the list of suspects."

"What else have you determined?" Alynna asked, hoping to change the subject.

"Well, sounds like it was the champagne," Nick continued. "Did you see who gave it to you?"

"Someone just handed it to me. A waiter," she said.

Cady nodded. "We interviewed every member of the staff, except for one waiter. He called in sick today."

"Wait. No one else was poisoned? Just me?" Alynna asked.

"Yes," Nick confirmed. "We have yet to hear any other cases of belladonna poisoning from other guests."

"That's strange," Alynna said, her eyes narrowing. "That was the last thing I drank before I collapsed. After I drank it, I remember someone taking the glass from my hand, like yanking it away."

Nick contemplated what she said. "It could be the same waiter. He may have wanted to destroy the evidence."

Grant let out a soft growl. "I want him found. Today," he said in a deadly voice.

"Yes Primul," both Nick and Alex answered, bowing their heads.

"Let me help," Alynna said. Four pairs of eyes looked at her. "I'm a PI, I know these things. I can help track him down. Please." She wanted to find Frankie first, just in case. Grant looked like he was going insane from worry, and she didn't want him to do something he might regret.

Grant sighed. "We'll talk about it, okay? I want you to be one hundred percent first."

"I am better ..." she yawned. "Aw, fuck." She collapsed back on the bed. "Fine, I'll rest."

A knock interrupted their conversation, and Grant strode to the door to answer it. He spoke a few words to the person on the other side, then turned around carrying a big package in his arms.

"Alynna?"

"Yes?" Alynna remained on the bed, her arms over her face.

"Why did Liam Henney send you a basket of Campbell's Chunky Chicken soup?"

Alynna sat up and looked at the package in Grant's hands – a huge basket filled with the distinctive white and red cans wrapped up in a bow – and then up to her brother's confused face. She laughed out loud.

CHAPTER TWENTY

A week after the ball, Alynna felt fully recovered. The effects of fighting the poison left her tired, like she had been hit by a truck. Although she was annoyed at having to spend a few more days in the recovery room, she was glad she got out of moving her stuff from Gus' apartment to her new place in The Enclave.

She wasn't sure what to expect when she moved into the Lycan stronghold. She had lived in New York all her life and had never realized what was hiding right under everyone's nose. How could an entire community of secret werewolves remain hidden on the small, dense island of Manhattan for generations? She was also quite surprised The Enclave wasn't one building, but an entire complex of buildings taking up three blocks on Manhattan's Upper West Side.

There were three main clusters – North, South, and Center. Cady explained that, to outsiders, The Enclave looked like any ordinary collection of buildings. Inside it was more like a mini city with an underground system that connected all the buildings and could be fortified if necessary. Cady also added that a bit of magic was involved in keeping

The Enclave secret from non-Lycans and those not associated with the New York clan. A few decades before, a witch who owed the New York clan's Alpha a favor, Alynna's great-great grandfather she learned, put a spell over the complex that repelled outsiders. When people walked by, they simply felt the need to go the other way, completely ignore it, or even forget about it. There had been some close calls, but the magic held even after decades. Lycans, Cady warned, did not mess around when it came to the place that protected their pups.

When Cady had brought up the issue of where she was to stay in The Enclave, Alynna wanted to have some semblance of privacy, so she declined Grant's offer to stay in his plush, five-bedroom penthouse in the Center Cluster. Cady found her another place, a loft apartment just below Grant's floor. It was roomy and had a great view of the Hudson River. Best of all, it was just hers. While she wanted to spend time with her brother, she also wanted a place where she could just be alone. And, with The Enclave having the best Lycan, technological, and magical security, Alynna no longer had to have security detail posted at the door or tailing her around as long as she stayed inside the complex.

Today, she found herself once again heading into Fenrir to meet with Grant and Cady to go over a few things and update her on the investigation into what happened at the ball. Patrick picked her up and brought her directly to the office.

"Good morning, Ms. Chase," Jared greeted. "How are you feeling today?"

"Good, thank you," she greeted the assistant back. "Is my brother ready to see me?"

"He's in there with the other Alpha, but he said you're welcome to interrupt them if you arrive early."

Other Alpha? she wondered as she opened the heavy

wooden doors that led to Grant's office. As soon as she entered, the four men sitting in the middle of the room stood up.

"Liam – Mr. Henney, Matsumoto-san," she said in a surprised voice. "What are you guys doing here?" She looked over to Grant, who gave her a sly smile.

"Alynna, glad you could make it." Grant motioned for her to come sit with them. "Liam and Takeda are here on some business."

"Boring business, I'm afraid. With Fenrir and Amata Ventures, my company," Liam explained. "I asked Grant if I could see you as well, to see if you were feeling better, and he said I should just come in this morning."

"Uh, cool," Alynna said, giving her brother a knowing look. "Sorry. I didn't mean to interrupt."

"Oh no," Liam said. "We're the ones interrupting. We should be on our way."

"Oh," Alynna said in a disappointed voice.

"Liam and Takeda will be here for the entire week," Grant said. "We're in talks about funding some startups he's working with. From what he's explained, there are some really great technologies out there when it comes to cancer research."

"Really?" Liam nodded at her. "That's great!"

"You'll join us for dinner tonight, I hope?" Liam asked. "I mean, it'll be all of us. With Ms. Gray."

"That sounds good." Alynna smiled. "I'll see you then?"

The two men said their goodbyes, and Nick escorted them out of the room.

"So, Liam Henney just showed up here today?" Alynna raised an eyebrow at her brother. "What a coincidence."

"Actually," Grant began, "Liam has been hounding me for a meeting for weeks. But, seeing as he seems to enjoy New York, I thought I'd finally invite him and listen to what he has to say."

"I see," she said as she sat down.

"Anyway," Grant poured her a cup of coffee, "how are you feeling?"

"I'm fit as a fiddle," she declared, taking a sip of the warm liquid. "Are you going to fill me in on the investigation?"

"About that ..."

"Grant," she said, a tone of warning on her voice.

"Look, I'm not going to stop you from helping. But, you have to tell us more about what you remember."

"I have, haven't I?" she feigned.

"Not everything."

"What?" she said. "Are you still going on and on about the woman in green? I told you all I know!"

"Are you sure?" Grant sounded doubtful. "I think you're hiding something."

"And I think you're barking up the wrong tree," she said, her cup making a loud clinking sound as she set it back on the saucer a little too forcefully. "I'll be conducting my own investigation on that matter and if I find anything, I'll tell you."

"Ms. Chase," Nick said as he rejoined them, "may I remind you that a week ago someone tried to poison you, and a few weeks ago someone broke into your apartment?"

"Could be totally unrelated," she retorted. *But unlikely*, she added silently. She did not believe in coincidences.

Grant sighed. "Alynna, please don't be stubborn about this."

She crossed her arms. "What did you find out about the waiter?"

"His name's Fred Allman, and he's gone. Fled," Nick supplied. "We tracked down his apartment, and it was empty. His clothes were all gone; his landlord and neighbors don't know anything and haven't seen him in a week."

"Hmm ..." Alynna said thoughtfully. "Definitely suspicious. Do we have names or numbers of relatives, girlfriends? Have we checked his social media accounts?"

"We're working on it," Nick stated.

"Good. You can keep me updated, and I can start looking up records on him. What?" she said as she bit into a croissant. Both men were looking at her strangely. "Look, this is what I do. You do your Lycan thing and I'll do my PI thing, okay?" She finished the croissant and stood up. "Well, I guess I'll see you ..."

"Alynna, wait." Grant put a hand on her arm. "Nick, give us a minute?"

"Yes, Primul," the other man said and silently left the room.

"What is it?" she asked.

"We need to talk about other things."

"Oh." She picked up another croissant. "What is it?"

"First, Alex will be back on your regular security detail."

She took a deep breath. "Okay."

"I couldn't interfere anymore, and Nick was starting to get suspicious. After all, Alex rushed to you when you collapsed and stayed throughout the night."

"What?" she asked, confused.

"Well, as soon as you fell, he rushed in and brought you to the ante room. Frankly, we couldn't get him to leave."

"Excuse me?" she asked, swallowing a mouthful of pastry.

"Yeah. I was too busy worrying about you, but Cady said one of the other security guys tried to get him to leave the room and Alex almost bit his head off."

Holy crap.

"There was so much going on we left him alone. He never left your side, only when you went into the clinic and Dr. Faulkner insisted everyone stay out. Anyway," he continued, "my hands are tied. You said so yourself, I shouldn't interfere."

"I know," she said quietly. "And it's okay. Really, I'm ... over it."

He gave her a smile. "I'm glad. And if Liam is helping you ..."

"Ugh!" she let out a frustrated groan. "Can we please not talk about my love life?"

"Oh, it's love, now is it?" he teased. When Alynna grabbed one of the pillows on the couch, he put his hands up in defeat. "Okay, okay, no meddling! But," he said in a serious voice, "I also wanted to know if you've thought about what you want to do, now that you're officially part of Lycan society. Do you have ideas? There's no pressure, especially with what happened."

"No, I ...." She paused. "I've been thinking about it and have had some thoughts, but nothing concrete. Is that okay? I can pay rent on the apartment or ..."

"Oh no, Alynna, it's not that," he said. "The apartment is yours, your right as a part of the New York clan. As long as you decide to live in The Enclave, you'll always have a place there. I'm more worried about you. You don't seem like the type to spend your days idle, going to lunches and shopping."

She shook her head. "No, I want to do something. I just don't know what."

"Take your time," Grant said. "And if you need advice, just ask."

"Thank you. I'll definitely think about it."

———

Alynna opened the door to her new apartment, kicked off her heels, and slunk down on the couch. It had been a long day, her first full day doing anything since she was poisoned. She had gotten her appetite back, although to be honest she never really lost it, and dinner had been at an amazing sushi place that impressed even Takeda. Both Liam and Grant had an early day, so they called it a night by ten p.m. They dropped off Liam and Takeda at their hotel, but before they left, Liam asked Alynna to dinner at some point during the week, an invitation she gladly accepted.

"What am I going to wear?" she said out loud to no one in particular. She had all those nice dresses she and Cady had shopped for at Bergdorf's. That seemed like years ago, not weeks. She sighed and stretched her calves out. She wanted to dress to impress tonight, so she wore her little black dress and stiletto heels. She'd have to find the right outfit for her dinner with Liam.

She couldn't quite bring herself to get ready for bed yet, so she picked up a pile of folders on the coffee table. Nick had been quite surprised at the request, but he indulged her. The files pertained to all the "Lycan Requests" Nick had gotten so far for this year, about six or seven. Most were petty things – car break-ins, stolen property – she could see how these didn't need to go to Grant's desk. However, there were a couple that caught her eye. One was a Lycan-owned small business downtown, a dry cleaning shop that was getting frequently targeted by robbers, and the other a custody battle between a Lycan mother and a human father. She took the first file and began to read it thoroughly.

A knock on the door broke her concentration. *Who could it be at this hour?* she thought. *Probably Grant.* He said he was bringing work home tonight and maybe he couldn't sleep.

She stood and walked to the door, not bothering with her shoes. She unlocked the door and opened it slightly.

"Alex," she said softly. "What are you doing here?"

Alex stood in front of her door, wearing a black tank top and jeans, his hair wet from a recent shower.

"May I come in?" he asked.

She let out a breath and then closed the door, unlatching the chain so she could open it. "It's late. What do you want?"

He strode inside and she closed the door behind her. "Well?"

"Nice place." He looked around and walked into her open living room/kitchen area.

"Thanks, it still needs some work." God, he smelled good. And he looked damn sexy. His shoulder muscles rippled as he bent down to pick up a magazine she had left on the table. His tight tank top showed off his muscled arms, and the way it clung to his flat stomach made her mouth water. She could almost see the outline of his delicious abs. And those tight jeans molded to his ass like they were painted on. *Get a grip*, she told herself.

He moved to her window, looking out at her view. He whistled. "Now that is a view," he said, turning back to her.

She crossed her arms. "What do you want, Alex?" she repeated. "Tell me now or get out."

Alex's eyes blazed like molten gold. He strode over to her, his long legs crossing the distance between them in short time. "You," he growled as his warm hands grabbed her arms, pulling her close to his chest. "I want *you*."

Alynna wanted to protest, but it was like her hands had a life of their own. She slid her fingers down to his waist, pulling his tank top up to expose his rippling abs. Jesus, she'd forgotten how sexy he was, the way his muscles moved under his warm skin. "Off," she said in an urgent voice. "Need to touch you ... now."

He complied, grabbing the bottom of his tank top and pulling it over his head. He stood there, his chest heaving. "Now your turn," he said.

She turned around and lifted her hair away. "Unzip me?" she said coyly, turning her head to look at him.

Alex took the zipper between his fingers and pulled it down deliberately, slowly exposing her creamy white skin. Alynna let the dress fall to the floor, and she stepped out of the pool of fabric, turning around to face him. She was wearing only her matching green lace bra and panties. She grabbed him by the arm and pushed him until the back of his knees hit the couch. She reached down and unbuttoned his jeans, shoving them down. She gasped audibly when she realized he wasn't wearing any briefs and he was already fully erect.

Alex tried to grab her, but she pushed him down on the couch and knelt between his legs. "Alynna ... I ... uhhh ..."

Alynna ran her tongue down the side of his hard cock before moving her head back up to take him in her mouth. Alex let out a groan at the sensation of Alynna's soft, wet mouth on his cock. He breathed deeply, trying to get a hold of himself. Alynna enjoyed teasing him, sucking on his dick like it was a delicious treat, her mouth providing tempting suction that only made his cock twitch and ache. He buried his hands in her hair and let himself be subjected to her torture.

Alynna reveled in the power she had over him, and her body was reacting exquisitely to his arousal. Her nipples were pebbled hard and her pussy gushed with wetness, soaking through the delicate lace of her panties.

Alex seemed to have enough, and he hauled her up so she lay sprawled on top of him and they were face to face. He captured her mouth in a fiery kiss. She moaned against his lips, parting her own to let his tongue snake inside her mouth to taste her. A hand moved lower and the sound of lace ripping told her that Alex made quick work of her panties.

He grabbed her legs, pulling them up, so her pussy was perfectly positioned over his cock. She sighed as he surged up into her, and she sank down on his hot, hard cock. The feeling of his member filling her was more than satisfying. It felt so right, even though she knew the whole thing was wrong.

She let out a growl and planted her knees on either side of him. Sitting up, she grabbed his shoulders and began to grind back and forth. He let out a soft shout, his hands grabbing her hips to help her with the rhythm.

Alynna felt her body tense, and soon she was right at the edge of an orgasm. She rocked on his lap, his cock sliding in and out of her. Sensing her tension, he snaked a hand between her legs, his fingers manipulating her clit, until she reached her climax. Her pussy tightened around him and he groaned as he felt himself orgasm, shooting his hot cum deep into her. He spasmed, grabbed her shoulders and roughly pulled her to his chest as he shot load after load of sperm inside her.

"Alex ..." she sighed, collapsing against him. He pushed her hair aside and kissed her neck.

Alynna breathed in his scent, the familiar scent that seemed to consume her whenever he was near. She moaned in protest as he softened and slipped out of her. She felt his arms wind around her and then lift her up. She hummed against his chest, feeling drowsy, and slipped off to sleep.

———

Alex's eyes flew open, and for a second, he forgot where he was. But, when Alynna's sweet scent hit his nose, the memories flooded back. Looking down, he saw Alynna's head laying on his chest, an arm thrown across his torso. He sighed and stroked her hair.

Why he went to her last night, he wasn't sure. Last time they came together it was rough and quick, his anger and jealousy getting the better of him. Then, seeing her collapse and then fight for her life was too much. He was wracked with guilt, knowing that if he had been doing his job, he might have prevented everything. He wanted to stay away, knew he should stay away from her, but he just couldn't. Something inside of him was pulling him to her, and he couldn't resist. Yes, he wanted her luscious body, purring and mewling underneath his, but he also wanted more.

But what he wanted and what he could have were two different things. This, the sex and her body, were things he could have for now. And he would take it, whatever Alynna could give him.

Turning his head toward the windows, he saw the sun peeking out from the clouds, painting the sky in pinks and blues. Gently, he moved Alynna aside, giving her a soft kiss on the cheek as he stood up. She stirred a little bit, but her eyes remained closed.

Alex walked down the steps of her bedroom loft, all the way to the living room. He picked up his discarded clothes, putting them on. This was the last time, he told himself. Surely by now, he'd had his fill of Alynna Chase. Because if he pursued this any further, he knew they would only end up getting hurt.

CHAPTER TWENTY-ONE

As soon as she got up and realized that Alex was gone, Alynna decided it was time to get on with her life. She had been presented to Lycan society, moved into The Enclave, and now she could get around somewhat freely in the city.

She spent most of the morning sorting through her email, letters, and packages. Lycans from all over the country were sending her letters and gifts, wishing her well. There were also many of them asking her out. Cady and Grant had warned her, but she didn't think they were serious. Apparently, she was the most eligible Lycan female in the world and many of her would-be suitors were not shy in making their interest known to her. She put all of them aside and decided to ask Cady or Grant the proper way to let them down.

After making herself some lunch, she worked through the files she was reading last night, taking notes and setting up her laptop on the desk she put in the corner of her main room. She was surprised to find the afternoon had gone by quickly, and she had to get ready for dinner with Grant, Liam, and a few of the VPs at Fenrir.

Alynna took a car to Fenrir, and they all went to a trendy restaurant in Chelsea. The group tonight was bigger than last night. According to Grant, they spent most of the day in meetings with Liam since Takeda had headed back to San Francisco earlier in the day. Things were going well, and Fenrir was definitely going to fund some of the cancer startups Liam was working with.

Alynna did her best to try to seem interested in what was going on, but all the business talk went over her head. She sat beside Liam, who included her in their conversations as much as he could, explaining details here and there.

Finally, it was time to call it a night. Grant said he had to head back to Fenrir, so Liam graciously offered to bring Alynna home. She gave her brother a smirk as he waved goodbye to them.

"Shall we?" Liam asked as he opened the door to his rented town car.

"Thank you," she said, stepping inside and sliding over the plush leather seat to make room for Liam.

The door closed and the driver started the engine. Liam gave the driver directions, then he put up the privacy window.

They settled in and the car started to move.

"I –"

"What –"

They both talked at the same time.

"Go ahead," he said.

"No, it's okay. What did you want to ask?"

"I hope you don't mind, but I have a question. It's okay if you don't want to answer it," he said. He reached over and slipped her hand into his.

"What is it?" Liam's hand was warm against hers, and his scent, that of lemons and limes, filled her nostrils. It was a pleasant scent for sure, though aside from warm fuzzy feelings, it did nothing else for her. Unlike ... "Please, go ahead and ask," she said, interrupting her own thoughts.

"Well, your mother ... the only thing I know about her is from the invitation that was sent from your clan. She was your father's True Mate? And she was a human?"

She nodded. "Yes. I didn't know about him until a few weeks ago. She died when I was sixteen."

"Oh, I'm sorry," he said sincerely. "What happened?"

She shrugged. "Cancer. Stage four. Nothing we could do about it."

"Oh, my father, too," he said, his eyes suddenly turning sad.

"Really?" she asked.

He nodded. "Stage four stomach cancer. The doctor gave him six months, but it was more like six weeks."

"I'm sorry," she said, gripping his hand tighter. "That's awful. You weren't prepared, were you?"

Liam shook his head. "No, it was very sudden. He was fit and active, and then it was like when he got the news ... he lost his will to live."

"I'm terribly sorry," she repeated. "Is that why you're trying to get funding for all these cancer startups?"

"Yes." He nodded. "That's part of the reason. I also wanted to do my own thing. Sure, I could work for the family food business, but well ... that's kind of my mom and dad's thing. They grew my grandfather's grocery business into one of the biggest restaurant supply companies in California. My mom still runs the day-to-day things. I kind of wanted to strike out on my own, you know?"

"Believe it or not, I do."

"Really?" he asked. "What are you going to do now?"

"I don't know. I mean, I have ideas." She bit her lip. "I hate having to shut down my Uncle Gus' agency, but like you said, that was his thing."

"Whatever you decide to do, I know you'll be great."

Before Alynna could reply, the car stopped. "Thanks. It looks like we're here."

"Yes, we are. I had a great time, as always." He gave her a boyish smile.

Alynna thought for a moment, then leaned over and gave him a kiss on the cheek. "Me too," she said before stepping out of the car. She quickly ran to the entrance of The Enclave, but before she went through the door, she looked over her shoulder. Liam's car remained in the driveway with the window down. He was grinning at her, touching his cheek where she kissed him. She gave him a playful wave and walked through the door.

When she was clear of the doorman and inside the elevator, she breathed a sigh of relief and allowed herself a smile. A rush of excitement ran through her, and she let herself enjoy the little bit of happiness.

It didn't last though, and she felt the wind rush out of her when she turned the corner to her apartment and saw who was standing there. He looked devastatingly handsome and sexy. Her heart melted.

"Alex," she said breathlessly.

———

"Did you enjoy your trip to New York?" Alynna asked as she took a sip of wine. The week passed quickly and most nights she would have dinner with Liam and Grant, then Liam would take her home. Finally, on his last night, Alynna and Liam finally found time to have dinner alone.

"I did, very much," Liam replied as he put his knife and fork to the side of his plate. One of the waiters quickly rushed forward to get the used dishes.

"Dessert and coffee, Mr. Henney?" the eager young man asked.

"Yes, please. Thank you," he said politely. "And please do tell Chef Durand that the meal was absolutely exquisite."

"I will, Mr. Henney," the waiter nodded and took the plates away.

"Thank you again for dinner," Alynna said. "This was excellent. I can't believe you convinced the chef to give us a private room!" She looked around at the richly decorated private dining room at Le Petite Lapin, one of the hottest and trendiest restaurants in Manhattan. The room wasn't big, it could probably sit eight people comfortably, but tonight it was only set for two. In the corner was a settee and coffee table, set next to a fireplace.

"Oh, Henri is a friend of mine," Liam replied. "He started out in San Francisco, you know. We used to supply him with the best ingredients for his restaurant."

As if on cue, the chef himself, Henri Durand, came in brandishing two dishes holding his special dessert. The waiter followed behind him with a carafe of coffee and two cups. They set the dishes on the small settee and the couple moved toward the small alcove. Henri greeted Liam with a flourish and showered Alynna with compliments before he excused himself to give them some time alone.

"Oh wow," Alynna moaned as she put a spoonful of pot de creme into her mouth. "This ... this is amazing!"

"Better than sex," Liam quipped.

"What?" Alynna nearly choked on the thick chocolate pudding in her mouth.

"*Mieux Que Le Sexe,* that's what Henri called it," Liam said, taking a mouthful himself. "Very apt."

She gave him a nervous smile. "Right." A stab of guilt surged through her. *What the hell am I doing?*

Alynna wasn't the type of girl who went on dinner dates with one man and had sex with another when she came home. Sure, it was mind-blowing, earth-shattering sex. She figured whatever this thing she had with Alex would burn out soon. But, try as she might, her body longed for him, wanted him. He had showed up at her door every night that week, and one time he was sitting on her couch when she got home and she didn't know how he got in. She tried to talk to him, preparing a speech in her head every day in case he came back, but when she opened her mouth to speak, his lips stopped her and they fell into bed – or on her couch, in her shower, on her kitchen table, and on the rug a couple of times. Every morning, he would leave at dawn.

And here was poor Liam, sitting beside her without a clue as to what was going on. And Alex? Maybe she did feel a little guilty, but she didn't know what the heck they were doing anyway.

"Penny for your thoughts?" It was Liam who spoke first.

"Um ... sorry. Just, you know. I have a lot on my mind."

"No worries." He put down his coffee cup and took her hands into his. They had grown comfortable over the past week, but their contact never went past hand holding or a goodnight kiss on the cheek. "Is it about your plans for the future?"

"Partly." She didn't want to lie. "I think I know what I want to do."

"What is it?" he asked.

"Well, I don't want to jinx it, but I'll let you know as soon as it takes shape, okay?"

He nodded. "Whatever you decide, I'm sure it will be good."

"Thanks." She blushed at his compliment.

"No, thank you. Also, I wanted to tell you, I've had a good time this week." Liam leaned over and Alynna froze. His breath was warm, his pleasant, citrusy scent enveloping her. She closed her eyes, waiting for the touch of his lips on hers, but instead, his mouth landed on her cheek.

She sighed as he pulled away from her. He gave her a small smile and did that adorable thing where he rubbed the back of his head with his palm.

"Liam," she began, but he spoke first.

"No, wait. I mean, may I say something?" She nodded and let him continue. "I think you're an amazing person, incredibly funny, whip smart, witty, and gorgeous. And I like you. A lot." He paused, touching her cheek. "But I can't help but get this feeling that you don't feel the same way."

"No, Liam, I like you, too," she protested.

"There's a but in there somewhere."

She sighed. "Yes, there's a but."

"I know. I mean, I can feel it. You're not here with me right now. It's like ... I know this sounds corny, but your heart isn't here."

Her jaw dropped at his perceptiveness. "No! I mean, yes. I don't like you in that way ... yet. Maybe I will?"

He gave her a small laugh. "Wow, thanks."

"I'm so sorry." She turned away from him, hiding her face in her hands. "I tried. I wanted to like you in that way ... to maybe fall in love with you. It could be so easy and simple."

"But you can't," he finished. "Because you're already in love with someone else."

His words hit her like a Mack truck. She couldn't believe Liam figured it out before she did. But he was right. She was in love with Alex. She sighed. "I'm sorry. I'm so sorry."

Liam gave her a sheepish smile. "No need to apologize. Do you want to talk about it?"

Her throat burned slightly, tears threatening to spill down her cheeks. "No." She shook her head. "Can we just talk about something else?" She turned away from him and discreetly brushed the tears from her eyes.

He cleared his throat. "Well, if you want a laugh, apparently the Lycan gossip vine has been burning all week."

"What?" she asked, puzzled. "What about?"

He laughed. "Believe it or not, you and me."

"You and me?" she said in an incredulous voice.

He nodded. "News even made it back to my mother. She wants to know when I'm proposing."

Alynna was glad she wasn't eating or drinking when he said that as she would probably have done a spit take all over his expensive suit. "You're joking."

"I wish I was," he said. "If you weren't ... er ... if you were available, you know I would have ... not proposed tonight, but I mean, I was going to ask if you wanted to try and work it out. Maybe even invite you to visit or live in San Francisco, since you wanted to do your own thing."

"That's very nice of you." She took his hand into hers. "I appreciate it, but New York is my home. My clan is here. My family is here."

He smiled sadly. "Can't blame a guy for trying, huh?"

"I'm –"

"Please don't say sorry again. There's nothing to apologize for."

Alynna felt terrible. Liam was a great guy, he really was. He just wasn't the one for her. She gave a silent prayer, hoping he'd find a great girl someday.

"Can I do anything at all?" It sounded trite, but she didn't know what else to say.

"Well, there is one thing. You must know how it is, being single and eligible in Lycan society."

She laughed. "Yes, I know. It's annoying. I can't even remember their names and they want to date me."

"Yeah, well, since I became Alpha, it's like I'm a piece of meat, a prize to be won."

"Ah, I see," Alynna said with a glint in her eye. "So, we don't admit or deny anything for now."

"And let the rumor mill work on its own."

"And maybe we can both have peace for a little bit," she finished. "Brilliant!" At least she could get some actual work done, instead of having to write replies and return all the flowers, jewelry, and other gifts she'd been getting from overeager Lycans.

"So, you agree? You don't mind? What about your ..."

She shook her head. "Don't worry about that. That's ... done. No one will mind."

"Great!" Liam kissed her on the cheek. "It's a little sly and cheeky. You should tell Grant, though. I don't want him to think I'm playing around with his sister's heart."

"Of course," she laughed.

"I'll be visiting a couple of times a month since I'll be dealing with Fenrir a lot," he mentioned. "It would be nice if we could be friends."

She smiled at him. "I'd like that."

They continued their small talk and finished their dessert. Liam was scheduled to leave New York just after midnight, so after dinner, they set out to the private airstrip where his jet was waiting. Alynna insisted on bringing him there, and when she cleared it with Nick he agreed, but only if she took one of the security guys with her.

"Ms. Chase."

Alynna's heart jumped into her throat when she saw who was standing outside the restaurant. Alex was dressed for work in a dark, professional suit. His face remained stoic, betraying no emotion.

"Alex," she said. "I –"

"Ready?" Liam asked as he appeared behind her. He put a hand on her lower back and guided her to the waiting car.

She scooted in, leaving room for Liam. Alex got into the front passenger seat, and they were on their way.

Liam seemed lively, chatting with her about San Francisco and when she should come for a visit. She tried to keep it light, and if the Alpha noticed anything wrong with her, he didn't betray it.

After thirty minutes, the car pulled into the airstrip, driving right up to the jet which was waiting for its lone passenger. Liam exited the car, walked over to Alynna's side, then opened the door for her. He helped Alynna out, and she tucked her arm into his as they walked toward the staircase.

"Thank you for seeing me off." He looked boyish and handsome with the wind whipping the locks of hair that normally fell over his forehead.

"You're my friend, of course I'm going to see you off," she laughed, patting him on the arm.

"Oh, we're friends, are we?" he laughed.

"Of course!" she grinned.

"Well," his voice turned serious. "As your friend, can I say one thing?"

Alynna nodded.

Liam took a deep breath. "It's just, well, if you want something, you should go for it. Whatever it is." He gave her a warm smile, placing his hands on her shoulders. "You and I both know how short life can be. Don't waste time living it with regret."

A vice-like grip squeezed her heart and tears threatened to spill down her cheeks again. "Liam ..."

"Is it ..." He didn't finish but glanced over to the waiting car.

Her shoulders sank, and he knew the answer.

"Don't wait. Tell him."

"I can't," she stated. "He won't ... it's not like that. He doesn't ..."

His lips tightened. "Believe me, he does." He gripped her shoulders tighter. "Let me show you."

"What do you – mmph!" She let out a small surprised squeak as Liam pulled her close and pressed his lips to hers. It was weird how one man could touch her and kiss her and elicit nothing more than brotherly affection, while another equally handsome man's lips could set her whole body on fire.

"Liam!" she exclaimed as he pulled away. "You shouldn't have done that!"

He gave her a smirk. "We gave quite a show, I think." As he ascended the steps, Liam gave her a little salute.

She waited by the stairs, not knowing what to do. The stairs were pulled away and the attendant told her she had to leave the tarmac or the plane wouldn't be able to take off. When she walked to the car, Alex was waiting, holding the car door open.

"Did you have a good evening, Ms. Chase?" There was a snideness in his voice she'd never heard before.

"Yes, Mr. Westbrooke," she sneered back. *Bastard*, she added mentally as she entered the vehicle. The car was filled with tense silence the entire ride home and Alynna quickly let herself out as soon as they pulled up in front of The Enclave.

Later that night, Alynna tossed and turned in bed, waiting for a knock on her door. But it never came. She slept by herself for the first time that week.

CHAPTER TWENTY-TWO

D espite the lack of sleep and the bags under her eyes, Alynna was determined to meet with Cady and Grant that morning. She took the files with her and met with the two of them in the redhead's office. It wasn't that she was intimidated by her brother's office, but Cady's was neutral ground and she knew if Grant objected, Cady would definitely defend her. She felt slightly nauseous that morning, which she chalked up to nerves and fatigue.

Before heading in though, she stopped by Nick's office and handed him an envelope with her research. He gave her a raised brow, then a nod of acknowledgement, which she guessed was his way of saying thanks. She shrugged and went into Cady's office. After Cady's assistant brought them coffee and pastries, they sat down on the couches in the corner.

Alynna took out the folders from her bag and put them on the coffee table. She opened the top folder. "Gardiner's Laundromat on 1st and 16th. Robbed six times in the last year. Police have no clue or leads, despite all the footage on CCTV cameras." The photo in front was of a Lycan man's face, severely beaten and bleeding. She opened another folder. A picture of a young Lycan woman. "Michelle Lapicola, mother of two human children. Her piece of shit husband cheated on her, beat her up for years until she finally found the courage to leave him. Now, he's suing her for custody, claiming she cheated on him and therefore is an unfit mother."

Grant looked at his sister with a serious look on his face. "These are our clan members who came to us because the authorities won't help them?"

"Uh-huh. But we should help them. I want to help them," Alynna stated.

Cady and Grant looked at each other.

"I know we're supposed to let the police or the lawyers handle this, but well, it's obviously not working. These people are part of our clan, so we should protect them."

"All right, all right," Grant relented. "You don't have to make a case for this. If this is what you want to do, then you should do it."

"– And if no one will help them and they can't trust – wait, what?" Alynna's eyes widened. "Did you just ... you said I could do this?"

"Only if you're careful and stay under the radar from police, the authorities, and the media."

She blinked. "Yes, of course. I mean, I always do. I don't go in with guns blazing. All I want to do is help these people, our people, the best way I know how. Like you do."

Grant smiled. "Well, there are other details to be taken care of, like more Lycan rules and procedures you should know. The High Council lets us deal with small things like this, but we are not enforcers, nor do we take justice into our own hands." Grant looked at the pictures and frowned. "I wish ... I didn't know. Or I did, but I just haven't had the time."

"You can't be expected to micromanage the clan. You're our Alpha. This is street-level stuff, Grant, my turf. You can take care of the big picture," Alynna stated. "There's a couple of cases like this a year and not all of them need attention. I'm not running around for every Lycan who loses his cellphone or wallet. It shouldn't take up too much of my time, which is why I've also accepted Liam's offer to be on the board of Amata. I'm also going to be investing my own money in some of the companies he's working with."

"I didn't know things were that serious between the two of you," Grant quipped.

Alynna laughed. "Yes, Grant, he's so serious about me he wants to put me on the board of his company," she said sarcastically. "With me having some interest in the company, he figures he doesn't have to come to New York as often."

"Ah, so it's not serious then?"

She gave an exasperated sigh. "Can we talk about that another time?"

Grant looked at Cady. "Would you mind if we took over your office for a moment?"

"Of course." The redhead stood up. "I have to talk to HR about something."

When they were alone, Grant turned to his sister. "I'm proud of you, Alynna. If he were here, Dad would be, too."

"Thanks," she said softly, a lump forming in her throat. "I can't believe everything that's happened to me, you know. And I know I can't go back to my old life. Too many things have happened and in a way, I wasn't really living a life of my own. More like going through the motions because I thought I had no other choice." She paused, her voice cracking a little. "It's all overwhelming. PI detective stuff, I can do. But board member stuff? Grant, I never even went to college."

Grant pulled his sister into an embrace and kissed the top of her head. "Listen, you'll do great. You're talented and smart, and you don't need a fancy degree."

"But most people who hold these positions, they have MBAs and stuff, right?"

"Yes. If you want to enroll in school, you should do it. But experience will help you. And you've got great instinct. If you need anything, you can always ask me."

Alynna smiled against his shoulder and hugged him back. "Thank you, Grant."

He let go of her and gave her a serious look. "Any other surprises or major announcements? I would like to have breakfast first before you announce you're going to join a rock band and tour the world."

"Oh good god, no! I don't think *I* could take any more surprises."

————

Nick Vrost liked to think he was good at what he did. What that was exactly, he couldn't say. As Beta to Grant and second-in-command in the clan, it was his job to protect his Alpha. That included protecting him from anything in the day to day running of the clan that could get Grant's hands dirty. And today was one of those days.

Maybe he did things that were slightly illegal, but he never hurt anyone innocent nor committed murder. Perhaps he skirted the law a little bit, but he thought of that as part of his job. Including what he was probably about to do today.

He hated to admit it, but Alynna was good. The envelope she handed him this morning contained screenshots from Fred Allman's social networks, which tagged him in Staten Island. It also included the name, address, and social security number of his mother. He was glad the dumbass was still in the state and didn't bother to go farther than his mother's house.

There was nothing out of the ordinary about the home in

the suburban area of east Staten Island. Nick didn't scent any Lycans nearby, nor traces of them. The neighborhood was one hundred percent human, which hopefully should work with him rather than against.

Nick snuck around the back of the Allman place and pulled open the unlocked door. *This guy was either an idiot or this was a trap*, Nick scoffed to himself. He walked down the basement steps quietly, stopping as he heard loud bangs and gunfire. He put his hand over his own gun in his shoulder holster and descended slowly.

The basement was dark except for the glow of the large HDTV. It was new and just unboxed, judging from the cardboard and wrapping material strewn about. A first-person shooter video game was on the screen, its player obscured by the large leather sofa which also smelled new to Nick's keen senses. *Definitely an idiot*, he thought.

Nick waited for a few seconds, watching the screen explode in blood as the player shot down a group of enemies. Just as the game was reaching its peak, Nick reached over the sofa, dragging the surprised man over the back and letting him fall to the floor.

"What the fuck!?" The other man ripped his headphones off and tried to stand up. Nick grabbed him by the collar of his shirt and shoved him against the nearest wall. "What the fuck do you want? My mom has jewelry and stuff upstairs; go take that and get the fuck outta here!"

"Is that what you think I'm after?" Nick was tempted to show his fangs to the boy, but of course he couldn't risk it. "Fred Allman?"

"Yeah, what?" he asked, still struggling to get away from Nick's grip. "Whaddaya want? Did Joe send you? I already sent him the money I owe him and the interest! Tell your boss to leave me alone."

"Joe didn't send me." *Loan shark*, Nick thought. "I'm here about the night at the Waldorf."

Though it was dark, Nick could scent the sudden fear from Allman, his sweat leaking out of his pores revealing his terror and panic. "Hey man, I don't know nothing about that!"

Nick shoved him harder. "We can do this the easy way or the hard way," he stated. "The easy way would be to tell me what happened and I leave. The hard way ... well, if you want to find out what that is, I'll gladly oblige, but I don't think you could stand more than five minutes of what I've got in store."

"All right, all right!" Allman cried. "What do you want to know?"

"You poisoned the glass you handed to the girl and then took away the evidence."

"No!" he denied, which made Nick throw him to the ground. "I ... I didn't poison her! I mean, it wasn't me!"

"But you put the poison into her champagne?"

"I didn't know it was poison," Allman confessed. "Look ... I got a call two days before the party. They said they would give me $25,000 dollars if I do this one thing." He scrambled to get up. "I just had to make sure this substance went into something she ate or drank. Someone at the party put a vial in my pocket at some point. Don't ask me who; we weren't supposed to stare at the guests. Then I put it in her champagne. That's all I know, I swear!"

"And the money?" Nick asked, a hard edge to his voice.

"Cash. Showed up in my mailbox. I had enough to pay off my debts to this loan shark I owed money to." The frightened man cowered. "Please don't hurt me! I swear I didn't know what it was."

"You idiot," Nick spat. "What else could it be? Did you think it was vitamins? Someone paying you to make sure she didn't get a cold?" He hauled him to the wall again.

"Look, I thought you said if I'd told you what happened you'd go away!"

"Who was it? What do you remember? Was it a man or a woman?"

Allman shook his head. "I don't know. The voice that called me on my cell was muffled. Could've been a man?"

Nick grunted in frustration and threw him over the back of the sofa. "Don't leave town. Don't even try to disappear. You know I'll find you. And if you alert anyone, you'll find out what the hard way is."

The other man nodded. "I swear ... I won't."

Nick turned and walked up the dingy stairs and straight out of the house. He parked his car a few blocks away, but he didn't have to turn around to know Allman was not following him.

As soon as he got in his car and started driving, he dialed Grant. *A dead end*, he thought. The Alpha wasn't going to be happy, but it was better to tell him sooner than later.

CHAPTER TWENTY-THREE

Alynna walked out of the elevators with a spring in her step. It was the first time in weeks she actually felt somewhat normal. Things were falling into place, and she found a new purpose. She stepped into the lobby of the Fenrir building, looking around for Tate Miller who brought her here. *Hmmm ... no sign of him.* Alynna shrugged and looked outside. It was a nice sunny day, and it had been a while since she had just walked around New York City.

Alynna waved to the friendly receptionist in the lobby and left the building. The weather was lovely, though she could feel just a slight bit of autumn in the air. She walked north on Madison, grabbing an iced coffee and two bagels at an Au Bon Pain café. After a couple of blocks, she turned west toward Central Park.

Normally the entrance to Central Park was teeming with people, but it was one of those strange, lucky days when it seemed the city wasn't crowded with tourists. She continued to walk through the park, meandering her way through the Pond, the Bethesda Fountain, and eventually, the Met. She wasn't following a particular route, just working her way through. She planned to cut across after the reservoir through Bridle Path and make her way to The Enclave.

Alynna took her time, enjoying the outdoors and being alone for a change. So much had happened, and she was still trying to process most of it. Now that she finally knew what she was going to do, she was mapping out all the tasks that had to be done in her head. She wanted to start with her new cases right away, maybe visit Gardiner's in the morning and then call Michelle Lapicola to see if she was free for lunch the following day. Then, if she had some time, maybe she should seriously start looking at college courses or programs she could take part time.

Alynna was so deep in thought that she didn't notice the three men following her. She was halfway across the park when she felt their presence behind her. Every hair on her body stood on end. *Stay calm*, she told herself. This was bad news. She clenched her fists and picked up her pace.

The path ahead of her seemed long, and there was no one else around. She wondered if anyone would hear her if she screamed. It was the middle of the day, which actually made it less safe than being out here at night. Since it was daylight, the already-spread-too-thin NYPD or park security probably wasn't sending anyone out here on patrol.

The footsteps behind her shuffled faster, and Alynna swallowed a gulp. *Now or never.* She broke into a run, getting ahead of the men behind her. Unfortunately, their longer legs made up for her small lead and one of them overtook her, effectively blocking her path.

Alynna threw her handbag at the man in front of her. "There's cash there, about $300 dollars and my phone. Go ahead and take it. Take all of it."

The man in front of her was well over six feet tall and built like a brick wall. He was completely bald, with tattoos running all over his arms and shoulders. "That's not why we're here, girly."

"I don't wear jewelry." Alynna gritted her teeth. "We can go to the ATM. You can have everything; I won't try to scream." She turned to his friends, who were not as large or tall, but still imposing. She considered getting off the path and running up to Ninety-Seventh Street, which might be her best chance, but being unsure where she was exactly, she might run into a wall or face a big drop down.

"We don't want your money," the ringleader said. Before Alynna could think of what else they could possibly want, he raised his hand, showing her the syringe he was holding. "Now, just stay still and we won't hurt you. We just want you to come along with us and go for a ride."

"Ride with you? Drugged? Are you insane?" Alynna shouted. The men came closer, and the feeling of being trapped was very real.

The man holding the syringe quickly lunged at her. *Fuck it*, she thought. Instinct took over, and she dodged the larger man. Her would-be kidnappers probably thought she'd just comply, so it was obvious her move surprised them. She wasn't sure what she was doing, only that she had to run. But before she could step off the path, one of the other men grabbed her arm, pulling her back.

Alynna screamed in pain as she was hauled against his body and his hand came around to muffle her mouth.

"Just hold still!" the leader ordered.

There was something inside her, an inner voice that seemed to speak to her. *Protect ... must protect ...*

As the large man approached, Alynna's eyes rolled and she went limp for a few seconds. The man stuck the needle into her neck, but before he could plunge all of the sedative into her skin, Alynna's eyes flew open and she let out a snarl.

"Holy fuck!" the third man, who was standing next to the leader, shouted in surprise. "What the fuck is wrong with her eyes?"

"Help me!" the man who held her sputtered. "She's fucking stronger than she looks!"

Alynna struggled against the arms holding her, trying to shake them off. The leader threw the syringe to the ground and wrapped his own beefy arms around the other man's, trying to subdue her with his strength.

She made one last push and grunt, then was able to break free as both men toppled to the ground.

"What the fuck!" one of them shouted.

Alynna breathed in and out. Her eyes blazed in anger while her arms elongated, the muscles underneath shifting and growing.

"Fuck! What is ... *that*?" the man on the ground cursed.

She could feel herself transforming, her skin stretching and her bones moving. The change felt like it took forever, but in truth it was only a few seconds. It wasn't painful, but it was a new sensation. Instead of blacking out like the other times she shifted, she remained fully aware of the change. Black and dark brown fur sprouted from her arms, legs, and all over her body. Her clothes ripped as she grew. It felt exhilarating and freeing. *Protect ... save ... must protect ...* She had never heard the voice before, but she knew it was her inner wolf speaking to her.

When she was fully transformed into her Lycan form, she pounced.

———

Alex waited outside the Fenrir building across the street where he could see the entrance clearly, but not too close. He wore a dark baseball cap to shield his eyes from the sun, as well as obscure his face from view.

He'd been waiting since that morning. Despite being off-duty for the day, he wanted to be there. He wanted to be near Alynna. Miller told him he was driving her to Fenrir for a late morning meeting, so he took the subway and planted himself across the street. Right on schedule, the black town car pulled up in front of the entrance and Alynna stepped out. Alex felt his heart skip a beat at seeing her again. Jealousy twisted inside him, remembering how the San Francisco Alpha kissed her before he boarded the plane. He knew he had no chance. He never did, and he had to remind himself of that. He asked Nick if he could take the overnight shift as soon as they got back to The Enclave, knowing that guarding the Alpha was the only thing that would prevent him from storming into Alynna's apartment and trying to wipe Liam Henney's scent from her and cover her with his own.

Just before noon, he saw a flash of black hair. It was definitely Alynna, but no car had arrived to pick her up. She started walking north. *What the hell was she doing? Why was she alone?* His jaw tightened, but rather than running across the street to confront her, he pulled his cap lower and started to tail her.

Alex made sure to stay at least a block behind her at all times. Her heightened senses, plus her PI instincts might alert her to a tail. He followed her north, hanging back when she stopped at a café and waited until she stepped out. *Where the hell was she going?*

He nearly lost her when she went into Central park. As the crowds grew thinner and thinner, he didn't have much of a cover, so he hung back even farther. *She's probably gonna try to cut across and walk back to The Enclave.* Alex couldn't believe the Beta or the Alpha would let her out alone, not after what happened at the ball.

He followed her until they were almost at the top of the Reservoir, then he felt a vibration in his pocket. *Shit.* She would hear him if he picked up the phone, so he let her get ahead of him but kept his eyes on her as he stepped off the path.

"Westbrooke," he answered, not bothering to check who it was. It was his work phone, so it could only be one of the guys or the Beta.

"Alex," Nick's voice was tense. "Sorry to bother you on your day off. Are you at The Enclave?"

"No problem, Al Doilea," he answered. "I'm not at The Enclave. What can I do for you?"

"It's Alynna. She's missing again. We found Miller – he was subdued and locked in the trunk of the town car. The receptionist said Alynna walked out into the street and she didn't see what happened after."

The hair on the back of Alex's neck stood up, his heart starting to pound. He had a terrible feeling. "She's here ... I mean, I'm in Central Park and I followed her. She's ahead of me, probably cutting across Bridle Path to head back to The Enclave."

"You saw her? What are you – never mind. Grab her and bring her back to The Enclave right now."

"Yes, Al Doilea," he said. "Wha –" Before he could continue, he heard a scream. "Fuck!" Alex breathed deeply to try and calm down, but his body tensed. Something was wrong, he knew it. *Keep her safe ... keep them safe ...*

He was stunned. His inner Lycan never spoke to him while in human form. Only during transformations, and that was very rare. Even when he was fully shifted and could control himself, the wolf only spoke in growls or single words.

"Alex?"

He snapped out of the trance. "I have to go. She's in trouble," he growled softly as he dropped the phone to the ground. His human legs would be too slow to help her, and his wolf was already rearing to get out. He ran toward Bridle Path, shedding his jacket, shoes, pants, and shirt as he fully shifted into his Lycan form.

Alex's wolf form was over six feet tall when it stood on its hind legs. His muscular body was covered in dark brown hair with streaks of light blond. His eyes were a pure molten gold color, and his fangs were long and sharp. He controlled his wolf expertly, pushing its legs as fast as he could. He sniffed out Alynna's scent – the familiar, wonderful scent – until he came upon her just off the Bridle Path.

He didn't see Alynna exactly, but he knew it was her. The black wolf, almost an identical copy of the Alpha's except half the size, was pinning someone – a man – down on the ground as its jaws snapped at his head. The man's shoulder was bleeding profusely.

He howled at the other wolf, and its shaggy head snapped up. Green eyes – Alynna's unmistakable eyes – looked back at him. She whimpered, and then walked over to him.

Alynna nuzzled his neck, staining his fur with blood. *It's okay*, he wanted to say to her. She let out a last whine, then lay down on the ground. *She's probably tired.*

The black wolf closed her eyes, then slowly began to shift back into human form. Limbs and torso began to shorten, as did the long snout. Fur retracted back into the skin, which turned from black to milky white.

Alex looked around for something for Alynna to wear, but all her clothing had stretched and ripped. He quickly retraced his steps and gathered his discarded clothes. He rushed back to Alynna, covering her naked, shivering body with his jacket.

Alynna's eyes flew open and she sat up, clutching the jacket around her. She hunched over and heaved, emptying the contents of her stomach onto the soft grass. She wiped her mouth with the jacket sleeve before putting it on.

By the time she had the strength to stand up, Alex had fully transformed back into his human form and had dressed in his pants.

"A ... A ... Alex," she cried out as she felt another wave of nausea and sank to her knees.

"Alynna," he said softly as he knelt down beside her and gathered her into his arms.

"They tried to ... they wanted to drug me." She hiccupped. "I transformed, but I didn't black out! I could control myself ... I mean the wolf. It spoke to me, too."

Alex pulled her tighter. "I know ... I know," he soothed.

She pulled away, then looked at the man lying on the ground. "Wait. Is he ...?"

He didn't want to let her go, but she started shaking when she realized she might have killed someone. He kissed her forehead and walked over to the other man. Kneeling down beside him, he put a finger to his wrist. The pulse was weak, but it was there. The wolf's jaws had punctured the man's shoulder, but it didn't sever a major artery. He grabbed the nearest scrap of cloth he could find, Alynna's shirt, and pressed it to his wounds. He wanted to let the bastard die, but not only would that cause a lot of trouble for the New York clan, he knew Alynna would be haunted by the death even if it was done in self-defense.

"Alex?"

He looked up. Alynna's face was marred with worry as she looked guiltily at the man on the ground.

"You didn't kill the bastard," he growled. "He's alive. But I doubt he'll stay that way once the Alpha gets here."

It wasn't even five minutes later when Grant, Nick, and three other members of the Lycan security team arrived on the scene. The wounded man's condition didn't worsen, but just as Alex predicted, Nick had to restrain the Alpha when he saw his sister.

"Go tend to Alynna," Nick urged Grant, who looked like he was barely hanging on to his human form. "I'll take care of this."

Grant's eyes returned to normal, then he walked over to where Alynna sat on the grass still clinging to Alex. The younger man reluctantly let her go and let the Alpha gather her into his arms.

"I'm fine ..." Alynna's voice slightly cracked.

"I know," Grant said, kissing the top of her head. "But I'm not."

She sank into his arms and wrapped her arms around him, her body shaking from the ordeal.

Nick stood over the wounded man, contemplating if he should tear the man apart or let the authorities handle everything. The former choice would leave quite a mess, so he let out a sigh and took out his phone, dialing the personal number of the Deputy Police Chief of New York City.

Soon, Cady had arrived along with Dr. Faulkner and one of his nurses.

"Alynna!' she exclaimed as she wrapped the half-naked younger woman in a blanket. "Let's get you out of here." The redhead looked over at Nick who was still on the phone, and he nodded his agreement to her.

"No wounds? Concussion?" Dr. Faulkner asked.

"No. I'm good, just ..." She stood up, but before she could say anything else, she puked on Grant's shoes. "Sorry!"

"I'll live." Grant smiled weakly as he helped her stay up.

"Are you sure you didn't hit your head?" Dr. Faulkner took out his pen light and shone it into her eyes.

Alynna nodded, but it sent her head spinning again. She held onto Grant to steady herself.

"Let's take you back to The Enclave." Grant lifted her into his arms.

"No! Alex! I want to stay with Alex!" she said in a panic. Her heart pounded wildly at the thought of being separated from the other man.

"Shhh ..." Alex came up to her and stroked her hair. "Let them take you back and make sure you're okay, please? The Beta needs me to stay here and help first."

"Will you come as soon as you can?" She looked at the younger man and then to her brother, who gave her a reluctant nod.

"All right," she replied weakly, laying her head on Grant's shoulder. She breathed in her brother's comforting ocean-spray scent and closed her eyes before the world went black again.

CHAPTER TWENTY-FOUR

Alynna's eyes flew open. For a second she felt fear and terror. Three men were attacking her, and one of them had put a syringe with some drug in her neck. She screamed, and the dim lights grew brighter as the door flew open.

"Alynna, dear, calm down," Dr. Faulkner's voice was soft and reassuring. "You're safe. You're at The Enclave."

The young woman's breathing evened, and she fell back against the soft pillow on her hospital bed. "Yes ... I remember. Sorry, Dr. Faulkner. I didn't mean to scream my head off and frighten your entire ward."

"Yes, well, you've had quite a day. I'm sure everyone would understand if you were shaken," the older Lycan assured her.

She smiled at him weakly, then noticed he seemed hesitant. "Dr. Faulkner, is there something wrong? Did something happen to me when I shifted?"

He smiled back at her. "No, everything's fine. In fact, you're in fit health."

"But?" She knew there was a but.

"You're healthy for someone in your condition."

"What condition?" Alynna looked confused.

"Well, my dear ... you're pregnant."

"No, I can't be." She shook her head and opened her mouth to protest but snapped it back shut. Pregnant. The word rang in her head, her memories flooding back. Her cravings, her body changing. The voice in her head. *My wolf said it had to protect ... not just me, but us.*

"I take it you didn't know?" the older man asked hesitantly.

"No. I mean, it doesn't make sense! I was on birth control and you said being Lycan I can't ..." she trailed off.

"Well," Dr. Faulkner began, "we know it's hard for Lycans, but not impossible."

The whole last week with Alex ... of course it had to happen at some point with the amount of sex they had. However, since finding out about her Lycan biology, she stopped taking the pill since they ran out about two weeks ago.

"Is there anything I can do for you?" Dr. Faulkner's face was a mask of concern. "I know I'm a Lycan, but I'm still a doctor. I'm bound by my oath to give you the best care. Medical privacy laws will allow your decisions to remain ... private."

She whipped her head at him, and her inner wolf growled at her as if it understood his meaning before she did. "Yes, I mean ... please, can you call Grant in here? And, uh, Alex Westbrooke, if he's around."

The doctor seemed taken aback at the mention of the other man's name. "He's –"

"The father, yes," she confessed. "I should tell them."

The doctor nodded.

"Wait," she called out. "Um ... just in case, could you make sure Cady's here too?" She thought for a moment at what her brother's reaction would be when he found out. "Er ... and Nick also, I guess." Nick's cool head would prevail, and he would be good backup just in case Grant overreacted.

"There's something else Alynna, something you should know."

She let out a breath. "I don't know if I can take any more revelations, Dr. Faulkner. If it has to do with Lycan stuff, can you tell me with everyone here? I waive my privacy privilege just for them."

The kindly older Lycan nodded. "All right, I suppose it will save us the trouble of informing everyone anyway."

———

"Everything all right?" Grant asked as Nick walked into the waiting room of the medical ward.

"Yes, Primul," Nick answered. "Don't worry about it. Deputy Chief Andrews said he'll take care of everything. They'll report it as a robbery gone wrong. No one will know Alynna or any of us were on the scene."

"Good." He gritted his teeth, his eyes steely. Cady stayed beside him, her hand on his arm.

"How is she?" Alex suddenly burst into the room.

"You!" Grant shot to his feet and grabbed him by the collar of his shirt. "What were you doing following her? Did you lead those men to her?"

"Primul!" Alex exclaimed, putting his hands up in self-defense. "No! I was keeping her safe! I saw her walk out of Fenrir without an escort."

"Grant!" Cady followed the Alpha, putting her hand gently on his arm. "He helped her. He saved her." Grant loosened his grip on Alex.

"I think she saved herself," Alex declared, pride evident in his voice. "Primul, she transformed, controlled her wolf, and took the guy down."

"That still doesn't explain why you were following her in

the first place when you're not assigned to her. Are you stalking my sister?" Grant's voice had a dangerous edge.

"No, Primul. I love her," he blurted out. "I'm sorry. I do. She and I ... we were having an affair."

The room went silent. Cady's mouth opened in an unlady-like manner. Even Nick looked surprised.

"Yes. She told me." Grant crossed his arms. "What are you going to do about it?"

Alex seemed aback by his question. "I'll leave her alone. I know it's not my place. We shouldn't have slept together. She's your sister and that was disrespectful of me."

Grant looked at him with piercing eyes. "You love her, huh?"

He nodded. "But I know she doesn't feel the same way. She deserves someone who could give her everything. Someone like Liam Henney." He looked at Nick. "Al Doilea, I'll have my resignation letter to you before the end of the day. I'll head back to Chicago as soon as I settle some business here."

Before anyone could say anything, Dr. Faulkner entered the room. "She's awake. She didn't black out, just passed out due to fatigue."

"Can we see her now?" Grant asked.

The older Lycan nodded. "Yes."

Grant started to walk toward Alynna's room.

"Wait, Alpha," Dr. Faulkner called out, then turned to Alex. "She wants to see you, too. Actually, all of you."

"Let's go see her then," Grant said.

They followed him to the private room where Alynna was staying. "Are you okay?" He rushed to his sister's side.

"I'm fine," she laughed weakly. "I was just super tired."

"You said you wanted to see all of us? What is it? Do you remember something about your attackers?"

"Um, no. There's something I need to tell you, yes, but first I need to ask ... is the man who attacked me dead?" She looked nervously at him.

"All taken care of," Nick interjected. "They have him at the hospital in police custody. So far, he's stable. The Deputy Police Chief is a friend to the Lycans. He's going to make it seem like the man was trying to rob someone, but the victim fended him off with a knife, then fled. We cleaned up any evidence we were there."

"He saw me transform," she confessed. "He's gonna talk and it's all going to come out."

Grant took her hand and squeezed it. "No, Alynna, it won't. We're prepared for these kinds of situations. He won't remember. Or at least he won't remember if he was hallucinating or if it was real."

Before she could ask, Nick explained. "A confusion potion. We have a limited supply in store and they're a bitch to get a hold of, seeing as witches don't like us, but we keep it handy. It doesn't erase memories but definitely makes them unreliable. We administered it before the cops and paramedics came. He'll probably be hallucinating about dinosaurs and aliens for a few days, too."

She sighed in relief. "There were two others. They got away. They didn't want my money or my purse. They said they wanted me to take a ride with them and then injected me with a sedative. I can work with a sketch artist or identify them through photos if you need me to."

Nick nodded. "That will be helpful." His brow crinkled. "It's obvious someone wants to harm you or get rid of you altogether."

"We won't stop digging until we find out who," Grant gritted through his teeth. "So, what else did you want to tell us? Why did you ask for all of us?" He shot Alex a look.

"Well, Dr. Faulkner said ... he said that ..." She looked at the older Lycan and nodded.

Dr. Faulkner cleared his throat. "Alynna is expecting. We'll be welcoming a new addition to the New York clan."

Alynna heard a growl and in a flash, Grant leapt toward Alex, his hand encircling the man's throat. "You motherfucking asshole!" Grant roared. Alex barely protested, letting the Alpha's hands tighten around his neck.

"No! Grant, don't kill him! I love him, please!" she cried, jumping off the bed to grab her brother's arm, frantically tugging at his bicep with all her might.

Grant reluctantly let go and Alynna rushed to Alex, checking his throat which was already starting to bruise.

"You will marry her," Grant snarled, straightening his coat.

"That was never a question, Alpha," Alex sputtered.

Alynna wrapped her arms around Alex. "Alex, I'm sorry! I didn't know!"

"Shhhh ... don't cry, baby doll," he soothed her. "It'll be fine."

"You don't have to marry me no matter what Grant says," she protested. "This is the twenty-first century. A woman can raise a baby on her own."

"But why would I let you do that when I love you and want to be with you forever?"

"We can work it out," she continued to babble. "You don't even have to do anything ..." She stopped short. "What?"

He chuckled and tipped her chin up. "I said I love you. I want to be with you and raise our pup together. If you'll have me." He gave her a searing, passionate kiss that made her knees weak.

When they finally pulled away, Alynna had an incredulous look on her face. "What? I thought you didn't want to be with me!"

"I did. I mean, I still do. I wanted you so bad, it hurt," he confessed. "But it wasn't meant to be, you know? You're the Alpha's sister, and I'm just some Lycan nobody who's got no prospects."

She started to protest, but he silenced her with a kiss. It felt so right, being with him, that Alynna almost forgot they weren't alone.

"I knew the Alpha wouldn't approve, not wholeheartedly. Not with your status, your position. You're too valuable, Alynna, to be wasting your time on me."

"No! Don't say that!" She pulled away from him.

"It's the truth. But," he knelt in front of her, "I promise you and the Alpha I will do everything in my power to be worthy of you. If you'll have me."

The room was hushed. Tears sprung from Alynna's eyes. "Of course! I love you, Alex."

"I love you too, Alynna." Alex sprung to his feet and gave her another heated kiss.

Time seemed to pass slowly, but the happy couple was interrupted by someone awkwardly clearing their throat. They pulled away and turned to the others in the room. Cady had tears forming in her eyes, Grant stood frowning with his arms crossed, and Nick, surprisingly, had a smug look on his face.

"Sorry to interrupt." Dr. Faulkner took a piece of paper out of a folder he was holding. "But there's something else."

Alynna sighed. "Okay, give it to me, Dr. Faulkner."

"Well ... I had some suspicions, but I won't know for sure until I get the tests back. Alynna, do you know how far along you are?"

She thought for a moment. "I can't be more than ... uh ..." She looked sheepishly at Grant and turned red. "The night of the ball? Two weeks, give or take?"

Dr. Faulkner shook his head. "No, my dear. You're about seven weeks along."

"Seven weeks?" Alex exclaimed. He did the mental math.

"That would mean ..." She looked up at him. "The first time? That weekend?"

Grant made a strangled sound, but Cady dug her fingers into his arm to keep him quiet. The Alpha gave protest, and Nick muffled a laugh.

"Ah, so you could say that was the time you two ... er ... were first together?"

Alynna fell silent, but nodded.

Dr. Faulkner's face lit up. "I think we have to look into the possibility that the two of you are True Mates."

It was Alex who stumbled back at the news. Alynna laughed and grabbed onto her newly-minted mate. It made sense. "Alex smells particularly good to me. Like, you all smell okay to my senses, but when I get a whiff of him, it's like ... it's like I'm home."

Alex spoke up. "I feel the same way when I scent Alynna," he stated. "It's er, arousing, yes, but something else, too. I can't say why, but she makes me feel different."

"When we first met, I felt hot temperature-wise," Alynna said. "I remember my skin tingled when he touched me, then the rest of me was on fire, but in a good way." Alex nodded in agreement. "That must have triggered my first shift. And, I think, when I transformed today, my wolf was telling me I had to protect the baby."

"Me too," Alex said. "When I heard Alynna scream, my wolf started to go crazy and I couldn't control the shift."

"That's probably why your body fought off the Belladonna poisoning, Alynna," Dr. Faulkner theorized. "It was rejecting the poison to protect your pup."

Cady, Grant, and Nick all looked stunned. "Could you find out for sure, Dr. Faulkner?" Grant asked.

The older Lycan nodded. "Yes, I could. But I think we pretty much can say it's true. Alex and Alynna are True Mates. Possibly the first of this generation. This is amazing and good for our research, too. I mean, if Alex and Alynna wouldn't mind us taking some samples from them and possibly their pup when he or she is born. It could be the key to solving Lycan infertility."

Alex and Alynna embraced and kissed again. "Whether we are or we aren't, it doesn't matter," Alex said, beaming at Alynna.

————

After a few more minutes, Alynna asked everyone if she could have some time alone with Alex. Grant reluctantly agreed but nodded toward Alex in perhaps the first gesture he made in acceptance of his sister's new beau. After all, Alex and Alynna were True Mates, a fact that would certainly turn the Lycan world into a tizzy, and more importantly, the father of his heir apparent.

"You think the Alpha will ever warm up to the idea of us?" Alex asked as he laid down beside Alynna on the bed.

"Of course," she assured him. "Give him time."

"He loves you. You know that, right? Even though he's only known you a short time." Alex cuddled her closer.

She smiled. "I know. And I love him, too."

"And you love me, huh?" He grinned.

"Yes, you goofball. Even though you're a stubborn, obstinate Lycan who seems to think we're still in the dark ages." She laughed, then grabbed his hand and placed it on her belly. "I hope you don't take after your father, Horace," she sighed.

"Horace?" Alex recoiled. "No baby of mine is gonna be called Horace!"

She laughed aloud. "How about for a middle name?"

"How about we talk about it?" He leaned in and kissed her, but her eyes grew wide and she pulled away. "What is it?" Alex asked.

"Crap!" she cursed. "What about your girlfriend?"

"My girlfriend?" Alex looked confused.

"Jenna." Alynna looked deflated.

This time it was Alex's turn to laugh. "What gave you that idea? Oh," he said sheepishly. "*I* gave you that idea. Alynna, I'm sorry." He took her hand and kissed it. "She's not my girlfriend. She never was. We went out that one night, but I never slept with her. Actually, she kind of tricked me into going out with her. I've only been with you since our first time."

She sighed with relief, then punched him in the arm.

"Ow! What was that for!?" He rubbed his arm.

"For making me think I was a side chick!" she joked.

"Oh yeah? And what about Liam 'I'm-so-perfect-I-could-make-you-puke' Henney?"

"Oh, haha." Alynna punched his arm again, though softer this time. "He was in on it. He wanted to make *you* jealous."

"Hmm ... remind me to thank him next time I see him," he said. "Before I punch him in the face for kissing my True Mate."

"Tsk, tsk," she tutted. "You Lycan men and your violent tendencies."

"Hey, I'm the one who's nursing a hurt shoulder!"

"Oh you baby! I didn't hit you that hard!"

"Why don't you kiss me and make it better?" he asked sweetly.

"I'll do whatever you want to make it better," she said before pulling him in for another kiss.

"Are you really going to make me do this?"

"Yes, I'm really going to make you do this." Alynna smirked and handed Grant the keys.

Grant grabbed them from his sister. He opened the passenger side door to his Maserati. "Get in."

She smirked at him again as she stepped into the sleek car. He walked to the driver's side and entered, putting the key in the ignition and letting the engine roar to life.

The ride to the courthouse was pleasant, and although Alynna begged Grant to drive faster, he kept his restraint, telling her someone in her condition shouldn't be trying to break the speed of sound. She pouted and crossed her arms, which made Grant rev the engine. And maybe he did go over the speed limit a little bit, just enough for his sister to break into a smile.

They arrived at the courthouse with no need for meter quarters as Patrick was waiting by the steps to dutifully drive the car away to a private parking garage. Grant offered his arm to his sister, and she took it, following him up the steps.

After getting clearance from Dr. Faulkner, Alex brought

Alynna to Chicago a few days after her attack to meet his parents. Gene and Mary Westbrooke were quite delighted, though also startled at the sudden appearance of their son who toted his new girlfriend along. The same girl who also happened to be the much-talked about Alynna Chase in Lycan circles.

They spent three days in Chicago, and on their last night Mary Westbrooke cooked them a wonderful dinner featuring all of Alex's favorite dishes like pot roast, potatoes, and apple pie. Afterward, when they were all on the porch having coffee, Alex knelt in front of Alynna. He opened a small velvet box which held his grandmother's marquis-cut diamond ring and asked her to marry him. She wholeheartedly said yes, and Mary Westbrooke started bawling her eyes out. Just when Mary was ready to stop crying, the newly engaged couple also told them about their impending arrival, which made the overjoyed grandma-to-be reach for a fresh handkerchief.

Alex and Alynna wanted to get married right away, preferably before she started showing. Neither wanted a big fancy wedding and so, in two weeks, they were able to obtain a license and get permission for Alex's family and friends to come to New York. On a beautiful mid-Autumn day, they were set to marry at the New York City Courthouse.

The bride wore a tea-length off-white gown, kitten heels, and held a bouquet of fresh cut daisies tied with a green ribbon. Her brother escorted her down the modest aisle, where the dapper looking groom was waiting along with the maid of honor and best man, Cady Gray and Nick Vrost. Alex's parents and two Lycan friends from Chicago stood on the left side, and Callista Mayfair, her husband Jean-Luc, and Dr. Faulkner and his wife stood on the right.

After the ceremony, they all drove back to The Enclave where all the Lycans in New York and a few more from

Chicago, including their own Alpha, were waiting to celebrate with the happy couple. The garden behind Center Cluster was dressed up in fairy lights and paper lanterns, and long tables were set up with white tablecloths and beautiful floral centerpieces. Alynna didn't have to deal with all the arrangements, thanks to her maid of honor's efficiency and good taste. Everyone welcomed the wedding party and soon, the reception was in full swing.

With Cady at the helm, everything was absolutely perfect. The wine and champagne were flowing, the food was amazing, and the speeches kept short and sweet. There was one thing Alynna insisted on – instead of cutting a traditional wedding cake, they had a specially-made four-tier key lime pie cake from Elsie's Diner. Each table also had a different type of pie. Cady looked at her with a puzzled look when Alynna requested this, but somehow, thanks to her dazzling efficiency, she made it happen.

"Happy?" Alynna asked as she snaked her arms around her new husband's waist from behind. They snuck away from the crowd after the pie-cutting and made their way up to the private terrace overlooking the garden. She nuzzled at his back, his warm scent filling her senses.

"Why wouldn't I be?" He turned around and gathered her into her arms. "I have a beautiful wife, a pup on the way. Life is good."

"Mmm ... better than good." She pressed her cheek to his chest.

"And Grant finally stopped looking at me with murder in his eyes," Alex joked.

"Well, I think he realized he's off the hook for producing an heir for the time being," she laughed and looked down at the garden space. Her brother was surrounded by a gaggle of Lycan women, all single and of proper breeding age. He looked uncomfortable, but as Alpha, he had to do his duty and entertain the guests.

"Hmm ... it seems like a dream," Alex confessed.

"That your child could one day be the Alpha of the New York clan?"

"Yeah, well, he's still gonna be a White Sox fan," he quipped.

"Shut your mouth, you heathen!"

"Make me!"

She pulled him down for kiss. She moaned as his delicious scent filled her nostrils, wrapping itself around her very soul. After a few moments, they pulled away.

Alynna sighed and burrowed back into her husband's embrace.

"What I meant was," he continued, "being with you and having a family seems like a dream. One I never thought I'd have."

"I know." She thought about her past, her mother, Uncle Gus, and her life struggling on her own. For the first time, she wasn't alone. She was surrounded by friends, family, and her new husband. Still, Alynna shivered slightly, both from the light nip in the air and because of what was looming ahead.

"I won't let anyone hurt you." He kissed the top of her head and held her tight. "And you're pretty much invincible, at least until the baby is born."

"True," she said quietly. But that only made her feel slightly better. There was someone out there who wanted to hurt her and her new family. She would find out who before they tried anything else.

"Hey, lovebirds," a voice called out from behind. They turned toward the balcony doors. Cady was standing there

looking absolutely stunning in her purple fl[o]
honor gown, her hair falling in soft waves arou[nd]
"You can't hide out here forever! You have gue[sts]
She cocked her head and then disappeared [past] [the]
door.

"Duty calls," Alynna quipped.

"After you, Ms. Chase," Alex joked, extending his hand in front of them.

"That's Mrs. Westbrooke to you."

He laughed and picked her up, spinning her around. "Whew! I thought I'd have to be Mr. Chase from now on."

———

Dear Reader,

Thanks for reading! But the story's not over yet.

We still don't know who tried to kill Alynna.

Plus, there's all that yummy tension between Nick and Cady.

To continue the story, turn to the next chapter to get a sneak peek at the next installment of the True Mates series starring Nick Vrost and Cady Gray. It's now available on Amazon at your favorite online retailers.

Also, I have BONUS SCENES from this book, featuring Alex and Alynna in Chicago, PLUS their Christmas Holiday Story.

Want to get it (and some free books?)? Just join my newsletter here to get access:

ALICIA MONTGOMERY

*://aliciamontgomeryauthor.com/mailing-list/

You'll get access to ALL the bonus materials from all my books and my **FREE** novella **The Last Blackstone Dragon.**

Happy Reading!

Alicia

ABOUT THE AUTHOR

Alicia Montgomery has always dreamed of becoming a romance novel writer. She started writing down her stories in now long-forgotten diaries and notebooks, never thinking that her dream would come true. After taking the well-worn path to a stable career, she is now plunging into the world of self-publishing.

 facebook.com/aliciamontgomeryauthor

 twitter.com/amontromance

 bookbub.com/authors/alicia-montgomery

SNEAK PEEK: BLOOD MOON

BOOK 2 OF THE TRUE MATES SERIES

Cady Gray sighed softly as she watched the newlyweds on the makeshift dance floor. Alynna threw her head back and laughed as Alex picked her up and twirled her around. She smiled as the young couple embraced and began to slowly dance when the DJ put on a more subdued love song.

Was it really just a few weeks ago when Alynna Chase arrived in their lives? The young private investigator had thought she was fully human for 22 years and that she was virtually an orphan. Alynna was at Blood Moon, a club that catered to Lycans, when she met Alex Westbrooke. Apparently the young woman transformed into her Lycan form accidentally upon meeting the young man and ran away, but Alex tracked her down. Of course, she was brought in to see Grant Anderson, the leader and Alpha of the New York Clan. They initially thought she was an intruder, someone from another clan who had come into their territory without permission. They discovered, however, that not only was she a full Lycan, but also Grant's half-sister by his father Michael and his True Mate,

Amanda Chase. Unfortunately, Michael had died in a car accident before he could bring Alynna into the New York Lycan society. Although it was a difficult adjustment for the young woman, she managed it masterfully, and it also turned out Alex was her True Mate.

It was a beautiful reception and she had to give herself a mental pat on the back, since she put everything together in about two weeks. Alynna had left all the planning to her, giving her free reign on what to do for decorations, music, and food (except for her strange pie request). Cady went to work the moment the couple came back from Chicago and announced their engagement. There was much to be done, and she did have some help from Callista Mayfair, Grant's mother, who was more than happy to lend a hand. The older lady seemed disappointed Alynna didn't want a big wedding with all the fanfare, but was quickly appeased when she learned why the couple didn't want to wait months to get married (and overjoyed at the prospect of being a grandma, which Alynna had confessed weirded her out still, given that the baby would technically be her former husband's grandchild by his mistress.)

She truly was happy for Alex and Alynna, not just because they were True Mates, but because they found each other and what seemed like real happiness. They also were already expecting a Lycan pup - with instant pregnancy an effect of being True Mates. Although Cady might have projected a pragmatic image, she was a romantic at heart. But, would she ever find someone of her own? Not necessarily another person who would hold the other half of her soul, but someone she could come home to after a long day, and maybe a child or two to bring more joy into her life. She shook her head. *No, I shouldn't think about it.*

"You look like you're still working."

Cady froze at the familiar voice. One that never failed to

make her nervous. Or giddy. Or both. "I am working. Aren't you?" she answered without taking her eyes off the dance floor.

"Of course," Nick Vrost stepped up to join her where she stood right beside the dance floor. He was dressed smartly in his formal black suit, cut in the Italian style that suited his long, lean, but powerful frame. His blonde hair slicked back with gel, though a tendril had fallen over his forehead. "My work is never done. But that's the nature of being Beta and head of security."

"We are in The Enclave," Cady replied, turning her head up to look at him. "I'm sure you can relax while we're in here."

Ice blue eyes regarded her. "I will if you will."

She laughed. "Fine. I'll have a glass of champagne." Cady turned to head towards the refreshment table, but a warm hand wrapped around her upper arm. "Actually, I was thinking we could dance, Ms. Gray."

"Oh," Cady gasped quietly. In all their years working together, she couldn't remember Nick Vrost ever touching her. His large hand was calloused and warm, the grip strong, yet gentle on her arm. The sensation of his bare skin touching hers shot tingles through her, spreading heat along the line of her body. She sucked in a breath, his cologne filling her nose. She thought back to that night he brought her home after the incident at Blood Moon. *Hmmm...fir trees?* She wondered what brand he wore that made him smell so...different and sexy. The scent reminded her of Christmas, her favorite time of the year.

Suddenly, a dizzying feeling overtook her. Her knees buckled slightly, which only made Nick grab her with his other hand, his arm wrapping around her waist. "Are you ok?" he asked. His face was mere inches from hers.

"I'm fine. Just overwhelmed, I guess." Cady straightened up, which only brought her closer to Nick's broad chest and she got another whiff of his cologne.

"Not too overwhelmed to dance with me, Ms. Gray?" Nick asked hopefully.

"No. But only if you call me Cady. Which I think you can do, after all these years."

"Ten years, to be precise, Ms.— er, Cady," he faltered. "Alright, but you should call me Nick, then."

Her name sounded strange coming from his mouth. She realized he had never said her first name aloud.

"Of course, Nick," she replied, giving him a smile. She let him lead her to the dance floor, and when they found an open spot, he placed his left hand on her waist and took her small hand in his right one. They swayed in time to a slow song the DJ had just put on. Small tingles shot along her left palm where their bare skin met.

Nick was surprisingly a good dancer, able to keep with rhythm and lead Cady along. "I didn't know you danced, Nick," Cady remarked. "I'm usually at the same parties you are, I don't think I ever saw you dance with anyone."

"We hardly have any parties where I'm not working. Didn't think it was appropriate."

"And now?" the redhead inquired.

"As you said, there's nothing to be worried about. We're inside The Enclave, and we are here as Best Man and Maid of Honor. I think it's actually our duty to have a good time." Nick twirled her efficiently, and when he pulled her back, Cady found herself pressed up against him even closer.

"You do that quite well," she breathed out slowly.

"Thank you. My grandmother insisted I learn to dance when I was younger," he said wryly.

Cady was a little bit surprised at the revelation. That was perhaps the only personal thing Nick had ever revealed to her in all the years she worked alongside him. "Well, I'll have to thank her for making sure you didn't step on my toes."

Nick cracked a sad smile. "She passed on, some time ago."

"Oh, I'm sorry." She couldn't help herself when she saw the sadness in his eyes, and touched his cheek softly.

He turned towards her hand and closed his eyes, his lips barely touching her palm, his breath warm tickling her skin. Her head felt light and she was afraid she'd faint. Cady swallowed a gulp of air, trying to steady herself.

"It's alright, it's been a while. She—"

"Can we cut in?" A bright, cheery voice interrupted Nick. Alynna Chase (now Westbrooke) and her new husband stood behind them.

"How could I say no to the bride?" Cady quickly disentangled from Nick. She was partly relieved, feeling somewhat nervous at how close she and Nick had been. But, a small part of her was disappointed.

"Thanks, Cady," Alynna turned to Nick. "May I have this dance, Nicky-boy?"

The taller Lycan gave her a wry smile. "Of course, Mrs. Westbrooke."

Alynna laughed. "C'mon and show me those moves."

Cady watch as the young woman took Nick's hand and dragged him away to the center of the dance floor.

"Sorry, you're stuck with me for a bit, Cades," Alex joked. "I'll try not to step on your toes too much."

"You should have warned me, I would have put on my hiking boots!" Cady laughed as the younger man took her hands.

The DJ had put on a slightly faster song this time, much to Alynna's delight and she laughed aloud when Nick spun her. Nick was an excellent dancer and twirled her around expertly.

"You're not half bad," Cady remarked to her current dance partner. She and Alex had an easy friendship, and she had been drawn to his good nature, despite him being an outsider.

"Yeah, well I'm no Nick Vrost," he teased. He turned his head to watch his new wife and his Best Man / boss dancing. "Did you know he could dance like that?"

"I didn't, actually." *There's lots of things I don't know about him*, she realized.

"Really? After all this time?" Alex seemed surprised.

Cady shrugged. "I was as clueless as you are."

"Not that clueless," Alex smiled down at her. "But you can be slightly dense."

"What?" Cady asked incredulously.

"I'm joking, I'm joking," Alex defended. But then his voice turned serious. "But you know, if there's something you want, you should just go for it." He looked over at the other dancing couple.

Cady's eyes widened and then her mouth opened to say something, but quickly shut it.

A spark lit up in Alex's eyes. "So you do have feelings for him?"

"I don't know what you're talking about," Cady retorted in a slightly deflated voice. Despite not truly knowing Nick Vrost after almost ten years, she couldn't help it. She guarded herself and her feelings carefully, and even though his disposition towards her all these years remained formal and chilly, she knew it was truly too easy to fall in love with him. If she wasn't halfway there already.

True Mates 2: Blood Moon
Available at your favorite online retailers

Don't forget to join my newsletter to get access to the latest news and bonus content and my **FREE** novella **The Last Blackstone Dragon.**:

http://aliciamontgomeryauthor.com/mailing-list/

Printed in the USA
CPSIA information can be obtained
at www.ICGtesting.com
LVHW101124080124
768071LV00027B/104